*To Debbie
Take a Journey
rest of Jimmie's life.    June*

# REDEMPTION SUITE

*June Titus*

JUNE TITUS

Copyright © 2023 June Titus
All rights reserved
First Edition

Fulton Books
Meadville, PA

Published by Fulton Books 2023

ISBN 979-8-88982-829-7 (paperback)
ISBN 979-8-88982-830-3 (digital)

Printed in the United States of America

# DEDICATION

*Redemption Suite* is dedicated
to my late grandson

Andrew J. Hoyt

July 21, 1996 to March 18, 2023

Andrew struggled with life after a severe head injury at age two, resulting in epilepsy. He believed that everyone had a great potential. Andrew emerged from very difficult circumstances trusting God's grace for his life and eternal destiny, believing we can all find Redemption and eternal life.

Psalm 91:14–16

"Because he holds fast to me in
love, I will deliver him;
I will protect him, because he knows my name.
When he calls to me, I will answer him;
I will be with him in trouble;
I will rescue him and honor him.
With long life I will satisfy him
and show him my salvation."

# Acknowledgements

Many people have encouraged and contributed their input into the writing of *Redemption Suite*. I appreciate their wisdom. Thank you, Jacqueline Allen, Charlotte Burke, Kathryn Fisher, Peter Koch, Elizabeth Reinker, and Will Watt.

# PRELUDE

Nightmare
*June 5, 1939*

*Arnie after me…King Kong's face…breathe hot with moonshine…knife—fire surging up through me…ton of bricks…unwashed…reeking…speaking words from hell… Help me, Jay-Lee…hel…ll…p…*

"Oh! Oh!" Jess screamed. She took a deep breath, and another paroxysm surged through her tiny form. "It's my birth pangs! Oh, Jay-Lee, my sweet twin, why can't you be here with me? Why did this happen?"

Jess got up from her cot in the cold, damp early June morning and went to get Mrs. Smithers. She knocked on the woman's bedroom door. "Ma'am…it's time. I'm havin' my pains."

Mrs. Smithers, her landlady and midwife, crawled from her bed and threw her wrap about her. She hugged the girl and took her back into the little room where Jess had been for the last few months, set up what she needed to assist in the birth, and five hours later…

"You have a beautiful little girl, Jess. Here, you want to hold her? What will you name her?"

Tears ran down Jess's cheeks as she took the baby in her arms but handed her back to Mrs. Smithers without cuddling the infant. "No. She isn't mine to hold or name, ma'am."

The nightmare continued in real time.

# OVERTURE

*Tampa, Florida*
*December 25, 2009*

The music in Lynelle Van Sant's soul went beyond the music she played. Her parents had not called her Lynelle, nor did they go by Van Sant. At age twelve, however, her former name no longer existed for her. If music represented Lynelle's life, then it had more than its share of minor requiems. On the other hand, joyful triumphs of life had added beauty and created a magnificent soul-spilling melody on everyone she met. To have been a part of Lynelle's life afforded an opportunity to find the music in one's own soul. Today, December 25, 2009, would be a special carol that celebrated her release from seventy years of hiding and a return to who she was meant to be.

You might say Lynelle Van Sant had been born at age twelve, but how does a girl begin to tell the story of a life that starts at age twelve?

# First Movement

# CHAPTER 1

## *"I'll Fly Away" by Albert E. Brumley*

*Lenoir, North Carolina*
*June 8, 1939*

Twelve-year-old Jess heard the whimper of her two-day-old baby from the next room. The midwife crooned to the baby as she fed her. In Jess's mind, she smelled the baby scent, felt the touch of the miniature hand on her face and the labor pains. *How can such a tiny thing—only five pounds—cause such pain, such fire?*

Tears wet the pillow beneath her head.

*Baby...not mine to hold and keep... Never call me Mama...someone else her mama. Leave. Now. In the middle of the night. I'll wander, be a runaway. I know women in the hills...birthed their young'un in the morning, tended the garden in the afternoon, and milked the cow before they made supper for their man.* "I can do this," she said to the pillow.

Then she thought about Jay-Lee and how she would never to see her identical twin again if she ran away. *How can I do it?*

She cried as she rocked back and forth on her cot, cradling the damp pillow in arms that ached to hold the baby, to feed her. She thought of how they had lost Ma and Pa. She would rather her baby never know her than to lose her the way they lost their parents.

She made up her mind. She would not stay. *After all,* she thought, *she's not some dolly to play with. She needs a real mother. I'll leave here, forget the baby—the past—my twin Junie Lee—Jay-Lee—my brothers. Forever. Life begins today.*

Terrors welled through her sore body—dread to stay and dread to leave. She feared the baby's father would learn of her whereabouts and follow her. *He'd hurt me again. Arnie Frampton will never hurt me again! That's the last time his name will cross my thoughts. From here on, he remains nameless.*

Quiet settled over the house again. Once she heard the midwife snore, Jess gathered her resolve to run away. Although grateful for the midwife's hospitality, the time to go had come. She spread the covers over the cot where she had slept for the last few months, pulled a hair brush through her thick curls and, without further thought, laid the brush back on the dresser.

Her focus centered on what to take with her more than on her hair. She piled on all the clothes she could wear and gathered what she could stuff into a pillowcase—extra undergarments, her one good dress, a sweater, a nightie, and clean rags. She picked up the scrap of paper with the poem her sister had handed her when she left school in April. She read it once more:

> I'm gonna miss my twin, so hurry back.
> When you're not my right arm, I'm way off track.
> But in these days while we're apart,
> I'll hold you ever close within my heart.
> Junie Lee Vance

Then she wadded the scrap of paper into a little ball and shouldered her tote. *Heavy! But got to take it.*

Jess tiptoed into the kitchen. A lamp from the street shed enough light so she didn't need to light the oil lamp. She lifted the lid on the cookstove and tossed the little verse onto the embers. There were enough live coals remaining to turn the wad of paper to ash before she replaced the lid. *The past is now ashes.*

*Food.* She drank some milk right from the bottle in the icebox and looked about the room while she drank it. Asparagus stalks, fresh from the garden yesterday, stood in a tub of water on the table. She took four stalks. She cut off several hunks from a round of hoop cheese on the counter and wrapped them in waxed paper. She helped herself to leftover cornbread on the back of the cookstove, still warm from last evening. All this food she added to her pillowcase.

She shivered, sucked in a deep breath, and listened again for the baby and her hostess. Not a sound. She slipped out the back door, went to the privy, and then set off to her life as a runaway, trying to forget her baby—a part of her—left behind.

She turned her eyes toward the west as though she could see the mountains in the dark, inhaled deeply, and turned away. *Got to get far away from the mountains—and him.* To think about him made her want to throw up. *Anywhere I can't hear the cries of the precious young 'un.* She hesitated in her thoughts. *I'm a runaway.*

She hummed to herself, "I'll fly away, fly away, oh glory, I'll fly away…"

Jay-Lee and she had talked about running away when they were ten years old after reading *Huckleberry Finn. But enough of the past. Stop it!* Except for the old runaway idea, she had to put the past behind her. Now at four o'clock in the morning and dark, she started down the road. Early in June, the sun would not be up until six.

*I'll head away from the mountains. If I leave now, maybe I can get out of town by sunup. Which way would Jay-Lee go? Wish we could run away together.* She stamped her foot. *No! No! I must not think of her.*

As she made her way away from the life she had known before, she shifted her pillowcase tote bag from one shoulder to the next. The support from her crepe-soled saddle oxfords lent at least a little comfort to her journey even if they were secondhand.

She threaded her way along a little creek for an hour when she came to where the creek flowed into a larger river. She didn't know the name of the river, but she followed it. The sky had begun to lighten up. Because she didn't want anyone to find her, she hugged the undergrowth along the river like a box turtle.

She grunted. "I can't go any faster. I'm plum tuckered out from birthing the baby. Bleeding too, and drat it. It hurts."

She soon came to a bridge across the river. Seeing the deep waters roiling beneath her brought to mind how to end her misery.

"How about I jump in the river…no reason to live, is there? If I'm dead, nothin' else to fear. Can't swim." She stood staring, tears welling then spilling. Stepping farther onto the bridge to the edge, setting down her bag, she held onto the flimsy railing, and stared at the roiling water. *It would be easy.*

There had been heavy rains for the last week, and the river was swollen but not to flood stage. The water looked deep. She stood there for ten minutes in hopes she might drum up courage to cast her frail frame over the railing and into the water. She tried to empty her head of all but jumping in the river.

"No!" a voice said. Surprised, she looked around. *Did I say that?* "No, it's not right." She stepped back. "God…if there is one."

Her mind dredged up the horrors of the last nine months, things she didn't want to think about, but the thoughts intruded and overcame all other senses. The God thought held on stronger than the urge to end it all.

But after her ten-minute reverie, her surroundings caught her attention, and her self-talk faded. The joyful sounds of birds lifted her spirits. A mockingbird gave a concert on a tree on the far side of the bridge. Wild roses perfumed the air and mixed with the aroma of food from a nearby store. The odors interrupted her thoughts. A light in front of the store reflected off a truckload of watermelons. A woman in the back of the truck tossed the watermelons to a man, who stacked them in front of the store. They sang an Uncle Dave Macon song, "Watermelon Smilin' on the Vine." The familiarity brought a smile to Jess's face.

She shuddered at the thought of what she almost had done. She knew killing herself would be wrong. *I heard that in Sunday school.* She took a deep breath to dismiss what she had considered.

Her thoughts now turned to her stomach—it growled. *Reckon the watermelon folks'll be after some breakfast. I don't have any money, so maybe a bite of my corn bread.*

As Jess tucked herself behind a tree and munching on the dry bread, she noticed the truck had a different license plate from the North Carolina plates. The colors were opposite, red on white rather than white on red, a 1939 Florida tag.

"I can go to Florida and be far away."

She watched until all of the watermelons were unloaded. Aromas of fried ham and coffee made her stomach rumble, so she bit off another hunk of the corn bread and fantasized. *Mm, mm...hot cornbread slathered with sorghum molasses.*

After the couple unloaded the truck, they went inside the store. Since no one else lingered about, concealed by undergrowth, she edged by the truck and started down the road.

"Wait! How about I take a ride to Florida instead of a walk?"

With wary steps, she inched toward the truck and around the back side and peeked in the back. She saw a big canvas tarpaulin cover and straw. *Perfect.* She climbed over the back bumper and slid beneath the canvas. With her tote as a pillow, she nested on the straw. *Guess this is my bed.* A sweet watermelon aroma saturated the straw, but she looked in vain for a stray hunk of the melon. While no fit bed for a tramp, let alone a girl, she dozed off for a few minutes.

Then she heard the doors to the truck open. The couple had returned. She held her breath in fear they would see the movement of her chest beneath the tarp.

With her head up against the back of the cab, she could hear the chatter of their voices as if she were in the back seat of a car.

The man bragged. "Shore made good on that deal, didn't we, Siney?"

"Oh, Ollie, what a great breakfast. Them biscuits was better than Mama's, and that's sayin' a lot. Always helps when ya git a free breakfast, a jug of coffee, and bag of donuts on top of cash. Feller paid in cash dollars too. Even with the country jes' gettin' back on its feet, I still don't trust them bank checks." Siney rattled the bag of donuts.

"Hey! Don't rattle the sugar off our dessert."

Once Ollie started the engine, the girl could hear only brief snatches of the conversation. Her stomach growled at the thought of a bite into a sugary treat. As the truck bounced along the unpaved road, her bed became a lumpy, bumpy pallet. It reminded her of a hayride they had gone on last Halloween as the straw poked at her bare legs. The truth dawned on her at last. Running away had gone beyond an idea. Reality had set in.

Fearful her ride might hear her through the back of the cab, she muttered softly, "So much for comfort! I'm libel to bleed to death. It might be an adventure, but I'm leaving—leaving my mountains, my baby, my sweet twin. Don't cry. Don't think about it. Ever." A groan escaped her lips, and tears ran down her cheeks.

But she did begin to think about the baby again. She longed to hold the tiny infant in her arms and thought up a little ditty to distract her mind and to keep from crying.

> Donuts are sweet, coffee is strong,
> To leave my baby can't be so wrong.
> Straw beds are scratchy, canvas is rough.
> Life as runaway's bound to be tough.
> Where do I go? What'll I do?
> Who knows if this ride will ever be through?
> Though I am hungry, might as well dream
> of string beans and taters and peaches and cream.

Throughout the long morning, she kept from starvation with small bites of asparagus, cheese, or corn bread. Although she had no grasp of how long a trip to Florida would take, she had a vague concept her food needed to last more than one day. With no liquid to wash the food down, she ate the asparagus to supply moisture.

As the sun beat down on the truck and the heat rose beneath the canvas, Jess became more and more miserable. Her legs itched from the straw and truck bed grit; blood ran down her leg. Heat, smells, and thirst compounded her misery. She longed for the icy water of the little creek near the school back in the mountains and fantasized how the cold water would cool her feet. She didn't want to think of those days, but the context of her life revolved around the wonderful days back in the mountains. She thought about the good times—*duets on the piano, tricks played on the other girls, teachers, the boys when the twins would switch identities*. Then her eyes teared up again.

Since she didn't want to think of the past, she imagined the future. She wondered whom she would be wherever she ended up. *I'll have to make up a person to become. I'll make up a new name. I can be Lynn—without the Jessie. Lynn or Lynelle. Yes, Lynelle! What about a last name? It'll come to me.*

# Chapter 2

## *"Way Down Upon the Suwannee River" by Stephen Foster*

When the sun stood high overhead, Ollie pulled the truck into a gas station, filled up with gasoline, and had the oil checked. Then he parked the truck under a tree.

As the pair left the truck to go inside, Ollie belched loudly. "Them donuts didn't last long. Reckon they got some chili dogs and fries in here? Smells like it to me."

Siney rolled her eyes. "Ya know, Ollie, yer downright crude. But shore does sound tasty. Looks like they got a fan in the window, so it'll be cooler if we eat inside rather than in this hot ol' truck."

Although hunger dogged her, the thought of chili nauseated "Lynelle," the name she wanted to convince herself she had become. With care, she lifted the canvas to peer at the couple through the slats in the side of the truck; she breathed in fresh air she hungered for in her confinement beneath the tarp. She could see the couple were young, maybe in their twenties.

She also saw an outhouse. "Aah, that's what I need." As soon as Ollie and Siney went into the gas station, Lynelle slipped over the opposite side of the truck away from sight of the gas station and made a beeline to the outhouse despite her weakness.

It had been cool when they left Lenoir. Now, however, the flat country's sticky heat had added sweat to her already soiled clothes. She disrobed, tossed the worst of them into the hole, redressed with the outer layers, and replaced her bloomers and padding. Although her dress was soiled, she didn't want to put on her good dress—one she had hand-sewn herself.

With no place to get water in the outhouse, she longed for a drink of water. She needed to clean herself too. When she emerged, she spied a little brook on the other side of the truck, a little muddy from a recent rain. She checked to see if anyone lingered about. When she saw no one, she edged toward the brook, sank her face into the water, and lapped it like a dog. Once she slaked her thirst, she plunged her arms and legs into the brook. Ahhh! She cleaned up as well as she could and hurried back to the truck.

The lack of traffic helped her make it back into the truck bed without discovery. As she slipped beneath the tarp, she heard Ollie and Siney emerge from the gas station and head for their turns in the privy.

Soon, they were back, and the truck knocked along the road again—a test for her already sore body. She shook her head. *Reckon my driver got nary idea he's toting such poor produce as me.*

As Jess contemplated her new name, Lynelle, she dozed off and on for hours but never a sound sleep. Toward evening, they arrived on a smooth road. When she peeped out from her hideaway, the girl could tell they were headed due south because the sun flamed on the western horizon on the right-hand side of the truck. Her dark-blue eyes lingered on the beauty of the colors splashed across the sky and thought about the sunrises back home in the mountains.

She made up a ditty about the sunset.

> As the sun sets in the west, when day is done,
> and wonder if you'll ever have won
> a life finished with the sun
> with beauty, in spite of being on the run.

Lynelle hoped they would stop soon so she could get a good sleep, but she worried they would pull off to the roadside and crawl into the back to sleep. *They'd have me arrested!*

Ollie drove until long after the sun had set and on into the night. In the wee hours of the morning, he pulled off the road. Lynelle held her breath again. She dreaded discovery. But no, they left the truck with a small cardboard suitcase and went into some roadside cabins.

Lynelle could not see much beyond the lights in front of the cabins, but as soon as they had gone into their cabin for the night, she crawled out of her hidey-hole and walked around. Although there were picnic tables and trees close by, she saw no place except trees where she could relieve herself. In the dim reflection from the cabins, she saw a hand pump and bucket in the picnic area. "It'll make do."

After a good drink, she soaked her head.

*Ay, la! Forgot to put my hairbrush in the tote. No toothbrush either.*

She wetted her hair down and finger combed it to get the straw out.

With her thirst quenched, she carried the bucket back into the trees out of sight of anyone who might be about, far enough away from the cabins and off the road so no one could see her. She cleaned up as best as she could. By now, her blood-soaked, sweaty clothes stuck to her, so she discarded some more in a trash barrel but not the dress.

*I'll be plumb naked before we ever get to Florida! Least ways, I still got stuff for…*

She didn't want to think of the horror she wanted to escape.

After another long gulp of water, she crept back to the straw and ate the remainder of her cornbread. She had broken off a twig from a bush and picked at the food stuck in her teeth. Then she curled up on the straw and fell asleep in moments. She slept until the predawn sky lightened.

*Come on, Jess—Lynelle. Tend to yourself before the waggoneer pulls himself outta bed and finds ya.*

Before she could make her move, however, her chauffeur and wife put their bag into the truck. The sun had not risen yet. She held her breath in hopes they would go into the diner next to the cabins so she could relieve herself. They did.

As soon as they were inside, she snaked over the side of the truck and back to the picnic area, conducted her needed business, and got back into the truck. She grabbed the last stalk of asparagus and ate it. Again, she had evaded discovery.

When the couple returned, they carried with them a jug of coffee.

*Wish I had a sip of their coffee even if it's chicory.*

Lynelle heard Ollie say they were now in South Carolina. She could picture South Carolina on the map she remembered from her geography at school.

He went on to say, "Reckon we'll be into Georgia by lunchtime. This here road is good, and with the truck empty, we'll make good time."

Siney whined. "Can't be too soon to get to Florida."

Ollie started the motor, and the two of them sang. "Way down along the Swannee River, far, far away…"

Lynelle knew the song well. She could play it on the piano. She hummed a third part with them, unconcerned they would hear because of the noise of the truck, and drummed her fingers on the truck bed like a piano.

*Maybe I can find a place to live along the Suwanee River, huh?*

She cried again because she wouldn't have a piano. She excelled and loved to play piano. The midwife had an old spinet she played until the baby came.

This second day of travel went a lot easier than the first one because they were riding on a smoother road. The truck still rattled so loud at times she couldn't hear Ollie and Siney at all. When she could hear them, however, she put her ear close to the back of the truck. The voices of other humans comforted her.

She heard Ollie say something about Key West. She had a vague knowledge of Key West from US geography. It was the southernmost point of the United States. She thought, *If Key West is all the way to the bottom of Florida, it would be "far, far away." Maybe I can go there.*

The couple stopped for gas and lunch. She looked through the slats. The place had a privy and a water fountain. She made her move with haste and back to the truck, but fingers of hunger grabbed her stomach. She had eaten up everything she brought with her. She longed for a scrap of bread. In response to her realization the food was gone, her stomach gnawed and growled.

She wondered if they could hear her belly growl through the back window of the truck. As she crawled in, she saw the bumpy road had bounced a piece of watermelon loose from somewhere. She grabbed it and sucked out the juice as she ate the flesh down to the edge of the rind. Then she ate the rind. It didn't matter that it was filthy.

The girl sensed they had gotten off the good road and were on an unpaved road again. Now they headed west.

It must have been midnight or later when she heard them yell, "Florida!" Soon afterward, they stopped at roadside cabins for the night. This time, not only a picnic area but also real toilets with running water served the site. As soon as they were settled in their cabin, the girl once again left her nest and took care of her needs. She saw a sign over the office: "State Line Cabins." She wandered about the picnic area, delighted to find blackberries. Loads of them. She ate until her stomach no longer growled. She cleaned up again in the restroom and went back to the truck bed.

She slept off and on all night. Her body, sore from the bumpy ride and hard surface of the truck bed, kept Lynelle asleep a lot longer than she had intended. When she crawled out and went to the restroom, she hurried but not fast enough. Just as she had started to scrub the purple stains from her face, she heard the truck doors close and the engine start.

"Oh, no!" she nearly screamed but caught herself. Instead, she whispered to herself, "Missed my ride, lost my bag, so I guess from here on, I'm a beggar."

# Chapter 3

## *"Come Thou Fount" by Robert Robinson*

*Florida*
*June 9, 1939*

Lynelle stood in the doorway of the outhouse and watched the truck travel southward. An old song came to mind: "I'm prone to wander, Lord, I feel it…"

"La…what'll I do? I'm in Florida, but where? And my rags are in that ol' pillowcase—and my beautiful good dress!" Tears joined the blackberry stains on her cheeks.

She looked down the road in the direction the truck went. The headlights reflected off the trees and the road. There were no houses. All she could see were trees and a long road ahead.

The notion of walking, walking, and walking overwhelmed her. Panic rose from her belly to her neck. "How am I gonna survive? Just jump out in front of the next truck and end it all."

The God thought reemerged as she looked southward at the road.

"Well, I suppose I could be a beggar around here as well as anywhere. They say beggars not only beg. They steal."

As she continued to look down the road where the truck had now disappeared, she repeated her new name. *I'm Lynelle. Lynelle who? I'm a beggar… I'm a beggar, and my name's Lynelle, but I mustn't steal 'cause I'll go to hell!*

Light glimmered in the east. She went back into the restroom, stuffed her bloomers with paper towels, and stuffed another pile into her dress pocket.

Her thoughts were drawn to her stomach. Hunger focused her attention on the cabins. No light shone in the office window, and she saw no one up and about. Lynelle noticed a soda machine and a trash can in front of the office. She sidled up to them with caution. A trash can revealed a half-full bottle of ginger ale. She took it. She found a discarded bread wrapper lying on top with the two heels in it. *Hooray! Good that some folks don't like bread heels.*

She hid back in among the blackberry canes while she ate her stale bread and washed it down with the flat ginger ale.

As she munched on the stale bread crusts, she said, "Hate to think I'll have to get food outta garbage cans in order to live. There must be a better way."

She almost gagged, bringing to mind her ma and pa dying of food poisoning.

"I shoulda jumped in the river in Lenoir. Who do I want to kid? Guess the joke's on me. I reckon I'm killin' myself one day at a time. But what can I do? Someone is bound to catch me and send me back to North Carolina. I need to stay hidden while I'm on the road. If I run into someone who asks questions, what'll I say? 'Excuse me, ma'am. I'm hungry. Can you feed me?'" A mocking laugh punctuated her monologue.

As the sun edged over the horizon, her attention turned away from her pessimistic reverie. She heard the sound of geese, and her eyes caught a glimpse of movement across the road. A bright glint hit her eye. The glint came from a pond as sunrise reflected on the water. A family of wild geese had gathered at the pond. They preened and dunked their heads along the edges, looking for tender aquatic plants for their breakfast. She hid behind a tree and watched them for a while. Seeing the young goslings along with the mature geese reminded her of families. *Something I'll never have. How about I walk into the pond and not come back out?*

She saw no one around and edged across the road. She stood beneath a large tree and tried again to summon courage to go into the pond and not come back out. How long she stood there she could not have told, but again, the geese distracted her as they assembled for a flight. They skimmed out into the middle of the pond and took to the air with loud honks.

The flight of the geese returned her to her resolve to go on—to maintain her own flight to a new life.

Lynelle turned back toward the southbound road. Long strands of gray growth, strange to her, swayed in the morning breeze from huge trees. These trees arched over the road and met like a tunnel. Unfamiliar with Spanish moss or live oaks, she thought it looked like a fairy land as the sun glinted on the damp strands of moss. She entered the magical tunnel and walked southward. *Maybe my fairy godmother will rescue me.*

Soon, the magic disappeared, and she feared someone would spot her on the open road, so she kept to the edges of the fields and undergrowth. Although traffic had been light, if she heard a vehicle coming her way, she hid until they drove by. She trudged on southward.

It had only been three days since the birth of her baby, and her weak body limited how far she could walk. She would walk about a quarter mile, take a rest behind a tree, walk some more, and rest. She was thirsty, wringing wet with perspiration, and miserable. With such slow progress, she made little progress.

Again, random thoughts… *Does it matter? My only destination is to get as far south as possible. I'm not used to this heat. Never had it this hot on the mountain. Don't think about it. Hope I can find a place—maybe a house with some laundry on the line. Get some clean clothes—rags…baby diapers.*

The thought of diapers caught in her throat. *The baby…oh, my sweet little baby. Never to see her again. Never to see Jay-Lee and our brothers again. How can I live? I might as well jump out in front of the next car headed this way.*

Back in the trees again, she huddled behind a huge tree with branches sweeping the ground. She sat down on a huge limb low along the ground and sobbed uncontrollably.

## JUNE TITUS

When she gained control, she took stock in herself. Filth covered her. Her milk had come in and oozed down the front of her dress. This dress, an everyday dress, had been well made by her own hand…ruined… *Rurrn'd,* she thought in her mountain dialect. She had made the dress in school last fall—all hand-stitched, a colorful calico print with a white collar. Her shoes that were supposed to be brown-and-white saddle shoes had taken on the appearance of a pig farmer's work boots. Her fingernails were black, her mouth tasted like the pigpen back home smelled, and her hair felt like a tangled mess of chicken wire.

"We always brushed each other's hair each night before we went to bed…oh, Jay-Lee." She sobbed again. Her head itched—a lot.

She scratched one spot, and then another would itch. "Reckon it's cooties!" Now instead of the tears, she laughed—hysterical laughter. The idea of head lice seemed to set her resolve to go on to find a place, beggar or not.

*Hey, Lynelle!*

"Who me?"

*Yes, you! You don't need to feel sorry for yourself. Get back on the road.*

But the first step she took she stepped on a hill of fire ants. "What the…?" She did the first thing on her mind. She grabbed paper towels from her pocket and sat back on the tree limb, removed the shoe and sock, and rubbed off what she could see on her leg and her shoe. She tossed the towels and the sock on the ground behind the tree limb. She beat the offended shoe on the tree limb in hopes she could knock off any unseen ants. Then she took off the other shoe and sock and put the sock in her pocket with her paper towels from the outhouse. She examined the shoe and beat it on the tree limb again to loosen any ants.

Her leg burned with fire, so she did what she would have done back in the mountains had she run into a patch of burn hazel. She got a gob of mud from the nearby stream and rubbed it over her leg. "I hope that works."

Her mud remedy seemed to cool the fire on her leg. With the shoes back on her feet, sockless, she traveled down the road again.

Familiar flowers—purple daisies, ditch lilies, and lots of clover—sprinkled here and there alongside the road, brought a smile to her face. Other flowers too, although foreign to her, encouraged her. And more blackberries. She picked a large handful of the berries and ate them as she walked along.

She remembered something about blackberries. *Hey, old granny women back in the mountains always said blackberries were good to control blood after a baby. Reckon it's a good thing I found some.* She grabbed another handful at the next patch, gaining a few briar scratches in the process.

She walked off and on all day. By dark, she had made little progress. There were some little farms back off the road but no places close by where she might steal some laundry to clean herself without being seen. By now, she had walked less than five miles, but she thought she must be halfway to Key West. She wanted real food. Her diet of blackberries, remnants of someone else's discarded bread, a few swallows of ginger ale didn't begin to fill her stomach. She stopped from time to time and filled the empty ginger ale bottle with water from the little stream alongside the road.

The sun had set. In the dusky evening, she sought for a refuge so she could sleep. Blissfully unaware of the dangers of wild animals, she crawled into the crook of a huge low tree limb and slept. After a few hours' sleep, a noise awakened her. She opened her eyes to stare into the eyes of a raccoon. She let out a squeal, and the critter took off as her babies pitter-pattered after her, their shadows reflecting in the moonlight. After her heart stopped pounding, she couldn't get back to sleep. The 'coon's visit got her wondering what other critters were out there, so she went out onto the road and walked again. "Hope I'm still headed south."

At first, a half-moon guided her steps, but then as morning approached, a storm threatened. Along with the threat came desperation. She had used up all the paper towels except what she needed for pads. She stepped back into the trees, got some leaves, and cleaned off where blood had dripped down her legs. As she looked down the road ahead, she cried out, "I have got to find help. So, God, if You are out there, help me."

# CHAPTER 4

## "The Old Country Church" by J. D. Sumner and James W. Vaughn

*Farmer's Corner, Florida*
*June 10, 1939*

Lynelle's eyes opened wide at the vision in front of her. What she saw ahead looked like a church steeple above the trees. She walked about a quarter-mile and came upon some buildings: a gas station, a general store, a post office, a little brown country church with a steeple and bell, a four-room school, several houses, and a bakery.

Although too early for the stores to be open, hunger urged her on. She edged her way toward the bakery. The baker must have already begun to bake fresh bread because a yeasty aroma tantalized Lynelle's stomach into a loud growl. The sign on the front read "Van Sant's Bakery. Closed."

She had no money to buy bread. "If I wait by the door till it opens, I can beg."

As she walked up the path to the door, it hit her. *Hmmm, Van Sant. Close to Vance.* "That's who I am—Lynelle Van Sant." A light glowed from within. Lynelle crept to the window. She could see an older woman inside. The woman carried fresh bread and other baked goods from the back and placed them in a glass front display case.

A big red dog met her and wagged his huge red feather duster tail. He barked then added a growl like the one in her stomach and nuzzled his welcome into her hand. The touch of the beautiful Irish Setter with a graying muzzle comforted her.

The woman lumbered to the door to see why all the commotion. Perhaps in her forties, she could be counted as neither plain or pretty, but her pleasant face made her seem beautiful to Lynelle. She presented herself as an impressive figure, tall and big-boned with a plump tummy. She wore her gray-blond hair pulled back into a long braid and wrapped in a neat bun behind her neck.

"Settle down, O'Hara. What's got you so riled up this morning?"

Then she spied Lynelle, half-hiding in the shadows. The woman's blue eyes penetrated the little beggar. "Bakery's not open yet, young'un. Come back at eight o'clock."

The woman turned back to go inside and then spun about and shot a suspicious glare at the girl standing before her. "Wait! What in the world? Who are you? What do you want?"

Lynelle didn't miss the woman's eyes as they ran over her body head to toe and back to the milk stains on the front of her dress. She realized the woman could see everything. No way could Lynelle hide the milk stains or the blood.

Lynelle usually spoke in her mountain dialect, but she knew how to speak with proper English. She used her best grammar and most polite voice. "Sorry to bother you, ma'am, but I'm hungry. I would like to have a piece of bread. That's all. Well, maybe if you have some old rags? Then I'll be on my way."

"You get in here, you little beggar! You look like you're 'bout to keel over. You come on in here and tell me what's goin' on." The woman crossed her arms and glared down at Lynelle.

"Who are ya?" she repeated. "I ain't seen ya around here before. Are you some of that bunch from over next to the swamp? Now come in here and tell me what's goin' on."

"Beggar? I reckon I am." Lynelle cautiously entered into the room. "I'm sorry, I'm so dirty, but…"

With her head down the beggar stumbled a response. "I'm…uh…L…I'm Lynelle."

She looked at the woman with fear in her eyes, but she plunged forward with the idea that had popped in her head when she saw the name on the store. She hesitated a moment and then stamped her foot as though she had stomped her fear. With shoulders held straight, she said, "I'm Lynelle Van Sant, same…" She pointed to the sign on the bakery, as though daring the woman to challenge her.

The woman's shoulders shook. She pressed her lips together to stifle a laugh, shook her head, and cocked her eye at the little wayfarer. Then she broke out in boisterous laughter.

Once she got her laughter under control, she spoke in a no-nonsense voice. "Likely story! Not that I believe you, Lynelle Van Sant, but if you like it, I won't argue with ya. Come in here. If O'Hara says yer okay, who am I to argue with him? We know all about strays, don't we, old boy?" she said as she ruffled his fur fondly.

O'Hara responded with a bark.

As calmness seemed to float around her, Lynelle Van Sant knew at that very moment Jess no longer existed.

The woman motioned for Lynelle to follow her and led her to a huge kitchen behind the store. "Likely story!" she repeated, "but we'll let it go for now. So where did you come from anyway?"

Not waiting for Lynelle to answer, the woman led her to a powder room and gave her a washcloth and towel. Then she grabbed a dish towel and handed it to her. "Reckon you'll know what to do with this till we have something better." She gave her a paper sack. "Put yer trash in this poke and come out. I'll give ya some food."

Lynelle did the best she could to clean up before she went back to the woman in the kitchen.

The woman pointed to a table.

With a wary look at her rescuer, Lynelle sat down.

The woman put a glass of cold milk and a slice of hot bread slathered with butter in front of her. "Here, eat this."

The woman sat across from Lynelle, lit a cigarette, and watched her. She took two or three drags before she stubbed it out in the ashtray. "Tryin' to quit," she mumbled.

Lynelle gulped the milk and took several bites of bread before she answered, "I hitched a ride on a watermelon truck, but the people didn't know I hid back there. They spent the night up the road at those state line cabins, but they left before I finished in the outhouse.

I walked all day yesterday and slept a little on a big tree branch close to the ground. Well, I slept until a raccoon and her brood woke me up. Thought I might try to walk to Key West."

The woman jerked her head back shot her eyes wide open. She handed Lynelle another slice of bread with butter and jelly on it. "You're lucky a raccoon and not a wild cat woke you up. You were fixin' to walk to Key West? Why, it'd take you all summer, but from the looks of you, you'd die before you got to Jasper!"

Lynelle had no idea where Jasper might be located. She said nothing until she finished the bread. The baker lady refilled her glass with more milk.

"I'm runnin' away from a bad boy who hurt me."

The woman stood, watching her visitor. She nodded as she leaned against a Hoosier cabinet, but she said nothing for a long time. She scrutinized Lynelle, nodding either up and down or shaking it side to side while Lynelle ate the second slice of bread and butter and finished her glass of milk.

After several minutes, the woman sat down again at the table across from her and looked her straight in the eye. "Okay, darlin', if you're Lynelle Van Sant, then I must be your old maid cousin, Florence Van Sant. You call me Aunt Flossie. I hate the name Florence. Your momma's dead, and your daddy can't take care of ya anymore. You ain't got no other kin. You've been sick, so you've hitched a ride down here from Georgia to live with me."

She waited until the made-up tale sank in and looked upward toward heaven. *Help me, Lord!*

Then she went on. "I can see you musta had a baby. What? A week ago?"

"Monday."

"Okay, that's only four days ago. Good grief!" She wagged her head side to side.

"So we need to take care of things and get you settled. Reckon I'm a pushover for strays like O'Hara out there. But since I need some help around this place… Maybe I'm a fool, but if yer a good girl and behave yourself—like you don't steal from me—you can live here with me, work this summer in the bakery, and then go to school in the fall. I ain't got any young'uns, and I could use the help."

Lynelle's eyes bugged out, and her mouth dropped open.

Flossie laughed. "Good thing there ain't flies in the house, or they'd be dessert for yer bread and milk."

Then Flossie gave another hearty laugh. "Maybe someday you and me, well, we'll drive down to Key West. I ain't never been there, but why not? All right, Lynelle Van Sant, or whatever your real name is, we will need to work together on this. To be honest, I don't have any kin folk or anyone else, let alone some cousin up in Georgia. I might need you as much as you need me. So first, you need to tell me who you are, and maybe we can work out something."

Lynelle hemmed and hawed a bit, took a deep breath, then plunged into her sad tale—if only a brief skeleton of her story.

"I'm…I used to be Jessie Lynn Vance. I went by Jess." The way she related her tale reflected how dead she felt inside. She talked in a rote fashion with little emotion in her voice. "I decided to drop the Jessie, call myself Lynelle. Since Van Sant and Vance were pretty close, I'd like to use it…uh… if you will let me?"

She became more animated. "I never heard the name Van Sant before, and it sounded elegant. The boy who hurt me didn't act right—slow-witted. I had his baby on Monday. The baby will be adopted and have a good home back in the mountains with folks I know of"—she shook her head as she lowered it—"but I had to get away."

She lifted her head, and with pleading in her eyes, she said, "I don't ever want to talk about it again. I want to change my life."

Flossie remained quiet and allowed Lynelle to gather her thoughts.

The girl hesitated a moment, and then with a glimmer of hope on her face, she looked at the woman and shrugged. "May I be your niece—cousin? I want to start a new life."

Flossie nodded and took a deep sigh. "Okay. First, it is fine for us to call you Van Sant. Easier when folks ask questions. If you stay here, you will be known as Lynelle. I think it's such a pretty name."

"Lynelle. Lynelle Van Sant. Yes! I'm Lynelle Van Sant!"

"How old are you?"

"Twelve. I'll be thirteen in August."

"Good grief!" Flossie shook her head in disbelief. She drew in a deep sigh. "Okay, thirteen would place you in seventh or eighth grade. Have you been to school?"

"Oh, yes. Our parents died when we were six years old, and we went to a mission school and stayed with a family close to the school. We were in seventh grade, but I couldn't finish the year, because—well, you know."

Flossie Van Sant nodded. "You keep saying 'we.' Who is the 'we'?"

At last, Lynelle cried. She sobbed nonstop for several minutes. *How can I tell her I left my right arm in Crossnore—my twin—my Jay-Lee?*

Flossie patted her on the back and smoothed over her matted hair for a few minutes and then left her alone to work through her tears, while she went to the store front to open up for the day. With all in order for the customers as they came in, she went back to the girl.

Dry-eyed now, Lynelle stood when Flossie came into the room. "Ma'am, what should I do now?"

"Well, the first thing, Lynelle, is you need to drop the 'ma'am' and call me Aunt Flossie," she said with a smile. "Good idea. Don't you think?"

Lynelle smiled back and nodded her filthy head.

"Next, we get you into the shower and see if you can remove a few layers of watermelon juice and straw and other things. Maybe you will look a bit more human." Flossie restrained a giggle and scrunched up her nose, more than suggesting Lynelle didn't smell too good.

Lynelle giggled with her as she followed this new aunt up a narrow, angled staircase to the second floor. Lynelle saw two closed doors at either end of the hall, a smaller sitting room in the middle, with a desk, a couple of chairs, and a well-worn Bible on a little table. Across from the sitting room, an open door showed the bathroom.

Flossie saw Lynelle look at the Bible. She nodded. "Ya know, Lynelle, I think God led you here to me for His purposes."

Lynelle swallowed but didn't respond. *I'm not sure God has anything to do with this. A good God wouldn't have let this happen to me.*

Flossie, noting the girl's lack of response, shook her head and pointed to the one door at the front. "There's the bedroom where you'll sleep. I'm in the back. I sit here in the early evenings and read before I go to bed.

"Okay, now here is the bathroom. You need to take a shower."

"A shower? I...I never...we had a tub."

"Nothing to it. I'll show you. It's a lot healthier than a bath because it'll wash yer dirt right down the drain."

Aunt Flossie showed her how to turn it on, adjust the temperature, and then she pulled a curtain around the tub. "There you are. You'll love it.

"When you are done, put on this old robe—mine thirty pounds ago. Here are some clean cloths you can use for pads until we get some store-bought ones and a pair of my old bloomers. Too big, but here's a couple of safety pins to fix them. Since you don't have clean underclothes, when I close up the bakery at noon, I'll run over to the general store and buy some things you will need right away. I won't be gone long. Now you need to get yourself clean from your baby so you don't get an infection."

Lynelle's face turned red to even think about this intimate conversation, yet she yielded to the mercy of this wonderful new cousin or aunt—she didn't know which. She didn't know what to say, so she nodded.

Aunt Flossie wrinkled her nose again at the malodorous clothes and reached out her hand. "Here, give me your stuff, and I'll be able to find some duds at the store the same size. Oughta pitch these in the incinerator with the contents of that paper poke."

Lynelle undressed and dumped the clothes in a little pile on the floor. She turned her naked body away from the woman and hesitated. Tears hung on her eyelids. She took a deep breath and explained "we."

"Ma'am...Aunt Flossie, 'we' means my twin sister, Junie Lee, and me. I always called her Jay-Lee. It hurts to think about her, but how can I ever forget her? What must she be suffering with me gone away? When I left, she said, 'With you gone, it will be like I've lost my...I called Jay-Lee my right arm—my identical twin! I don't want to talk about her."

The woman's face paled, and compassion set deep in her eyes. "Oh, darlin'! I know kinda how you might feel. We weren't twins, but I had a sister, Francie, eleven months older'n me. We were close as twins. We did everything together. We all had the Spanish influenza back in '20. She and Momma both died. Daddy and I got well, but there's not a day gone by that I don't think about her. But as the years go by, it sometimes gives me comfort to think about her. I know she's in heaven waitin' for me."

Lynelle's tears started up again.

"Are you sure you don't want your sister to know you are all right?" Aunt Flossie asked.

Lynelle shook her head. "No, ma'am. It will be better if she thinks I'm dead."

Flossie's jaw dropped as she pondered how to respond. "So why would she think such a thing? Oh no—can't be so. Lynelle, you can always talk to me and share anything you want. I can't judge you for what you believe you needed to do. But please talk to me when you ought to chat. I can't take away the hurt, but I can listen."

"Thank you, ma'am."

Lynelle shook her head as she crawled into the shower with caution. *She doesn't need to know I almost jumped in the river.*

She thought of another verse she should write about her life. *Who am I? Why am I here?*

Flossie closed the door and let out a "Whew! What have I done? I'm nothin' but a sweet old cream puff! Sheesh!" She walked away and let Lynelle alone.

The bell clanged from the front of the bakery, and she trudged down the stairs and back to work and served several customers over the morning.

It didn't take Lynelle but a moment to decide she loved the shower. She scrubbed her body with the ivory soap and let the water run over her tired body. As she slid the soapy washcloth over her slippery-clean skin, the soreness left, and her mind traveled into a fantasy land. She thought, *Is this real? Can I be the niece, cousin, or whatever she wants me for me? What will I do with my music? Will I ever play the piano again?*

As the filthy water flowed out of the tub and the fresh water rolled over her hair and body, she spied a bottle of Drene shampoo on the shelf by the bath soap. *Reckon it's okay to use this shampoo on my hair. I always used cake-soap, but this says it'll make my hair shiny.*

Lynelle let the water soak and wet her hair all over. Her thick, tight shoulder-length curls were matted. She might need help to wash her hair. She thought of how she and Jay-Lee always shampooed each other's hair. Then her hair had fallen to her waist, long and beautiful. Jay-Lee had cut it for her before she went to Lenoir. Lynelle chided herself for thinking about Jay-Lee again.

She scrubbed and scratched and squeezed and rinsed until the water ran clear. Although her hair felt clean, the tangles were worse than before. As she crawled out of the tub, she glanced in the mirror on the opposite wall and screwed up her nose. "Look like the wild man from Borneo!"

She wrapped a towel about her hair, pulled on the oversized padded bloomers, donned the bath robe, and headed to the bedroom Aunt Flossie had said would be her own room. She froze when she opened the door and gasped when she went into the bedroom. "Oh! It's beautiful!" She looked around to see the room. She closed her eyes and wondered if she had slipped into a dream. Would it disappear when she opened them again? She took a deep breath, opened them again and, pinched her arm to make sure of her senses. She took it all in before she made another step into the room.

The walls were covered with light-pink wallpaper with tiny roses scattered all over it. A bay window faced the road out front. White louvered shutters that could be opened or closed went all the way to the top of the windows, and lace curtains hung on either side of each window with a valance all around the top. In front of her the oak furniture included a tall wardrobe and a large bedstead with a backboard that reached the ceiling. A hand-crocheted counterpane covered the bed with a deep rose blanket showing through. She turned the other way and saw a tall three-drawer dresser topped with a hat box on one side, a mirror on the other, and a vanity with a carved oak mirror. The vanity had a pink dotted Swiss skirt around it with a padded seat tucked in front of it covered in deep rose velvet. To round out the room, a white wicker chaise longue padded with the same rose velvet sat in one corner.

*I never dreamed I could ever stay in a room this beautiful—even one night. And now it's to be mine? Is it real? If there's a God, maybe He sees me after all.*

Tears came as she thought how much she wished Jay-Lee could be here too. *No! No! No! Can't think of her. Ever. Never.*

Lynelle hated to shut her eyes. *If I close my eyes, it will all disappear when I open them back up. I'll be back in Lenoir or in the back of the watermelon truck.* She pulled the covers back and put the towel she had wrapped about her head onto the pillow. She didn't want to close her eyes as she sank into the softness of a feather bed, but her eyelids were heavy. Her world soon disappeared.

# Chapter 5

## "Wildwood Flower" by Joseph Philbrick Webster

*June 1939*

Flossie hummed "Wildwood Flower" most of the morning. *A wildwood flower's what the little gal reminds me of. She's a dainty trillium or a violet. Aye la!* In between customers, she checked on Lynelle. Each time she had checked, the girl continued to sleep. At last the clock struck noon, and it was time to put the closed sign on the bakery door. Her customers were used to half-days on Saturdays, and she had been busy selling fresh bread, cakes, and dinner rolls all morning and cookies—especially her famous molasses cookies.

She sat at the kitchen table with a cup of coffee, picked up her cigarettes, and smoked two back to back. Then she looked at the pack and tossed them into the trash basket. "I quit! So there! Can't have a young lady around here to take up my bad habits."

Flossie's routine included grocery shopping every Saturday afternoon in Jasper. But she needed clothes for Lynelle first. The almost naked and destitute girl had to have some clothes to wear. The trip to Jasper could wait.

One could walk to any place in Farmer's Corner in minutes. The trek to the general store took three minutes if Flossie walked at a normal pace. O'Hara followed beside her and gave a pleasant bark to each neighbor as they passed. He knew them all. They were, for the most part, youngsters, some about the same age as Lynelle, who took advantage of the warm, breezy June day. They had no concern with how to live.

Flossie shook her head at the contrast. *A far cry from the horrors the poor girl has put up with.*

"Hey, Miss Flossie! Nice day today," one of the girls called to her from a porch swing. Another group of barefoot boys with baseballs, bats, and gloves hailed her as they turned down the path by the post office headed to the field where they liked to play. Sarah Heller and her daughter, Joyce, were on their way to the church to clean for Sunday service. They waved. Everyone knew everyone else in Farmer's Corner—all respectable and sociable neighbors.

Flossie knew it would be a challenge to avoid the gossip. "But I will!" she said to the dog. "I might be a Christian lady, but I'm not above fibbin', and we shore made up a lulu, didn't we, O'Hara?"

O'Hara curled up on the porch floor of the store as Flossie went inside. More neighbors greeted her. Burt Heller, Sarah's husband, and Jimbo Connelly sat at a table with dominoes lined up as they did every Saturday afternoon.

Burt had to get his digs in about his bachelor companion. "Lookin' mighty fine today, Miz Flossie. Ol' Jimbo here might be willin' to take ya to Jasper tonight for a movie, providin' ya bring along a good cherry pie. Hear he's partial to 'em."

She looked down her nose and said, "Good afternoon to you too, Burt. Jimbo."

She went to the dry goods side of the store and found what she needed for Lynelle: undergarments, a cute blue-and-white gingham pinafore, a white puffed-sleeve blouse, some socks, a package of Modess pads, a toothbrush and a tin of tooth powder, and some hair barrettes. She took her items to Fanny Miller, the clerk, and whispered, "My niece has been sick and come to stay with me leastways till she's better. She's from up in Georgia and doesn't have nice things. Thought this dress would look cute on her with her dark hair."

"Oh, it is cute. It's like Shirley Temple or Judy Garland. I hope she gets well soon. I didn't realize you had kin folks over there. Where in Georgia? I have kin in Valdosta."

"A little dirt farm—west—close to Alabama. It's my cousin's daughter, but I call her my niece. Poor girl, her mother died a couple of years ago, and Hank is too sorry to care for her. I'm delighted to have her here."

Flossie had no cousin, at least not there in Georgia as far as she knew. Flossie continued with the scenario she had begun a few hours earlier with Lynelle. She paid Fanny, gathered her purchases, nodded at Burt and Jimbo, and went back to the bakery, O'Hara again at her side.

Lynelle remained sound asleep while Flossie shopped and on into the afternoon. Flossie washed the clothes, even the dress the girl had on when she showed up at the bakery door, and hung them all out to dry. With such a warm and breezy day, the clothes dried within an hour. She ironed the dresses, folded the undergarments, and took everything upstairs to the girl's room.

At two in the afternoon, Flossie stood in the doorway to Lynelle's room. *Hate to waken her, but it ain't good for her to sleep all day and then be up half the night.*

"Lynelle?" she whispered. The girl's head moved a little, but she remained asleep.

Then louder, she said, "Lynelle, it's me, Aunt Flossie. You should try to get up and get some food to eat."

"Huh? Lyn…oh, where…where am I?" Realization dawned on Lynelle. "Oh, yes. Yes, ma'am. I'll get up. This bed is so wonderful." She rolled out like a snail to Aunt Flossie's snickers.

"Yes, it is comfortable. As far back as I remember, I've always slept in the back room. My parents' used this bedroom, and I got a notion to redecorate 'bout a year ago. God brings these kinda notions when they're needed. Glad for ya to live in it."

Lynelle rubbed the sleep from her eyes.

"Now I got some clean clothes for you and some good pads. I hope the clothes fit. I had to do a lot of supposin.' As soon as you are up to it and can travel some, we will go to the stores in Jasper. It's been four days since you had the baby. I never had one, but I know a lot from when I took care of my friends when they had babies. I thought I'd become a midwife, but then I had to help Daddy in the bakery after Momma died. You must be sore, bleedin' a lot, and your breasts are sore."

Lynelle nodded and grimaced.

"You need to keep clean, and we can put ice on your breasts. If you start to leak before they dry up, we can put extra pads inside this brassiere I got you. Here. Try it on to see if it fits. I guessed."

Lynelle didn't know how to put it on because she had never had to wear one before. Aunt Flossie helped her. It fit.

"Good. Now go to the bathroom and clean up a bit, and put on a pair of these bloomers."

When Lynelle came back from the bathroom, Aunt Flossie handed her the new comb and brush for her hair. "Your hair looks like a rat's nest. I may need to help you. In fact, let me check and make sure you don't have cooties."

"It did itch right smart when I was walking down the road yesterday. The shower bath helped a lot. Hope you don't find any."

As Aunt Flossie went through Lynelle's hair section by section, Lynnie grimaced and grunted.

"Sorry. With your curls and as matted as your hair is, I know it hurts. I don't reckon you got any cooties. Shore hope we don't have to cut it none. Did ya use the shampoo by the tub? It makes my hair real nice."

"Yes, ma'am. Thank you. I looked in the mirror and thought I looked like the wild man from Borneo."

Flossie laughed. "Worse. Be an insult to Borneo. My daddy saw them once in a freak show. He said he didn't believe they were from Borneo. They looked American to him."

Lynelle laughed. It felt good to laugh. "You are funny, Aunt Flossie. It helps. I've been sad for so long. You mean there really was someone called the Wild Man from Borneo? I just always heard the expression about someone whose hair was all messed up or a fellow who needed a good shave."

Flossie teared up a bit and grabbed the hairbrush as she thought about her own daddy. "Come on, now. We gotta fix you," she added huskily.

Between the two of them, by suppertime, Lynelle looked like a new person dressed in her beautiful new outfit and her hair combed out, and Flossie didn't have to cut it.

Flossie looked with affection on her new ward. "You look adorable."

"Ma'am—oh, Aunt Flossie—it is so pretty. You know I feel like I'm in a dream in this nice house, and with such a pretty dress. I've never had many dresses and never new ones we didn't make ourselves. We made our own clothes in sewing class. I really like to sew. Sometimes we got good used clothes at what they called the Rag Shakin' store."

"What's Rag Shakin'?" Flossie asked with a laugh.

Lynelle held up the dress in front of her. "Where we went to school, Crossnore, they had a place where we could get a dress someone sent from off the mountain. I never had new clothes at all. Even got our shoes there."

She continued with her wonderment. "And the bedroom is like a place for a princess. I reckon I'll wake up tomorrow and still be in the watermelon truck after all."

"No, darlin', it is real. You are a gift to me, and I'm a gift to you. By the way, I didn't burn your clothes. I washed 'em, and you can wear 'em 'round here. If you made that dress, you done a beautiful seamstress job on it."

As they ate supper, Flossie outlined some of her plans for Lynelle. "I know you said your birthday is in August, but we will need to get a birth certificate for you. Oh, yes, I know someone who can do this for us." She grinned. "Don't ask, and I won't tell. We can change your name and the date of your birth. You will have a whole 'nother identity."

Lynelle's mouth dropped with astonishment. "How can you give me a new identity?"

Aunt Flossie rolled her eyes and grinned. "How about today, June tenth, as your thirteenth birthday? The way you're built, you need to say you're a little older than twelve."

Lynelle shrugged. "What about school records? If I go to school, they will want those records, won't they? I almost finished seventh grade."

"I thought earlier about the lulu of a tale we're a-spinnin', and now it's growin' bigger 'n' bigger. But we can't stop now. Your life depends on it, Lynelle. We have to agree on our story and know it backwards and forwards."

"Yes, ma'am. I read something in school Mark Twain wrote about truth. He said, 'If you tell the truth, you don't have to remember anything.' But I'm not about to argue with you. What can we do to make it work, Aunt Flossie?"

"Well! I'll be! You are one smart young 'un! I know about Mark Twain. Got his *Tom Sawyer* back there on the shelf in the parlor." She pointed toward the back of the house. "But I got some ideas."

Lynelle shrugged. "Yes, ma'am. I'm already in this too deep to stop now!"

"How about we say you were taught at home by your mama with books they got from a school when they bought new ones? Might work. The teacher can test you to see where you belong."

Lynelle shook her head in amazement. It crossed her mind that to live a lie could get them in a lot of trouble... *Trouble with the law and, worse, with God, and I've ended up smack-dab in the middle of a lie.* "Okay, how can you do this? I'm thirteen. Where do I come from?"

"Oh, your daddy—my cousin, the one I don't have—is a Georgia farmer. Fallen on hard times with the Depression. The farm is way out in the country, so you never went to public school. Your mama taught you till she died last year. You got sick, so your daddy sent you here to live with me. Think you can live with our made-up history?"

"I suppose it's as good as the one I want to forget."

The aroma of soup beans, collard greens, and corn bread drew them to the kitchen table.

During supper, Lynelle said, "I haven't eaten food this good for more than a week. The lady knew how to cook, but I didn't feel like eating for the last few days. I nearly starved before I got here. Lived on blackberries and a couple of crusts of bread back at those cabins."

Flossie teared up and shook her head.

After they ate and Lynelle helped clean up the kitchen, Flossie flipped off the light in the kitchen. "Now let's go into the parlor and listen to the radio."

# Chapter 6

## *"Old Dog Tray" by Stephen C. Foster*

Lynelle felt well, but exhaustion had caught up with her. She wanted to go back to bed, but Aunt Flossie led the way to what she called the parlor.

Lynelle had not been beyond the kitchen in the downstairs, but when she followed Aunt Flossie into the parlor, she had another surprise.

Lynelle sucked in a big gasp. "A piano! Oh, Aunt Flossie, you have a piano."

She went to it and started to lift the lid over the keyboard but hesitated.

"Go ahead. I call it Ol' Plunker. Would you like to learn to play?"

"I know how to play." Lynelle gave Flossie a big grin, sat down on the stool, and without hesitation, played one of the pieces she had learned at school from memory, "Fur Elise" by Beethoven. The piano had remained in reasonable tune despite disuse, and Lynelle played the piece with perfection and great emotion.

When she first started to play, O'Hara howled, but he quieted down in a few minutes. Flossie laughed. "The dog howls whenever I turn on the radio, but then he calms down. Don't worry. You won't have competition."

Flossie sat on her rocker and nodded in time to the music.

A closed hymnal rested on the music rack. Lynelle opened it and played beginning in the front. She went through each hymn and sight-read even the ones she had never played before.

Flossie must have known all the songs because she hummed along with every one of them, off-key from what Lynelle could tell.

Lynelle played for the next twenty minutes, but when she got to "What a Friend We Have in Jesus," she slammed the book shut and closed the lid on the piano. She got up from the piano stool, plopped down in an overstuffed chair, and faced Aunt Flossie.

Flossie cocked her head as if to question the girl, but she kept quiet and allowed Lynelle to gather her thoughts.

After a long but significant pause, Flossie diverted whatever had disturbed Lynelle and introduced a new idea. "Well, honey, it's a might early, but I think bed would be in order for you. I will be off to Sunday school tomorrow, but I don't think you should go out yet. You sleep as long as you want. Fix whatever you want for breakfast, and I'll see you after I get back from the church house."

"Yes, ma'am."

"Monday, after I close the store, if ya feel like it, we'll go to Jasper and get groceries and some more clothes for ya. How's that sound?"

"Oh, yes. I'd like to. Do you have a car?"

"Of course, I have a car. I have a 1929 Packard, and you'll never ride in a better car."

Lynelle's eyes popped. She looked around the room at the nice furniture and then back at the piano and again thought, *I am in a dream.*

"And, Lynelle, you may play the Ol' Plunker anytime you want. The beast has been silent too long. Daddy played the piano and named it Ol' Plunker. He played ragtime as well as hymns."

Flossie thought for a few seconds—a frown on her face. Then she had another inspiration. "Lynelle, yer mama had been a good pianist when your papa married her. She taught ya to play. Our story of you growin' up in the backwoods might seem strange if we don't add a piano story since ya play so well."

Lynelle shrugged and shook her head in disbelief.

Flossie picked up a red composition notebook with an Indian chief on the front and a pack of pencils and handed it to her. "I think it would be a good idea for ya to write a journal. Don't do one of them diaries. Moonstruck girls write diaries. Write a journal about what yer up to. I think it'll help ya through some of those bad spells when ya think about the past."

"Thank you, Aunt…Aunt Flossie. Good idea. I can write down the poems I have in my head. But I'm tired. Good night."

"Oh, I put a fresh nightgown out for ya. Sleep tight."

But before Lynelle lay down, she wrote in her journal:

> Who am I? Why am I here? I left behind
> all I've ever known—everyone I've known, every
> place I've known. Not certain where I'm headed;
> life behind is dreaded. Lost from all I own. Why
> bother? Why struggle?

It didn't take more than a few seconds for the exhausted girl to fall into a deep sleep. She didn't awaken until she heard the church bell ring at ten o'clock Sunday morning.

After she made up her bed and cleaned up a bit, Lynelle went to the kitchen and looked through the cabinet for something to eat. She found oatmeal and grits, but she didn't want to wait for either of them to cook. "Not today."

Aunt Flossie had left bread and jam on the table, so she slathered two slices of bread with jam and drank a glass of milk. That didn't satisfy her hunger, so she found a box of Kix. She had never eaten dried cereal before, but she ate some right from the box. *Good.* Then she ate some strawberries Aunt Flossie had left on the table.

After she cleaned up her breakfast, she went to her room and got the notebook Aunt Flossie had given her the night before. She wrote about her ride to Florida in the watermelon truck, the wonderful new "aunt," and the piano. She said little about how she felt but described the house and Aunt Flossie. She ended the entry with a poem.

I think I have entered a dream.
How can this be real?
How can I not feel?
I will awaken
in darkness and shaken
from sleep. It's a scheme
of the devil.
It's not on the level.
Is this new life too extreme?
A new name I'll take.
A new home I'll make.
A new life and day of my birth.
And a new relative,
who only gives love.
From here on we find my new worth.
(Lynelle Van Sant)

When Flossie returned from Sunday school, Lynelle, oblivious to anything but her music, sat at the piano producing beautiful sounds. She played from memory the various classical piano pieces she had worked on throughout the previous winter at school.

Sunday always meant a day of enjoyment for the baker of Farmer's Corner. Cooking up a nice Sunday dinner came first. Flossie pulled a rack of chicken pieces out of her refrigerator and sat them on the Hoosier counter. "How are ya at cooking, Miss Lynelle? I do love to eat. I always fix a big dinner on Sunday and eat leftovers the rest of the week. This is chicken week. We'll fry this one."

"I can cook. We had cooking classes at school. What would you like me to do?"

"Ah! That's the spirit. How about taters? Why don' cha peel a pot full? Taters are in a bin out on the porch." She pointed to the porch door. "Here's a pan ya can put 'em in and cover them with water till we're ready to cook 'em."

Lynelle peeled the potatoes, snapped some green beans, and put them on to cook. "Got some bacon grease to flavor these beans, Aunt Flossie?"

"Well, I reckon you do know how to cook. Here's the bacon grease." She handed her a tin half-full of grease. "How are ya on biscuits?"

"I hope you'll teach me your way. I make them, but they always turn out crumbly and dry. I do make good corn bread."

So went the dinner preparation, and in another hour, they were ready to sit down at the table and enjoy a nice meal. Aunt Flossie, in one day, had already made Lynelle feel like family and not a guest. A hymn she had heard back home at the little church on the hill came to mind. *I can't remember the name of the hymn—just the phrase "no more a stranger nor a guest, but like a child at home." Can this wonderful place be my home? Maybe there is a God who saw me and heard. I don't know. I do not know.*

After dinner and with the kitchen cleaned up, Flossie suggested a walk. "Ya know, after a gal has a baby, it's good to walk to get yer body back in shape. Good thing ya done all that walkin' on yer way here from the state line cabins even if you had to walk in the ditches. This afternoon is pretty, so I want to show ya one of my favorite spots by the river. Good place to go fishin'—the Alapaha River. Ain't far. Ya feel like walkin'?"

"It would be good, Aunt Flossie. I like to walk, but I hate to ruin my clean clothes. Will I get them messed up?"

"Nah…put on yer old dress, but keep them socks on I got ya yesterday. We won't do no fishin' today. You like to go fishin'?"

Lynelle laughed. "Not too happy when I have to put those night crawlers on the hook or to clean the fish, but I like to fish and eat them."

As promised, the walk invigorated them. The river had a nice pool at Aunt Flossie's favorite spot. She pointed across the pool at a ripple in the water. "Fish after bugs. Next time, we'll bring us a pole along. I don't think it's right to go fishin' of a Sunday even if it's fun and ain't work."

When they got back from their walk, they relaxed the rest of the afternoon. Flossie showed Lynelle where she kept her books. "Papa loved to read, and ya can read as much as ya want to. Once we get our baked goods made in the mornin'—and I'd like you to help me as soon as yer able—then ya can read, play the piano, or whatever ya want to do."

Lynelle picked a book she had not read before, *Anne of Green Gables*, and settled in the overstuffed chair and read. Lost in the story, it surprised her when Aunt Flossie called her to supper. Leftovers.

After supper, she played piano until Flossie stopped her. "Time for bed, gal. I gotta get up at four and get to baking. Sleep as long as ya want to, and if ya feel like ya can help me, ya know where to find me in the morning."

Flossie hugged her. She had not been hugged since she had hugged Jay-Lee goodbye four months past. She couldn't help but cry—a good cry. She felt like she belonged.

# Chapter 7

## *"Smoke Gets in Your Eyes" by Jerome Kern and Otto Harback*

Lynelle was filled with both anxiety and anticipation for the promised trip to Jasper. She was anxious about someone looking for a runaway girl, and on the other hand, she wanted to go to the stores and maybe have something new for herself for the first time in her life.

As promised, Monday afternoon after the bakery closed, Aunt Flossie got the Packard out of the barn and proposed a trip to town. "Ya feel like headin' out to Jasper?"

Lynelle's eyes opened wide, and she shot a toothy grin at Aunt Flossie. "Yes, ma'am. I feel good today. The ice helped, and I'm not—well, there's not so much blood. If I could survive a two-day ride in the back of a truck over all those roads and walk for another day, I can ride to town in your nice car."

Lynelle cleaned her saddle oxfords, donned her new dress, and combed her hair. She clipped it back away from her face with the new barrettes and looked at herself in the mirror. *Who are you? Not sure I recognize you. If I ever run into...*

She didn't want to think of the people from the past. *Those people do not exist.*

Once in the car, Lynelle almost felt as if she had entered an unreal world. She had ridden in wagons, trucks, and old Model-Ts, but she had not been in such an elegant vehicle. On the way to Jasper,

Lynelle looked at the scenery as it sped by in reverse. It seemed like the world whizzed by while she sat in comfortable room.

She didn't say anything for a while, but then she spoke her mind. She asked what had nagged at her since Saturday evening. "Aunt Flossie, I thought you smoked. Did you give it up?"

Aunt Flossie laughed and started to hum the popular song "Smoke Gets in Your Eyes" in her off-tune manner.

"Yep. Smokin's bad. Figured since yer here, I don't need them coffin nails anymore. Don't ever start. Makes yer clothes stink, yer breath stink, and yer pocketbook shrink!"

Lynelle let out a relieved sigh. "I never liked to smell it. Tried it once and got sick."

They stopped at the five-and-dime first. The store had a good selection of everyday dresses, skirts, and blouses appropriate for school, but with Lynelle's petite size coupled with her mature post-partum figure, the clerk took her to the ladies' half-size section.

Lynelle looked at the dresses, and her stomach sank. She pulled on Flossie's sleeve. "Aren't these dresses too grown-up for a schoolgirl, Aunt Flossie?"

"Hmmm, maybe. I don't reckon ya want to look like an old woman with a mop and broom."

Lynelle giggled at the image, not that she was unfamiliar with using a mop and broom.

Flossie snapped her fingers for the clerk. "We don't want nuthin' so grown-up. Don' cha have some more stylish clothes for chubby girls? Maybe some we can alter?"

The skirts and blouses fit a lot better and looked good on Lynelle. The clerk did lead them to find one nice dress that didn't make her look like a mop lady. Sweaters, underwear, stockings, and even a couple of hats, gloves, and a little purse rounded out her outfit except for shoes. Then they moved next door to the shoe store.

Lynelle's saddle oxfords were worn to the point where she needed to replace them. Her tiny foot fit like a glove into a brand-new pair of brown-and-white saddle oxfords and a pair of black patent leather Mary Janes.

"Oh, Aunt Flossie! I never had new shoes in my life, and now I have two pairs. Thank you, thank you! One for school, one for dress."

"Why yes, Lynelle. Ya need to look yer best for Sunday go-to meetin'!"

"Sunday go-to meetin', huh?" Lynelle thought, *Don't know if I want to go to church, but if that's what it meant to be her niece, I'll go to church. But what if...* She didn't know what "what if" concerned her, but in the back of her mind, she wondered if the police would be looking for her or if her running away had been put in some newspaper. *What about my good dress I left in the pillow slip? Suppose they come looking for me?*

After the shoes, the next stop was a dry goods store. "Since yer good with sewing, we'll get ya some material and pattern fer a good Sunday dress. I have an old sewing machine ya can use. Ya ever use one?"

"We had one at school, and I learned how. I did a lot of hand sewing like the dress I wore, but I made other things on the machine. I never used a pattern other than an old dress. I've seen them. I'd like to try, Aunt Flossie. I really would."

Lynelle chose a princess frock dress pattern with a flared skirt. It could be made with or without a Peter Pan collar. Flossie insisted two different kinds of material would be necessary.

"Aunt Flossie, do you like this peach linen? I could make the collarless dress with it. What do you think?"

"Perfect for yer coloring. Now how 'bout some yellow cotton for the other 'n?"

"I like it, and I could use white pique for the collar."

They got both materials with a good supply of thread, snaps, hooks and eyes, rickrack, and mother-of-pearl buttons. Lynelle eagerly anticipated sewing on her new dresses.

The new clothes were piled into the trunk of the Packard, things fit for a girl about to go to school—not a poor child who had given birth only a week ago.

"Okay, young 'un. Time to get some supper." Aunt Flossie led the way to the Old Jasper Hotel for dinner.

Restaurants were an unknown to Lynelle. She had been told that her mother and father had died from ptomaine poisoning after they ate apple pie at a restaurant in Asheville, North Carolina. She looked at the menu with skepticism and allowed Aunt Flossie to order for both of them. She ate shrimp and grits for the first time in her life, but when it came time to order the apple pie, she refused.

"I've never eaten at a restaurant before, but I know I can't trust an apple pie. It's not safe. We might get food poisoning from it. I'll stick to those cookies you made this morning if you don't mind."

"So! Ye've been into Flossie's Famous Molasses Cookies, have ya? Well, we'll go on back to Farmer's Corner and have us some cookies and milk for dessert. Four o'clock in the morning comes too soon to wait around here for dessert anyway."

They stopped at the grocery store after dinner and then drove home. Exhaustion had caught up with Lynelle. It didn't take long for her to nod off on the trip back to Farmer's Corner.

# Chapter 8

## *"Summer Time" by George Gershwin*

That first summer in Farmer's corner introduced Lynelle to the beauty of nature she had not known before. The mountains were beautiful, and she missed them when she allowed herself to think of them. On the other hand, Lynelle enjoyed her new home. Throughout the day, she loved the myriad of flowers Aunt Flossie had all around the edges of the house—crepe, myrtle, and magnolia trees, big live oaks with resurrection fern on the branches, and Spanish moss swaying in the breeze all along the road and in the yard. These were all foreign to Lynelle's experience, but Aunt Flossie told her the names of everything.

At night, she would sleep with the window open and listen to the chirp of the crickets and croak of the frogs. She listened to the owls' soft hoots in the tall trees. And songbirds awakened her in the morning to greet the day. A little wren nested outside her window. The little bird's cheerful song worked well for an alarm clock each morning. *I'll call her Winnie—gotta be a female with that voice.* These sights and sounds helped her bury the things she missed from back in the mountains.

Flossie explained to Lynelle why she wanted her to help in the bakery each morning that first week. "Honey, this will be a good way for ya to meet the folks who live around here. I want ya to go to the post office or the store too. Maybe then, by Sunday, you'll feel ready to go to Sunday school with me."

But Tuesday, the morning after the first trip to Jasper, Lynelle asked, "Aunt Flossie, I would like to start on my new dresses. I'm not too used to a sewing machine, and I never used paper patterns before, but I want to try."

Flossie took her to a small enclosed sun porch, a room Lynelle hadn't seen before next to the parlor. A table with a rack of threads, scissors, and other sewing needs took up most of the inside wall. A treadle sewing machine, a few chairs, and a bank of windows flooded the room with light.

Lynelle's eyes opened wide. "Oh! This is a perfect sewing room. I had begun to use a machine like this at school."

But her excitement over the sewing room put a knot in her stomach. She didn't want to cry, but the memory of Jay-Lee and sewing together came unbidden. She did not cry, but instead, she grabbed the pattern and opened it, delving into the project to push away thoughts of her twin.

She got busy and made the first of her new dresses. The sewing machine took a bit of practice, but she soon figured it out, and she could read the pattern. She chose the cotton material for the first dress and completed it in only two days.

"Oh, Lynelle! Ya did a fantastic job on it. I'll have to have ya make some for me. I always buy my clothes, but gee whiz! Yers is better than a factory-made dress any day!"

Lynelle grinned, satisfied she could please Aunt Flossie. She wanted to make the linen dress but wondered if maybe she should offer to help Aunt Flossie instead. As well, she needed to practice piano.

"Aunt Flossie, I'd love to go ahead and make the other dress, but maybe I need a break. I can help you a bit. I don't want you to think I'm lazy or selfish."

"Oh, dear girl! I do need ya to go over to the post office to see if there is any mail. Ya ask Hannah Thomas—she's the postmistress—if there's any mail for Flossie Van Sant. She's an old spinster, but she's a doll. She knows yer my niece. Saw her at the church house Sunday and told her you'd come in now and then to get the mail."

Lynelle screwed her mouth sideways. Although she had met a few ladies who had come into the bakery, she knew she had to engage in the community if she wanted to live there. *Gotta meet people some time. Guess this is it.*

O'Hara went with her that first foray into the community, and from then on, he accompanied her wherever she went.

Lynelle liked Hannah Thomas right away. Like Aunt Flossie, Hannah had remained single. She appeared ancient. She wore old-fashioned clothes reminiscent of pre-World War I with high-top shoes and an ankle-length dress. She wore her gray hair pulled back over her ears with a soft knot at her nape. She wore old-fashioned pince-nez eyeglasses on the end of her nose. Despite her old-fashioned appearance, she spoke with a genteel and soft voice, reflecting her Southern upbringing. She made Lynelle feel at ease right away. *Kind of reminds me of dear Dr. Mary Sloop at the Crossnore School.*

"Oh, you are Miss Lynelle, Miss Flossie's niece. Oh, you darlin' girl. We are so glad you have come to stay with our dear Flossie. I have wanted to meet you. Your aunt said you had been ill. I do hope you feel better with Flossie's good home-cooked foods. You should have some color back in your cheeks in no time. Welcome to our little community."

*Pale cheeks? Ill? Miss Hannah doesn't know the half of it!* She smiled and said, "Thank you, ma'am. I feel so much better. I appreciate all Aunt Flossie does for me."

There were a few pieces of mail for Flossie. Lynelle took them home, satisfied to have survived her first venture into the village. She and O'Hara went to get the mail or to post Flossie's mail every day.

On Thursday of the first week as she went to the post office, Lynelle met two girls who looked her own age. They were taller, but then Lynelle had always been small for her age.

O'Hara wagged his tail and growled his hello to them. This assured Lynelle they were friends.

"Hey!" They greeted her in one voice.

"You are Miss Flossie's niece, aren't you?" the girl with the brown hair and eyes asked.

"Yes?" She shrugged and then repeated, "Well, yes."

The other girl, a redhead with green eyes, introduced them both. "She's Joyce Heller, and I'm Maud Ellen Lee. You can call me Maudie. Your name is Lynelle, isn't it?"

"Uh—yes. Yes, Lynelle Van Sant."

"We oughta call you Lynnie. Everyone has to have a nickname."

"Hey, I don't!" her companion disagreed.

"Well, you don't 'cause you're a snob."

Lynelle laughed. "Sounds like you two are fun. What grade are you in?"

Joyce answered, "We'll both be in eighth. What grade will you be in?"

*Oh, oh, here comes the tale.* She tried to sound convincing. "My mama taught me at home until she died. She had a college education and taught school and piano before she married Papa. She taught me books and piano. That's one of the reasons Papa wanted me to come and live with Aunt Flossie, so I could get back to school and get piano lessons again. Aunt Flossie said the school would want to test me to see what grade I am. I hope I'll be in eighth grade too."

Maudie said, "We heard you playin' piano yesterday. You're real good. You oughta play for Sunday school. We don't have anybody now. Not since old Mr. Van Sant died."

"I don't know. I reckon the grown-ups might have something to say about it." Lynelle gave a nervous laugh.

"They'll be happy to have a piano player. I'll say something to Mother," Joyce reassured her. "She leads the singing."

Lynelle shrugged. "Nice to meet you both. I have to get to the post office for Aunt Flossie."

Nice to meet you too, Lynnie," Joyce said. "Hope you don't mind the nickname."

"I like it. Thanks." Lynelle, or Lynnie, waved goodbye to them as she went on into the post office.

When she got to the bakery, Aunt Flossie had a cake on the table frosting it with boiled frosting. "Guess what, Aunt Flossie?"

"You met the girls."

"How did you know? Well, yes, and they gave me a nickname. They want to call me Lynnie. How does Lynnie sound? Lynnie Van Sant."

"It's a good'n. Ya have to remember it, though—ya ain't had Lynelle long enough to get used to it. But I like Lynnie. Suits ya."

"It's Lynnie then. I am Lynnie."

Sunday came, and Lynnie put on her new dress. Her hands shook from nervousness, so she shoved them into her pockets. She was glad O'Hara walked to church with them.

Even when they went to church, the dog lay by the front door. He howled a bit when the first notes of singing floated through the door and then quieted down to a good nap for the next hour or so. This first Sunday, the church only had Sunday school and not preaching. Sunday school had four classes. The little ones were taken into a back room, the elementary children huddled off to one corner, the high schoolers in another, and the grown-ups, not involved with the children and young people, gathered in the front for their lesson. Some familiar things such as the songs they sang and the type of lesson taught made Lynnie to feel at home. Until...

Mrs. Heller, Joyce's mother, approached Lynnie with a *Gotcha!* look in her eye.

"Miss Lynelle, we are all so glad you are well enough to join us. I've heard you play when I went to the bakery." (Everyone in the village referred to as Aunt Flossie's home as the bakery.) "Would you be willing to play our closing hymn today? It has been so long since anyone played the piano, not since Miss Flossie's papa passed away."

Lynnie felt her stomach flop, and she looked at Aunt Flossie.

"Of course she'll play, Sarah. Won't ya, honey?"

Lynnie nodded and went to the piano. Mrs. Heller led the singing, and she announced the hymn. "Turn to page 46: 'There is Power in the Blood.'"

Lynnie knew the song, but when she went to play the piano, it had gotten so far out of tune it sounded dreadful. She played as well as she could, but her face turned red with embarrassment at how terrible it sounded to her.

No one seemed to notice, and they sang with vigor. Their loud voices almost covered the discord of the piano. Lynnie didn't say anything to Mrs. Heller when she praised her talent.

"Dear girl! You play beautifully! I think God sent you to us so you could be our pianist." She raised her eyes heavenward and said, "Thank you, Jesus!"

Lynnie, still uncertain if God held any interest in the lives of people like her, put on a sweet smile and said, "Thank you, Mrs. Heller."

When she and Aunt Flossie got to the bakery, she voiced her opinion of the piano. "Aunt Florence!"

"It's Aunt Florence, is it? Ya got a problem?"

"I do. If I have to play piano in Sunday school, y'all will have to get that old piano tuned. It is the most disgraceful piano playing I ever did. Blame it on the piano, not me."

"It sounded wonderful to me, but then I can't carry a tune anyway. I'll take care of it before next Sunday. Yer too good at it not to play."

A dark thundercloud shrouded Lynnie's face. "We'll see."

Monday morning, Flossie called the music store in Jasper and had a piano tuner come as soon as possible. He would tune it by the next Sunday. Good thing too. The preacher would be there Sunday. Lynnie would need to play for both Sunday school and the church service.

The piano tuner tuned the church piano, and then Flossie had him tune the one in their parlor. It pleased Lynnie to have two decent pianos to play.

So…a routine settled in for Lynnie at Van Sant's Bakery—up early and work in the bakery, sew, practice piano…

# Chapter 9

## *"Three o'clock in the Morning"*
## *by Julián Robledo*

Aunt Flossie did more than rescue a poor little waif; she created Lynelle Van Sant. The name Lynnie stuck and became the name everyone in the village called her. She felt safe and happy and able to forget about her past for days at a time. For the most part, it seemed as though she had disassociated her mind from her past. All summer Flossie had introduced Lynelle bit by bit to the community—first the post office, then the grocery store and church.

Lynnie enjoyed her routine. She made breakfast so Aunt Flossie could get the bakery started. After she cleaned up the kitchen, she practiced piano for an hour, after which she would help in the bakery, sew, do laundry, or clean house. She knew how to do all these things. As summer progressed her health had returned, and she showed no outward signs of a recent birth.

When Flossie arranged for the piano tuner, she also arranged for Lynnie to take piano lessons. So when August rolled around, the Saturday afternoon trips to Jasper included piano lessons from a teacher in Jasper. Now in addition to her hour morning practice, she would practice another hour each afternoon, sometimes two hours.

She would have been satisfied to remain in the house every day, sewing, practicing piano, and helping Aunt Flossie. Lynnie maintained a reserved image, but the sociable natures of Joyce and Maudie brought her into their camaraderie. She recognized the advantage of being out and about with these new friends, playing croquet or just sitting and talking.

Aunt Flossie had bought Lynnie a bathing suit, but since Flossie didn't enjoy swimming, she never took her. One hot day in July, Joyce and Maudie showed up at the bakery with their bathing suits.

Maudie announced, "Get your suit on, Lynnie girl! We're a-goin' swimmin'!"

"I...I can't swim."

"No excuse," Joyce countered. "I know Miz Flossie got you a new bathing suit. I saw it on the clothesline when y'all washed it and hung it out to dry. Put it on, grab a towel, and lets go to the swimmin' hole."

Lynnie complied with her friends' orders, but she refused to do more than put her feet in the water and sit on the dock.

Maudie prodded her. "Come on, Lynnie! Everyone learns how to swim. I can teach you."

"No. I'm happy cooling off in the water. I don't want to learn how to swim." She thought, *Every time I think of getting in the water, I think of what I almost did on that bridge in North Carolina or when I thought about walking into the goose pond up the road.*

"Your loss, chicken!"

Lynnie shrugged and swished her feet back and forth in the water from the dock. *There are plenty of other things to do without learning to swim. I have O'Hara.*

Truly, O'Hara, her buddy, wouldn't let her out of his sight as long as she stayed outside. He never followed her inside. If someone saw Lynnie, they saw O'Hara right there with her. Much as Lynnie liked her friends, life was only right for her so long as O'Hara or Aunt Flossie was there.

Then after her first time at the swimming hole, the nightmare returned. *Arnie after me...King Kong's face...breath hot with moonshine...knife fire surging up through me...ton of bricks...unwashed... reeking...speaking words from hell... Help me, Jay-Lee...hel...ll...p... Got to reach Jay-Lee. The closer she gets, the farther she goes—baby cries—endless horror—until...*

"Lynnie, sweet girl! Wake up. It's three in the mornin,' and yer havin' a bad dream." Aunt Flossie shook Lynnie's shoulder to stop the young girl's screams.

Nightmares were a frequent intruder in Lynnie's life with some version of the same story that involved Jay-Lee or her baby. Often, her right arm fell asleep because she had lain on it. Her tingling right arm triggered the nightmare.

As she awakened and rubbed the circulation back into her arm, she knew why it happened. She and Jay-Lee always called each other *my right arm*, and they would do a right arm swing and twirl one another in what they called their Twin Dance.

This prompted a reminder again of her notion to jump off the bridge. *I should have ignored the No! and jumped in the river in North Carolina. Who am I trying to kid? My life isn't going to be worth a rotten apple if I have to hide or cringe in the face of any stranger.*

The next time she went with Maudie and Joyce to the pond, she thought she might return later. *I'll jump off the dock and put rocks in my pockets so I'll not be able to come up from the bottom.*

She didn't return to the pond the rest of the summer. She always made the excuse "I need to practice my piano." And the practice on the piano did distract her enough to forget for a few hours.

The couple of times she and Aunt Flossie took their fishing poles and went fishing consisted of only going to the river. They caught some black bass one time and the next time a big catfish. Being with Aunt Flossie at the fishing hole was security. She could release her urge to end her life.

But this idea nagged her: *I don't have a life worth living if I must hide away and be away from Jay-Lee.*

Another idea crossed her mind. She had begun to shave her legs. *Razor blades. I could cut my wrists and bleed out.*

She positioned the razor against her left wrist, held it there for a long minute, put it back onto the sink, and ran to her room and cried into her pillow. *Why can't I do this? What makes me want to live? Is it the God thing that stops me?*

Flossie worried about her girl. She saw the frowns. She noted the wall she erected when she sat in church. *Ya don't reckon she'd harm herself, do ya, Flossie? Can't even tell my friends without tellin' them Lynnie's true story. Watch her, ol' gal.* She hovered over her like a mother hen. She prayed.

# Chapter 10

## *"It's a Sin to Tell a Lie" by Billy Mayhew*

How Flossie managed to create a new legal identity she never revealed. Lynnie did know when it happened. One Saturday, Aunt Flossie put her in charge of the bakery. "I gotta go off on some business this morning. I done all the bakin.' You sell it when they come in. Put the money in a cook pot on the stove, and I'll take care o' it when I get back."

When Aunt Flossie left, she was dressed in a long-sleeved shirt, overalls, and waders. She had a hat with mosquito netting to pull down over it.

Lynnie laughed. "Going to rob a beehive?"

"Ain't none of yer affair. See ya this evening."

By the time school started after Labor Day, Jessie Lynn Vance no longer existed. She had become Lynelle Jessamine Van Sant, birth date June 10, 1926, Early County, Georgia; mother, Myrtle Van Sant, deceased; father, Henry Van Sant, address unknown. It almost convinced Lynnie of the truth in the new story. After all, Aunt Flossie referred to it almost daily. Much as she begged, Aunt Flossie wouldn't show her the birth certificate she had contrived.

"You gotta wait till we need it."

"But if I can't see it, it isn't real, Auntie."

They volleyed back and forth at least once a week, but Aunt Flossie held her ground and wouldn't show it to her. "I'm a-waitin' till you go to school. Plenty of time."

"Yes, ma'am." She turned away in frustration but said no more.

Finally, the day arrived. School would start the day after Labor Day.

"Okay, Lynnie. I'm goin' with you to the schoolhouse to get ya registered. Since you ain't had formal education, the principal will wanna test you to see what grade to put ya in. I think yer smart, and there ain't no question in my mind you'll be in eighth grade."

With a big grin on her face, Aunt Flossie handed Lynnie an envelope with her birth certificate in it. "You can give it to the principal when we go have ya registered. And yes, you can look at it." Her generous abdomen jiggled as she attempted to restrain a laugh. "Now."

Lynnie gave Aunt Flossie a big hug and slobbery kiss, took a deep breath, and with her eyes bugging out, she opened the envelope and read whom she had become.

> Lynelle Jessamine Van Sant
> Date of birth: June 10, 1926
> Early County, Georgia
> Mother, Myrtle Van Sant, deceased
> Father, Henry Van Sant, address unknown

"Jessamine?" Her eyes opened wide. "Oooh, Aunt Flossie, that's pretty, though I've never heard of it."

"It's that yeller flower vine that grows in the woods earliest in the springtime."

"Well, it's perfect. So now, it is official, Aunt Flossie. I know who I am. I am Lynelle Jessamine Van Sant, but I go by Lynnie."

Farmer's Corner School, a four-room school, served grades one through eight. There were two classes in each room. The principal had a small anteroom office in the center of the building.

O'Hara followed them to the school. As they approached the school yard, Lynnie saw Joyce and Maudie. Since Maudie had been held back sometime in the past because of illness, both she and Joyce were in eighth grade. They waved and ran up to her.

"Hey!" Maudie called to her as they joined her and Aunt Flossie. "Ya gonna be in eighth grade?"

"I hope so. I think I'll need to take some tests. We will talk to the principal."

"We will hold us a prayer meetin' about it!" Joyce patted her new friend on the arm.

Lynnie raised an eyebrow. "Doubt if God's interested in whether I'm in eighth or second grade."

Maudie and Joyce looked at each other and giggled.

Miss Baker, the principal, did not live locally. She drove over from Jasper several times a month for official business at the school. She had other duties in the school district, but the first day of the new school year, she always started at the Farmer's Corner school. Flossie knew her from when she would come into the bakery each time she came to the village.

Flossie knocked on the opened doorframe. Miss Baker looked up from some papers on her desk. Peering over the glasses perched on her long nose, she acknowledged her intruders with a silent stare.

"Good morning, Miss Baker. I've brought my niece to school today. This is Lynelle Van Sant, my cousin's daughter. She has not had any schoolhouse education, but I think you will find she's smart as a whip from how her momma taught her."

Lynnie stifled a giggle. *Aunt Flossie is speaking in an educated voice. Wasn't sure she knew how.*

"No formal education? My goodness, where will we be able to place her?" Miss Baker looked up and down at Lynnie's slight figure. "She is small, but I can see she is becoming a young lady."

Lynnie's face reddened as she handed the envelope with the birth certificate to the woman. She swallowed and held her head up. "Ma'am. This is all I have. I think I may qualify for eighth grade."

The woman looked stern. "Eighth grade? You may be deluded, young lady. Formal education is a far cry from what I have seen from the so-called 'home schools' I have observed over the years." The educator shook her head at such presumption.

Miss Baker turned to Aunt Flossie. "Miss Van Sant, you should go on home, and I will give her a day of testing. We shall see. My supposition, from my experience with such students, will be fourth grade, not eighth."

Lynnie looked at her aunt with apprehension. She felt all a-tremble. *Hope it doesn't show. I don't want Miss Baker to think I'm afraid of her…but I guess I am.*

Flossie hugged her and whispered in her ear, "You'll do fine. You'll show the old bat!"

Lynnie grinned and whispered, "Bye, Aunt Flossie. I'll be fine."

With Aunt Flossie gone from the room, the principal went to her file cabinet, an ancient oak piece that squawked and squealed as she pulled out one drawer after another, and retrieved various folders, several of them. She withdrew a paper from each one and set them on a school desk in the corner of the small room.

Not even a semblance of a smile cracked her face as she handed them to Lynnie.

Wondering if the woman's face would crack if she smiled, Lynnie tried not to grin. Such thoughts removed her initial anxiety.

"Here are our seventh-grade final tests from last year. You will need to make at least an 80 percent, a B-minus on each of them, for me to place you in eighth grade."

"Yes, ma'am." With the papers in hand, she took her seat, and pulled out her pencil. She looked at the test on the top of the pile. *History.*

If Miss Baker thought the girl would stumble through these test papers and flag halfway through the morning, she would have a surprise. History came easily for Lynnie. She had always made near-perfect test scores in history, and Lynnie knew this one would be no different. She completed it in thirty-eight minutes and set it aside. She took up the arithmetic test.

These were easy. She had even taken some algebra in seventh grade. Although she took more time with the questions, by the end of an hour, she picked up the English exam. Again, an easy forty-five minutes. The geography she whipped through in fifteen minutes. At twenty minutes before noon, she scanned through the other three tests. *These look easy*, she thought. *I'll do them after lunch.*

She set the tests she had not completed aside and reviewed her questions on the other four. Then the lunch bell rang at noon.

Miss Baker stopped her. "Hand me what you've completed. You may leave for lunch. Do you know any of the girls here at school?"

"Yes, ma'am. I am friends with Maud Ellen Lee and Joyce Heller. They are both eighth graders."

Miss Baker looked down her long nose. Lynnie felt the woman's black eyes on her. *I'll bet her eyes can penetrate my gizzard.*

The woman spoke with an icy clip. "I am well aware these girls are eighth graders. I suppose you think because your friends are in eighth grade, you should be too. We shall see what we shall see. If you brought your lunch, you may go out to the school yard and eat, or you may go home. Do not take your papers with you. I will look over what you have done while you are gone. Be back here to finish your work at one o'clock. Not sooner and not later."

"Yes, ma'am."

Lynnie had not brought lunch. Aunt Flossie had told her to come home for lunch. O'Hara still napped beside the steps into the school, but he woke up when he sensed her presence. He and Lynnie joined Maudie outside the schoolhouse.

"Hi. Where's Joyce?"

Maudie laughed. "She got into a bit of trouble with Jacky Conroy, so she has to stay in and write an apology on the blackboard."

Lynnie covered her mouth and giggled.

Maudie grabbed Lynnie's arm. "Come on, I'll walk with you to your place. How're the tests? I'll bet Old Needle Nose gave you a hard time."

"Old Needle Nose? Sounds appropriate. So far they've been easy. I have three more to take, and I think I should do well enough to make eighth grade. Madam Needle Nose said I have to make at least a B-minus. Easy."

"Yeah, I could tell her how smart you are."

The girls parted, and Lynnie went into the bakery, had her lunch, and some of Flossie's Famous Molasses Cookies.

Now that Lynnie knew Aunt Flossie really did know how to converse as though she had learned her English lessons in school, she teased her.

"Auntie, I was shocked! I had assumed you learned your English from the swamp people. Sounded as though you might have actually gone to school when you were talking to Miss Baker."

Flossie laughed and patted Lynnie on her head. "Maybe I should begin speaking like I had some sense, huh? How 'bout if I try? Wouldn't want this school gal to be ashamed of her old auntie. Don't chide me though if I slip, which is most of the time."

"Promise." She took an extra cookie. "Yum!" She headed back to the school with the ever-present O'Hara.

The final three tests were easy, and she wrapped them all up by two o'clock. She stood with the three papers in hand and cleared her throat.

"Excuse me, Miss Baker. I have finished the tests. What should I do now?"

Madam Needle Nose had softened a bit over lunch. She spoke in a kinder fashion to her new student. "Sit down, Lynelle."

Lynnie sat back at the desk and waited for Miss Baker to scrutinize the papers. After about five too-long minutes, the woman looked up and bored her black eyes into Lynnie's. "I admit it surprises me to find you have finished so soon. And, Lynelle, you have done well. I have already corrected your first three papers, and a glance at these would suggest you are as far along in your studies as you claimed. You made 100 percent on geography, English, and history, 98 percent on arithmetic, and from what I see on spelling, health, and art, I think you will have made the grade. I want you to go to room 4, the seventh- and eighth-grade room, and knock on the door. You are admitted as an eighth-grade student."

Lynnie released the breath she had held back for most of the day. She nodded politely. "Thank you, Miss Baker."

A twinkle hinted at the edge of Miss Baker's eyes as she handed Lynnie a folded slip of paper with the name of the teacher, Miss Carter, on the outside.

Lynnie knocked on the door of Room 4. Jimmy Everett opened the door, wiggled his nose at her, and gave a theatrical bow as if to usher her into the room. Miss Carter said, "Thank you, Jimmy. Come in, Lynnie. We expected you."

If Lynnie expected a teacher like Miss Baker, she was in for a surprise. Miss Carter, although probably as old as Miss Baker, gave Lynnie a smile as she came into the room. She was short—eye-to-eye short as Lynnie. Her hair was snowy white, braided about her head in a loose crown and shone in the sunlight streaming in the window. Miss Carter's soft brown eyes were the thing that most attracted Lynnie's attention. *I like her already.*

"Lynelle, the eighth-graders are on the right side of the room, my left, and you may sit in the empty side of the desk on the outside row. Your seatmate is Bobby Everett. You met his brother at the door. You will find Bobby uses his talent to play his violin without the theatrical flair his younger brother shows. He can share the assignments with you for tomorrow." She nodded at Bobby. "And, Bobby, I know you will be as quiet as possible."

The teacher smiled at Lynnie. "Lynelle, your books are already on your desk. The eighth grade will have spelling class the last period. It will begin in about half an hour. Meanwhile, after Bobby gives you the assignments, look through the books while I finish up the seventh-grade lesson." Miss Carter turned back to the seventh graders.

So went the first day of school. As a student at Farmer's Corner grade school, Lynnie had started a new life.

It wasn't long before even Miss Carter called her Lynnie instead of Lynelle. She had found a smart student who was liked by all her classmates. Lynnie made the honor roll in every subject. Bobby, her seatmate, made her feel at ease, and his interest in music appealed to her. For a Christmas program the two played a duet of familiar Christmas carols.

Maudie had a bit of trouble with arithmetic, and Lynnie helped her so she would pass. Joyce hated science, and Lynnie showed her how to find something interesting in it. She knew Joyce liked to work in her mom's flower beds, so she showed her how learning about the science of flowers would help her know how to grow the best flowers.

When May came and eighth-grade graduation day arrived, Lynnie received an award for "best all-round student."

# CHAPTER 11

## *"Revive Us Again" by William P. MacCay*

*1940–1944*

The summer between eighth grade and high school mimicked the summer before. Lynnie helped around the bakery, practiced for hours on Old Plunker, ran errands in the village with O'Hara, sewed, and sat on front porches with her friends, Joyce and Maudie. O'Hara always went along.

When they sat on the Hellers' porch, Joyce would have her Victrola play popular records. She loved the Andrews sisters and played their records over and over, dancing on the porch in her bare feet. Her favorite was "Bei Mir Bist Du Schöen." When it came to the chorus, the three girls would sing:

> Bei mir bist du schön,
> Please let me explain
> "Bei mir bist du schön" means that you are grand.
> Bei mir bist du schön,
> It means you're the fairest in the land.

These words would prompt Joyce and Maudie into a discussion about the boys they knew who planned to fight in the war that threatened in Europe. They talked about the boys they knew who were on the football team at Hamilton County High, the high school in Jasper. They talked about Hollywood actors like Clark Gable, Cary Grant, and Gregory Peck. In short, they talked about boys, boys, boys.

Lynnie, tired of the conversation, snapped at her friends, "Don't you two ever get tired of boy talk all the time? I'll bet there is a lot of other stuff to talk about if we use our minds instead of—well, instead of our hormones."

Maudie interrupted. "Hormones? Come on, Lynnie. We are fourteen and fifteen years old, and like Pop says, 'budding young women.' We have all the female equipment, so isn't it normal to talk about males?"

Joyce added her two cents. "Yeah, admit it, Lynnie. You like Bobby Everett. Don't you dare deny it."

"He's intelligent and plays the violin. He has been my seatmate for a year of school. He is a nice kid who has been my companion in studies. Good grief! I'm not in love with him!"

Her friends laughed at her and went back to the conversation about the football team at the high school. Since Lynnie had never seen a football game, she wanted to know more about it. When the girls talked about what some football player had done in a game, she asked questions. At Crossnore, basketball, track, baseball, and soccer were the familiar sports.

So went the conversations whenever the girls were together.

Some days were too hot to do anything but go swimming, so they would head for the swimming hole, a pond at one of the farms close to the village. O'Hara loved to swim. Lynnie, once again, went along with the girls as she had the previous summer. She went for O'Hara's sake.

The boys and girls were not supposed to swim at the pond at the same time. Maudie laughed about the segregation. "It's cause the boys come down here to skinny-dip."

Lynnie's eyes bugged out. "Good grief! No bathing suits?"

But Aunt Flossie told Lynnie, "Don't worry about them boys being there when you are. They ain't allowed to swim with you girls. It ain't done. Least ways not around here."

One day when the girls were there, it was done. Jacky Conroy and Jimmy Everett sneaked to the pond anyway. They wore bathing suits and jumped right in with the girls.

Jimmy yelled at Lynnie. "C'mon, Lynnie! The water's warm. I'll teach you how to swim."

"No, thank you. I'll wade."

Maudie yelled back at Jimmy, "She'd say yes if your brother offered."

Lynnie's face turned red, but she didn't say anything. *Yes, I like Bobby, but how can I ever let a boy get romantic with me? I've been ruined. I can't be a real woman.*

She refused to try to swim no matter who would teach her. She had no fear of the water, but she didn't know how to swim and didn't want to learn. Again, she would wade in up to her waist or dangle her feet in the water from the dock, but no amount of coaxing could induce her to learn to swim.

Toward the end of the summer of 1940, anxiety about going to Hamilton County High crept into Lynnie's mind. She stopped her daily trips to visit her friends and spent more time on her piano. At the dinner table, she would play a mock piano instead of eating. Flossie gave her a strange look.

In truth, she was thinking about Jay Lee. *Will she be going to high school at Crossnore, or will she go back to live with our brothers?* This led her to think about the baby. *If I kept the baby, I wouldn't be going to school. Bet she's walking now—has teeth—maybe talking.*

Lynnie took a deep breath and played her mock piano harder.

"What's going on in your head, Missy? You haven't been out and about with the girls for two weeks. You ain't—aren't—fussin' about going to high school, are ya? You're gonna be an A student from the git-go. You are a Van Sant!"

*Huh? Does she really believe I'm a Van Sant? I don't know who I am. Or do I?*

Flossie wasn't about to give up. "Remember what Preacher Thomas said in his sermon last Sunday? He said somethin' like 'There ain't nuthin' too big for God to handle.' That goes for gettin' ready to go off to high school."

Lynnie made no comment, but she thought, *God didn't handle it too well when I got raped!*

Lynnie closed Aunt Flossie off and played the piano longer and harder than ever. Even the piano couldn't take her mind off the thought that life was not worth living. *I can't live this way. There is no future in my life. I can never...* She couldn't even think of what life might be in the future. *I need to end it.*

Over several days, her self-criticism built. One afternoon, she went to the pond alone. It had rained all day, and no one else had come to the pond. She took her shoes off and started to wade in where she knew the water was deep. *It's now, Lynnie or Jess or whoever you are.*

O'Hara grabbed her dress and yanked her away. He seemed to know her intention.

She collapsed at his side, hugged him in her arms, and started to cry. "O'Hara, I'm so messed up. I want to go to the new school, but I'm not sure if I can do it. It doesn't matter if Aunt Flossie has created Lynelle Van Sant. What if someone finds out who I really am? I like to think Jessie Lynn Vance never existed, but she comes to me and begs to be let back in every waking hour."

O'Hara licked the tears from her cheeks.

Once again, she pushed her notion that life wasn't worth living to the back of her mind. Once school started, she did even better than Aunt Flossie had anticipated, and the years flew by faster than she could have imagined.

Ninth grade melted into tenth grade. She played piano for the orchestra with Bobby at first chair with his violin; she played for both the junior and senior chorus even when she was in ninth grade. Lynnie worked hard to excel in both school and piano, but her diligence and push to succeed never quite enough dredged the thoughts of Jay-Lee or her baby from her mind or the fear of being found by the boy who had violated her.

She continued to have nightmares now and then, but to cope, she would immerse herself into her piano, sewing, and helping in the bakery. Flossie had to push her to get out with her friends. She did enjoy going with her friends to the football and basketball games at the high school. Joyce's or Maudie's dads took the girls to see all the home games.

The summer between tenth grade and eleventh brought a curious diversion to the community. The country, now embroiled in a war in both Europe and the Pacific, led the folks at home to seek relief at dance clubs and movies. Others turned to religion, believing that faith in God could give people hope in the shaky world. Religion in the little community of Farmer's Corner had always been centered on the "church house" as Flossie termed the building.

One day an evangelist, Preacher Tom Reese, with a big tent showed up south of the village on an open field. Tent revivals had been around since the early 1800s and became popular after World War I all over the South and even sometimes in the North. No particular religious group sponsored Preacher Reese, but he had the "hellfire-and-brimstone" approach to his message that appealed to people of several denominations around Farmer's Corner.

He would contact a local preacher and speak in the preacher's church. Then he began his tent meetings in the area. Farmer's Corner church had preaching once a month when Preacher Thomas made his circuit from the other churches where he preached. This evangelist had contacted him, and Preacher Thomas invited him as a guest preacher for his Sunday to preach.

At the end of the Sunday school, Preacher Thomas announced him. "Folks, we have a big treat today. My friend Preacher Tom Reese from up North Carolina way has planned a tent revival right here in Farmer's Corner. It is to start next Sunday night. I've asked him to join us today and give you a taste of his preaching."

As soon as he stood to take the pulpit, Lynnie huddled down in her seat and refused to play the piano. As soon as the preacher said amen at the end of his sermon, Lynnie hightailed it out of the church and went home before the invitation.

"What's all that fuss all about, Missy. You can't be sick. I can't believe you left and refused to play piano. He's lookin' for a piano player for the revival. It'd be a great opportunity for you."

"I recognize him, Aunt Flossie. I knew him from North Carolina. He can't see me. He's from—from back home. He's kin to the family we lived with at school."

"But, honey, you don't look at all like the little girl who showed up here two summers ago. He'd never recognize you."

Flossie took the mirror down from the wall in the hallway and put it in front of Lynnie. "Look at yourself in the mirror. Do you see the girl you were in here?"

"Well, maybe not. But what if he does? I can't go back, Aunt Flossie. I can't go back to where they know I had a baby. I can't go back to life the way it was before. I can't be what I was before."

Flossie ignored her tirade. "Did Preacher Reese ever hear you play piano?"

"No. We didn't have a piano at the house. I played the one at the school."

"Well, see there. Look, Lynnie, you are my niece. Even if you remind him of someone, you are not the same person. You are Lynelle Van Sant, and don't forget it. Play for the tent meetings."

Lynnie acquiesced and donned a hat each night with her dark curls tucked inside. She ended up as the pianist for the tent revival both weeks, and Preacher Tom Reese never had a clue. As soon as the service finished each evening, she got the list of gospel songs for the next night and left without hanging around. In truth, she never heard a word of his preaching.

Aunt Flossie often brought out points of his sermons. "Lynnie, wasn't that wonderful how Preacher Reese talked about Rahab, who in spite of her wicked profession, was used for God's glory. Like, whatever terrible thing happens in the life of a person, God will turn it to good if we let Him take control."

Lynnie nodded. She thought more about people she didn't know who came to the tent meetings.

On the last night of the revival, she had what could have been another scare. No, the scare didn't come from Preacher Reese. A young couple stood up front tuning their musical instruments. Lynnie recognized them immediately as the couple from the watermelon truck, Ollie and Siney. Although Lynnie had never heard of them, it turned out they had become popular gospel singers in the area from south of Jasper. Of course, they had never seen Lynnie before and didn't have a clue she had ridden in their watermelon truck two summers earlier. At least Lynnie hoped they hadn't seen her.

They sang neither the watermelon song nor "Way Down upon the Suwannee River" but a long repertoire of popular gospel songs. Ollie played the guitar, and Siney played a mandolin. It created a good distraction, and Lynnie enjoyed the diversion. At least, she didn't have to play all those revival songs Preacher Reese wanted her to play.

Lynnie's eyes bugged out, and she gasped. A younger version of Siney, a girl about ten years old, had come with them. *She's wearing my dress—the one I left in the pillowcase in the truck. Least it didn't get thrown out.* She couldn't concentrate on the remainder of the service and slipped out of the tent as soon as the service was over.

Lynnie didn't even tell Aunt Flossie their truck had been her ride to Farmer's Corner. There were some things even Aunt Flossie didn't need to know.

After the encounter with Ollie and Siney, however, she had another nightmare that night. *Ollie after me...face like Boris Karloff... breathe hot with moonshine...knife fire surging up through me...ton of bricks...unwashed...reeking...speaking words from hell... Help me, Jay-Lee...hel...ll...p... Got to reach Jay-Lee. The closer she gets, the farther she goes—baby cries—endless horror—until...bumping along in watermelon truck...Ollie's face...*

# Chapter 12

## *"Auld Lang Syne" by Robert Burns*

One sad event happened the end of May 1943, and Lynnie had just completed her junior year at Jasper. The day after the end of the school year, Lynnie and O'Hara resumed their daily walk to the post office. All of a sudden, a big truck, loaded and filled to the brim with huge cantaloupes, rattled through the village heading north.

Lynnie didn't get a good look at the driver, but O'Hara didn't get out of the way in time, and the back tires hit him. A cantaloupe bounced out of the truck and split open, but the driver kept going and never looked back. The severity of the poor dog's injuries indicated that he would not make it. He looked up to the sky with pleading eyes as the blood drained from the gash in his side.

Lynnie screamed, and Flossie came out to see what caused all the ruckus.

When Flossie saw him, she yelled at Lynnie to stay away from him. "He might bite ya if you try to help him. Wait. I'll get my pistol and put him down."

"No! No! Don't let him die. Don't let him die."

Villagers who had heard the commotion huddled around. They all loved old O'Hara. Joyce and Mrs. Heller ran to help. Jimbo Connelly, who usually lolled around at the store all day, ran to help. It was obvious to them all that the dog wouldn't make it.

Lynnie refused to give up. "Come on, old boy. Breathe. You can do it. I need you. Please don't die!" she pleaded.

The gunshot wasn't necessary. He was gone. Lynnie cradled him to her chest and sobbed.

Joyce tried to console Lynnie, but she couldn't be consoled.

Lynnie finally released him and rose to her feet. She went straight to her room and cried herself to sleep.

Hours later, she woke up and wrote a tribute to O'Hara in her journal.

> Ode to O'Hara
> My friend, my companion…
> You knew me better than my own heart.
> My shadow, my confidant…
> Where have you gone?
> To where I'll never have a part?
> Does heaven have such friends?
> Or is death the end?
> O'Hara, wait for me in another dawn.
> Lynnie

Jimbo dug a grave for O'Hara in the backyard, and they buried him with many of his friends standing by. Lynnie covered the grave with an armload of black-eyed Susans from the field behind the house where he loved to romp.

In time, Lynnie got through the crisis of O'Hara's demise. Flossie opted not to get another dog. Instead, she attempted to assuage Lynnie's heartache by logic and truth. "Honey, O'Hara was an old dog. I had him, what? I think ten years, and he may have been old when he showed up. He couldn't see well or hear anymore. It's a blessing to him that he's gone. You, the one he loved the most, were by his side when he went."

After O'Hara died, Aunt Flossie then did something she had not planned to do. She legally adopted Lynelle. "Lynnie, I figured I'd not adopt you because I ain't married—am not married. But us losin' O'Hara made me think we should be a real family. How about bein' my legal girl?"

Lynnie swallowed, her heart skipped a beat, and her mouth flew open. *To really belong?* With a wide grin, she ran to Aunt Flossie and threw her arms around her. "Adopted? Why yes. Yes, I really would. I'd belong then, wouldn't I?"

Flossie didn't make a big issue out of it, but she went over to the courthouse in Jasper, filled out papers, took the bogus birth certificate with her, and within a few weeks, Lynelle Jessamine Van Sant became her daughter and legally carried the name Van Sant.

They celebrated the event with a picnic down by the Alapaha with their fishing poles. This time they caught some largemouth bass and some blue gills.

Lynnie's year in school at Farmer's Corner had settled her in with the Hamilton County school system, and she had moved with ease into high school in spite of her fears. In spite of being the best all-round student at Farmer's Corner, the same did not transfer to her time at Hamilton Country. Now a senior at Hamilton County High School in Jasper, she excelled in each class. With her intelligence, talent, petite figure, dark curly hair, and blue eyes, she could have been the most popular girl in the class. That did not happen. Her reticence made her step away from any chance for popularity.

She spent time only with her friends at the football and basketball games. The Fighting Trojans weren't the greatest team, but the games were fun. Lynnie loved to watch the team and soon learned all about the game. In contrast to her girlfriends, her interest concerned the game and not the players.

"You all can drool over their muscles, but I like the strategy of the game. It is something like a good orchestra performance. All the team has to work together to win the game. Go, Trojans!"

Maudie tended toward frankness. "Lynnie, you are so weird!"

Lynnie wrinkled her nose at her friend and said, "Bosh!"

On the other hand, she played piano for each school event, even more than Mrs. Landon, the school's music teacher. Everyone in the county knew Lynnie Van Sant. Mrs. Landon also taught her privately in her home in Jasper. Lynnie had now advanced to the point where the teacher didn't feel like she had sufficient skills to teach her adequately. "Lynnie, you need to go to Jacksonville or Gainesville for more advanced lessons. To tell the truth, you are at the end of my expertise."

Lynnie's heart raced. She had thought about going to the city for lessons, but then reality sank in. "I don't think it would be possible, Mrs. Landon. Jacksonville is close to a hundred miles and Gainesville almost as far. With the war on and the gas rationed, I doubt we could get the gas to drive there all the time."

She mentioned Mrs. Landon's suggestion to Aunt Flossie.

"Look, honey, you are about to graduate, and then you can go to college and study piano. A few months without lessons won't do you any damage."

"College? Yes, I guess I will. I haven't even applied. Where would I go?"

"Well, Florida State College for Women in Tallahassee, of course."

Lynnie nodded and dreamed of being a college girl and then dreaded the prospect of being away from Aunt Flossie. She went to the school office and picked up some forms to fill out to apply to Florida State College for Women. She sent it in and would have forgotten it except for Aunt Flossie praying at the supper table every night, "And, Lord, we pray that Lynnie will be accepted at the college."

Lynnie rolled her eyes.

Lynnie's grades were exceptional. She would be the class valedictorian and be in line for a scholarship. Aunt Flossie's pride of her bloomed on her face when she talked to her friends about her girl.

"But, Lynnie," her aunt fussed and fumed, "you should have a beau. Don't the boys interest you at all?"

"Not in particular."

"You might think about it. After they graduate from school, most of them will go off to fight the war. They will need a girl back home. Think about Bobby."

Lynnie shrugged. She felt the heat rise in her face and her heart race. She turned away from Aunt Flossie. But she remained silent but thought, *If she only knew how I like Bobby, but I can't ever love a boy. Never.*

Bobby Everett not only played first chair in the high school orchestra, but he also played solos. Lynnie accompanied him. They would play the "hoedown" from Copeland's "Rodeo, Ballet Suite" for the spring concert. They often practiced in the Van Sant parlor. Aunt Flossie hoped they would begin to date. Bobby obviously liked Lynnie, and her aunt suspected those affections were returned but hidden.

The week before the senior prom at Jasper High School the next Friday night, Bobby made his move. He showed up at the bakery Saturday morning at 11:55, right before Aunt Flossie closed up the bakery for the day. He bought a bag of Flossie's Famous Molasses Cookies and dawdled around for a few minutes. Obviously, cookies were not on his mind.

"Where is your fiddle, Bobby?"

"I didn't bring it this time."

"And?"

"Uh…is…is Lynnie around?"

Of course. How could he have missed Beethoven's "Pathetique Sonata?" The vibrations caused the signs on the bakery wall to vibrate. It was the piece she would play for the spring concert in May.

Flossie pointed toward the back of the house. "Go on, Bobby." With her mouth awry, she cocked one eye and watched as he slipped through the kitchen and into the back of the house. She heard the piano stop for a while, and not too long afterward, a long-faced Bobby walked back through the bakery and gave Aunt Flossie a woeful look.

"No? Sorry, Bobby. You want me to talk to her?"

"Nah. You know what she said? She said she'd be proud to date me, but she had no interest in going with me or anyone else. She has no intention of going to the prom. I don't get it. I just don't understand. I thought she liked me."

"Bobby, you go ask the purtiest, most popular gal in your class to go with ya, and she'll jump at the chance. My niece will be the one who misses out, not you." Flossie patted him on the shoulder and gave him a couple more cookies.

After she closed the bakery, she went back to the living room where Beethoven shook the lamps and rattled the windows. When Lynnie got to the end of the piece, she looked at her aunt's scowl.

"What?"

"You know what," she snapped, "you might be smart and talented, but ya don't have a lick of common sense. Bobby Everett is the sweetest, nicest boy in the village, and you were downright foolish to say no—if not rude." She turned on her heel and went upstairs.

Later, as Lynnie looked out the window of her room toward Bobby's house, she muttered to herself, "She doesn't understand. How can I ever go with a boy after what happened to me? I'm damaged goods forever! Why didn't I jump in the river back in Lenoir? Why did O'Hara pull me from the pond? Why did I chicken out when I thought about cutting my wrists with the razor? Do I have feelings? I'm normal, but I have to forget them. Yes, I like Bobby a lot. I think about him too much. He treated me so nice right from the start, but I'm not worthy of him."

Ideas about suicide seethed beneath the surface again. The more she thought about Bobby, like daily, the more the thoughts of killing herself passed her mind, and the more she delved with vigor into her studies and her piano.

She wrote in her journal. "Not only do I think about Jay-Lee and hurt and think about the baby and hurt, now I think about Bobby and how I can never have a boyfriend or get married. It hurts too much to bear."

Up to this instant, she had excelled at the piano and made straight As in her classes. From this point forward, she drove herself not only to make As but also to make nothing short of 100 percent. And good piano would never be enough. She had to have perfect piano.

As Lynnie's grades rose to higher levels, and she fine-tuned her piano proficiency, she became even more isolated from her friends. Maudie and Joyce often stopped by to talk, but she always brushed them off too soon, and they would leave bewildered.

Then Maudie fell in love with the star football player, Harvey Roper. She had finagled her daddy into a purchase of a white evening gown for the prom. She planned to use it as a wedding gown as soon as she could convince Harvey they should get married.

Joyce didn't know Bobby had asked Lynnie to the prom. When Lynnie said no to Bobby, he asked Joyce as his date. She stopped by the day after the prom to tell Lynnie all about her date and the fun they had.

"Oh, Lynnie, I had so much fun. Bobby and I danced every song. He is such a gentleman. Better than his silly-nilly brother."

Lynnie gave Joyce a broad, if absentminded, smile. "Good for you. I'm glad you had fun, but Joyce, I have to practice. I'll see you in Sunday school tomorrow. Glad you stopped by." Lynnie said and turned back to the piano.

Joyce stared at her. "Hey, Lynnie. What is wrong with you? Are you mad at me that I went with Bobby? You know, I think you're sweet on him in spite of all those denials."

With a shrug, Lynnie gave her friend a breezy retort. "Oh, not at all. I'm just busy. Boys are the last thing I want. See you tomorrow."

Joyce shook her head and left.

Some of Lynnie's friends considered her a snob. Joyce wanted to remain friends and made it a point to sit with her in Sunday school and lunchtime at school. She also wanted to maintain the friendship in order to preserve a needed connection after Lynnie went off to college.

Maudie did not see Lynnie's attitude and isolation the same way and made it a point to voice her opinion. "Hey, she can be a snob if she wants to. Fine. I don't need her. I'm gonna get married and have babies. I am in love with Harvey, and I want to spend time with him. You enjoy her snubs if you want to." Maudie sat with other girls at lunchtime and sat with Harvey in church. If Lynnie noticed, she said nothing.

For the remainder of the school year, one day blurred into the next for Lynnie: final exams, spring concert, graduation, and then her valedictorian address. She had to write the speech and memorize it. Then she needed to fill out paperwork for college and try not to think about Bobby.

Back several months before, when Aunt Flossie suggested she should go to Florida State College for Women, Lynnie felt panicky at first. "Leave you, Aunt Flossie? Be in a city so far away? Even farther away than Jacksonville?"

When Aunt Flossie told her, however, the college continued as an all-women campus, she relaxed most of the time, and that is when she applied. So far, they had no confirmation of her acceptance, but she planned. She would major in piano proficiency and minor in music education. It would be good. She worried, however, that she might not be able to come home at all with the gas rationing during the war.

Graduation day came, and she gave a short speech with unexpected warmth, emotion, and an appreciation for the school. Her blue eyes sparkled in the floodlights. Dressed in her white cap and gown, she stretched her tiny figure as tall as she could and stood as a valid representation of the class of 1944.

> I want to address our school administration, teachers, and families today as well as my fellow students. The four years here at Hamilton County High School have prepared us for graduation, yes, but more, they have prepared us to commence on the rest of our life. A graduation is a move to another level of our life. A commencement is when we launch into what we do with our life. The world is our apple.
>
> Some of us will go to college; others with stay home and begin their lives here with jobs. They will have families and contribute to the community. Others will risk their lives for our country in this time of war. Each of us as graduates will pursue our goals, our purpose, and our future.
>
> Thank you, parents, families: You have encouraged us to do our best in school. Thank you, teachers: You have offered your wisdom in our pursuit of knowledge. Thank you, school administration: You have supported our educa-

tion to the best of your resources. We will need continuing guidance as we move ahead. We will need your support to precede with our dreams and goals. We will always need your support. Classmates, we will still need each other, each other's memories and friendships as we grow older apart from one another.

We will always remember Hamilton County High School. Yes, the world is our apple.

She closed her speech with a poem she had written:

The world is our apple with delicious days ahead.
There will be challenges in every bite,
and maybe times we must fight
to keep our chunk of fruit
or must grapple with decisions, but no need to dread.
The apple's there not just to take,
but rather we shall grow and share
and give our brand of flavor
for others who can savor
what we can contribute,
and we will make a world that's better
if we dare.
(Lynelle Jessamine Van Sant)

Loud applause followed her speech, and her classmates were stunned by the warmth she portrayed. Aunt Flossie stood, and tears streamed down her face as others stood with her.

The scholarship awards came as the last segment of the graduation exercises. As valedictorian, Lynnie received a full two-year scholarship from Florida State College for Women and another $1,000 from the bank in Jasper.

When Lynnie and Aunt Flossie arrived home, they stopped by the post office. Miss Hannah handed Lynnie the letter from Florida State College for Women.

Lynnie's eyes gleamed as she tore open the letter. "I'm in Aunt Flossie! I'm in." She gave her aunt a huge hug.

High school had finished. College loomed ahead, preceded by a summer of preparation—a summer of uncertainty. School, with all the work Lynnie had to do, kept her stable, but once she graduated, she felt as though her life had no further purpose.

On the other hand, her classmates were in pursuit of their new lives. Maudie and her beau decided to get married right away because he had joined the army. She moaned and whined until her daddy gave in and let them get married a week after graduation. She asked Lynnie to play for the wedding.

"Lynnie, I know I've ignored you for a few months. I didn't mean to," she lied. "but I've been so wrapped up in Harvey I couldn't think of anything or anyone else."

Lynnie hadn't even noticed Maudie's absence in her life. "I would love to play for your wedding. Believe me! I'm happy to have something to do this summer. What do you want me to play?"

The two friends put their heads together and came up with some beautiful wedding music. Plans went ahead for the wedding, and all the village would be invited. Joyce helped design and create the handcrafted invitations. Aunt Flossie would make the wedding cake.

As for Joyce and Bobby, they dated only once. Bobby enlisted in the Navy and left for Pensacola the week after graduation. He didn't even stay around for Maudie and Harvey's wedding. He came by the bakery with his violin the night before he left, and he and Lynnie played together for an hour before he had to say goodbye.

"We have to play the hoedown from *Rodeo*," Lynnie insisted. "It's a piece we can play to remember Jasper High."

They played the piece with perfection and tears.

As Bobby put up his violin, he said, "Lynnie, I don't pretend to understand why you wouldn't go to the prom with me, but I want you to know, you will always hold a place in my heart."

It surprised Lynnie that Bobby expressed how he felt, but she knew she could never allow herself to show her reciprocal sentiments no matter how her heart would break.

"Thank you, Bobby. I can't explain to you why I won't date, but you will always hold a spot in my heart. I won't forget you."

Bobby hugged her before he left.

Lynnie knew she'd never forget Bobby Everett.

The following Saturday after Bobby left, Maudie's wedding became the event of the summer. Joyce and her mother decorated the little chapel with pink roses, magnolia blossoms and leaves, and ferns. Aunt Flossie made a gorgeous wedding cake, and Lynnie played the piano. Maudie's friends created the most beautiful wedding Farmer's Corner had seen in years.

After the wedding, Aunt Flossie watched Lynnie with a heavy heart. "Lynnie, tell me how come you're mopin' about? Do ya miss your schoolmates and the structure of school? Are ya worried about college?"

Flossie suspected the truth: *Lynnie's heart has gone into the Navy with Bobby.*

Lynnie shrugged. "Didn't realize I'm moping about. Sorry. I'm not so much worried about college, but I think I'll miss this harbor in life's storms. I can't take you to college with me." She gave a nervous laugh and headed to her piano.

Aunt Flossie laughed and yelled down the hallway after Lynnie as she went back to her retreat at the piano. "Maybe I should pack up and go to college, too. Huh?"

Lynnie turned around with a quizzical look.

"Humph. I never even finished high school. Did ya know I got married instead? Got married to a drummer who came through here with his wares to peddle. He fed me a big line and then took off. Never saw him again. Daddy had it annulled. That way, I'm still a Van Sant."

Lynnie opened her eyes wide in surprise. "Auntie, you are full of surprises. Guess that's what I get for assuming. I figured we'd be two old maids living out our lives in the bakery." She returned to her piano.

Aunt Flossie glared at Lynnie. "No reason you have to be an old maid, a spinster."

# CHAPTER 13

## *"I'll Never Smile Again" by Ruth Lowe*

*August 1944*

A spinster was how Lynnie envisioned her future. Bobby had gone, and when he came to Lynnie's mind, she retreated to the piano. She avoided any of the pieces they had played as a duet. She pounded away at the piano, but she couldn't shake him from her mind.

She thought a lot about Jay-Lee too. *Did she graduate valedictorian too? She is just as smart as me—talented too. Maybe she'll go to college over in Boone. What about Jeb and Tommy? I'll bet Jeb's married now. He and Carrie Willson were getting serious… No! No! I can't think about them.* She made her resolve.

Two weeks before the beginning of college, Aunt Flossie and Lynnie were in the bakery. Lynnie acted in a chipper mood. She had joked around all morning. Flossie offered her a cinnamon roll.

"You only ate the almost-green banana and some coffee for breakfast. Here! Eat!"

"No, thank you. But you know, Auntie, if I stayed here instead of going off to college, I'd get so fat here in the bakery. Our goodies are hard to resist, aren't they?"

"As my ample girth gives testament." Aunt Flossie jiggled her plump tummy, picked up an envelope, and handed it to Lynnie. "Here, honey, I'll save ya the cinnamon roll while you go to the post office."

Lynnie hadn't gone half the distance to the post office when Flossie heard the squeal of brakes out on the street, and when she looked out the window, she saw a man get out of a rattle-trap truck and go to a form in the street. Lynnie lay sprawled out beside the road.

"Lynnie! Lynnie!" she called as she ran as fast as her large bulk would take her.

When she got to the road, she saw Lynnie hadn't been knocked unconscious, and she appeared unhurt. The letter remained clutched in her hand. The driver, a local farmer, had been on his way to Jasper. Flossie had seen him around, but she didn't know him well.

"She walked out in the road 'fore I saw her. It's a miracle I didn't hit her. 'Twas like some'un grabbed the steerin' wheel and tuk it away from me so I'd not hit her smack dab in front. Hit woulda kilt her fer shore! D'ye know the gal?"

Aunt Flossie got down on the ground with Lynnie. She cradled her in her arms. "Yes. Yes, thank you, God! She is my young 'un. I'd sent her out to the post office." She took the envelope from her hand.

"Lynnie, sweetie, can you hear me?"

Lynnie looked about in a daze. She didn't seem to have anything more than a bruised knee and an abrasion on her arm. "I'm all right, Aunt Flossie. I…I took my eyes off the road and didn't pay attention to traffic. Sorry to cause you trouble."

Lynnie looked at the man as he stood by his truck, hat in his hand. "Mister, thank you. Thanks for stopping."

"Don't be a-thankin' me, missy. Thank God. Yer angel tuk charge o' my steerin' wheel as sure as I'm a-standin' here. Jes' glad ya weren't hurt worse."

Aunt Flossie grinned at the truck driver, stood up, and lifted Lynnie. "Thank you so much." She nodded toward the bakery. "How about a sack of cinnamon rolls? Made 'em fresh this mornin'."

"Thanky, ma'am, but I gotta git goin' to Jasper afore the bank closes. Maybe on my way home if yer still open." He tipped his hat. "Good day, ma'am—missy."

When Aunt Flossie got Lynnie into the bakery, she examined her from head to toe to make sure there weren't any lacerations to stitch up or broken bones. She had stayed in one piece after all.

"I'm fine, Aunt Flossie. Don't worry. Sorry, I didn't get to the post office. Let me get cleaned up and I'll go."

"If you're sure. I can go if ya want to watch the store."

"No! I'm fine!" Lynnie snapped.

Aunt Flossie looked at her over the bridge of her nose. "Dadburn if you aren't one stubborn gal."

Lynnie wrinkled her nose at Aunt Flossie and strode out of the bakery and back through the house. She emerged in five minutes with clean clothes and her hair pulled back into a low ponytail. Curls popped out the sides like they had minds of their own. She grabbed the unmailed letter and said, "I'm off to the post office. Again."

Flossie looked after her and laughed at the mercurial teenager.

Lynnie knew about teenage mood swings, but hormones hadn't been what disturbed her. She had walked out in front of the truck on purpose. After five years of thoughts about suicide, except for the one time when the dog pulled her away from the pond, she hadn't made any attempts to harm herself. This time, she intended to go through with it. The truck created a perfect opportunity. Tired of life with ghosts waking her from her sleep, tired of constant thoughts about Jay-Lee, tired of thoughts about the tiny baby she had left back in Lenoir, and tired of thoughts about Bobby Everett, suicide seemed like the only avenue to escape. Like gnats around the pond on a hot summer day, these thoughts drove her crazy. She could escape only by spending hours on the piano. She was fearful to abandon her safe haven with Aunt Flossie. Yet school would start in Tallahassee, a hundred miles away, in two weeks. What could she do?

As Lynnie picked up the letter again she thought, *Aunt Flossie might know how to pull strings and get me a new identity with a forged birth certificate, but I know who I am, and I don't like me.*

*Blasted farmer, wish he hadn't been paying attention.* She shrugged and headed to the post office.

Lynnie sauntered along to the post office, mailed the letter, picked up the mail, and ambled back to the bakery with the few pieces of mail. No letter for her. *Only mail I've ever gotten was the acceptance letter to college. I've never received a personal letter in my life. Well, I never write to anyone.* With her limited circle of acquaintances, she never expected a letter.

"At least, when I go to college, Aunt Flossie will write to me."

Before she went to sleep, she wrote in her journal:

> I might as well live on the moon. I don't believe the farmer didn't steer the truck so he would not hit me. I don't have an angel. If I did, my life would have been normal. My life wouldn't have ghosts. I'd be with my family and not have to pretend I'm someone I am not. If I had an angel, it would have whisked me off to heaven when…

Her life had become a secret, and she had no family except Aunt Flossie, and in two weeks, she'd not even have her.

After the incident with the truck, she retreated into her quiet world again. She spent three and four hours a day at the piano. Since she no longer had lessons with Mrs. Landon, she made special arrangements of songs from song books and songs from the radio. She even composed some songs of her own. She struggled over her own compositions for, sometimes, two and three hours before she wrote them out on music paper.

Aunt Flossie left the door open between the bakery and the house so she could hear her play her music. "Sure will miss my gal when she goes off to college," she commented to Joyce's mother, who stopped in for some fresh-baked bread.

"I know you will. Joyce plans to stay home for now. She has a job at the grocery store. She said she doesn't want to go to college. I think she's serious about a boy who's been courtin' her since graduation. Does Lynnie have a boyfriend?"

Flossie Van Sant looked a bit sad, but she pasted on a smile anyway. "Lynnie is pretty much interested in her music. She wouldn't even accept a date for the prom. It will take her some time. Since she grew up in the country without any other young 'uns around, she's a bit behind in her growin' up process. I think college will be good for her. She won't look for fellows at college since it is a girls' school. Of course there'll be parties and dances with connection with other schools, but she won't have to have fellers in her classes."

Mrs. Heller shrugged and looked toward the open door where beautiful strains of "I Dream of Jeannie" were floating on the summer air.

"Thanks, Flossie. Lookin' forward to this bread and some of my fresh-churned butter." She left singing along with Lynnie's music, "I see her tripping where the bright streams play…"

As the last two weeks progressed, Lynnie packed her belongings, what she thought she would need for her first semester at Florida State College for Women. Her suitcase was filled with clothes and toiletries. A footlocker held her music, a few books, and some nice things friends of Aunt Flossie had given her for graduation. She had sewn some new skirts and blouses and, on Aunt Flossie's insistence, a beautiful peach satin formal she could wear to parties.

Flossie handed her a package. "Here are some dressy shoes to match your formal."

"Oh, Auntie! They are perfect."

As she packed, her thoughts returned to her baby. *Is my little girl happy up there on the mountain? She would be five years old now. I wonder if her mommy has taught her the colors and how to count?*

Somehow, in all the fuss of getting ready for her new adventure, her thoughts of her baby did not throw her into the usual "Life isn't worth living" mode.

As Aunt Flossie helped her pack, she thought in a different direction. *I hope Lynnie won't go wild when she gets away from Farmer's Corner.*

The thought prompted her to say, "I've heard how some of them girls get too sophisticated and start gettin' into bad habits. You remember your last five years here and the good upbringin' you had at that school in Crossnore."

"Oh, Aunt Flossie, I appreciate your concern, but you know how I study and practice. I don't even want a bunch of people around.

I know about the parties and the focus of those kind of girls. I don't want parties. I know, I know, I made that formal, and I'm sure I'll have an occasion to wear it, but all I want is an education. That's all."

"Maybe you should try to get into a sorority."

"No way! Too much social life!"

They went back and forth for days, and after she got nowhere with Lynnie, Flossie let it go with a final word of caution. "I hope you don't get a bunch of trashy roommates who don't know a thing about havin' good manners and how to get on in this life."

Fire came into Lynnie's bright-blue eyes. "Trashy, huh? How do you suppose I lived before my parents died?"

Lynnie had never talked about her parents and family or their way of life. Although she suppressed thoughts of those years, she never forgot it.

"You wanna tell me?"

"Yes!" She added a curse word. "I do. I want you to understand me and leave me alone!"

"Such language!"

"Well, I'm angry. Angry my life had to change. Don't get me wrong, Aunt Flossie. I am so grateful to you and all you have done for me, but you have to understand about me, and then I never want to talk about it again. Ever."

"Fair enough. Let's hear it."

Lynnie barreled into a long soliloquy of her life before Aunt Flossie. "We had no electricity or running water. The house sat up on poles with the underneath open. That's where Pa kept his hunting dogs and a pig! If we wanted to keep something cold enough so it wouldn't spoil in the summer, we kept it in the spring house. In the winter, we kept cold things on the porch. Our water came from the spring house. Ma had to build a fire outside under a big iron kettle and heat the water for our laundry and for our baths. We went to bed with the chickens because oil for the lamps cost too much.

"To go to the store, we walked over the mountain to a little store that only had the bare essentials, if that. We didn't have a nice shiny black Packard—not even a beat-up truck. Pa had a mule. The storekeeper took Ma's home-churned butter and eggs or her hand-made braided rugs, or Papa's handcrafted furniture, and traded them for dried beans, cornmeal, molasses, and on rare occasions, sugar, white flour, and fruit. Pa traded for moonshine too. I remember we each got a little sack of hard candy at Christmas. They heated the house from the cook stove in the kitchen and a fireplace in the middle of the house. My sister and I hadn't started school yet, but my brothers had to walk four miles to the schoolhouse. Ma made all of our clothes by hand."

Flossie had tears in her eyes as she fingered the beautiful material in Lynnie's store-bought dress.

"When they went on the only trip they had ever taken—the last one—they walked to the closest town to catch a bus for Asheville to visit one of Pa's kinfolk up in Asheville in the hospital. Then our familiar life stopped. They told us our parents had eaten some apple pie, and both of them got sick with ptomaine poisoning. We never saw them alive again."

She took a deep breath and plunged ahead. "Then we were sent to Crossnore School. At first, we didn't live at the school, not until my last year there. We lived with a family close by and worked for them for our keep. Life turned out better for us there. Once we moved into the girls' dormitory at the school—you talk about trashy girls for roommates—some of our girls came from worse circumstances than ours. We had a dozen of us in our loft at school. Sometimes it didn't smell good. Well, it stank."

Lynnie took a deep breath and relaxed her pent-up emotions. She giggled at the thought about all those country girls. As she giggled, Flossie joined her and said, "Lynnie, I understand. I won't say another word."

The big day came. To travel to Tallahassee from Farmer's Corner meant taking several different country roads until they were closer to the city. They went to Jasper and then through several little villages and towns. It would be a long morning of driving the little more than a hundred miles across north Florida.

Aunt Flossie backed the same shiny black 1929 Packard out of the garage, and Lynnie packed the trunk full of her things. Flossie had tears in her eyes. *My girl will be gone.*

Lynnie settled into a too-quiet, eerie silence. Flossie had the grace to leave her alone until she emerged from her dark place.

But once they were in the car and on the road for perhaps twenty minutes, Aunt Flossie asked, "Mind if I turn the radio on?"

Lynnie looked as though she realized for the first time she was in the car or on her way to Tallahassee. She shrugged and turned the radio on. Bing Crosby sang "Swinging on a Star," a song from the movie they had seen down in Jasper earlier in the summer, *Going My Way*. Flossie hummed in her usual out of key mode until Lynnie put her hands up by her head and made donkey ears. "Sorry if I acted like a donkey."

From then on, Lynnie's mood soared above her fears and misery. Flossie breathed a sigh of relief.

# Second Movement

# Chapter 14

## *"Grande Valse Brilliante" by Frederic Chopin*

*Florida State College for Women, Tallahassee, Florida*
*September 1944*

In 1944, Tallahassee remained a small southern town, less than 30,000 residents, despite the presence of the college and the seat of state government. Lynnie's journey from the remote mountain cabin in North Carolina to the backwater town of Farmer's Corner did little to prepare her emergence onto the college campus and the town around it.

When Aunt Flossie drove onto the campus, Lynnie's mouth dropped. "Aunt Flossie, it's huge! I've never been anywhere close to something like this."

The campus with grand brick buildings giving a cloistered appearance to Lynnie impressed the naïve freshman.

Although she had hopes for only one roommate, her assigned dormitory room would be with two other girls in Jennie Murphree, the freshman women's dormitory.

Lynnie and Aunt Flossie climbed the stairs to the second floor of the dorm. With a bag on each shoulder, they carried her footlocker between them. Through the open door, they saw a tall young lady with shoulder-length red hair arranged in a stylish pompadour. She turned from placing items into one of the chest of drawers when she saw Lynnie and Aunt Flossie. Lynnie thought the girl looked like Rita Hayworth.

"Hello! I'm Ruth Helton, your best friend for the next year."

"Ruth. Hello. I'm Lynelle Van Sant. Call me Lynnie. I have no doubt I will need a best friend since this is my rare venture out of the swamp."

Ruth looked puzzled and then giggled. "Swamp?"

"Oh, and this is my Aunt Florence."

Flossie cleared her throat and announced, "Flossie, please."

Her aunt's reply thawed the ice, and Lynnie smiled, winking at her aunt. She knew her aunt hated to be called Florence.

"Okay, I don't live in the swamp, close by, but I've never been in a real city. We are from a small village in the northeastern part of Florida, not far from the Okefenokee Swamp. I may need your help to navigate around here."

"Well, we're all novices. I came here from Norfolk, Virginia, so Florida is new to me too. We can navigate together."

The third roommate showed up with a huge pile of luggage. "Hey, y'all! I'm heah, so the pa'ty can sta't!"

A petite girl with straight black hair cut in the Imogene Coca style and dressed in red shorts and a white sleeveless blouse grinned at them. Lynnie looked at her aunt's pursed lips and scowl. Lynnie could guess what Aunt Flossie thought.

Indeed, Flossie thought, *Shorts! Bah! Showin' off them scrawny legs. She's gonna be a wild one.*

"Hey!" Ruth and Lynnie voiced simultaneously.

Lynnie ventured the first conversation. "I'm Lynelle Van Sant, better known as Lynnie. This is our roommate, Ruth Helton, and my Aunt Flossie. You are?"

The girl extended her hand and murmured in her best Georgia accent, "Hey, ah'm Liz Watson, from Cairo, Georgia. We spell it like Cairo in Egypt, but we pronounce it like the syrup, 'Kay-row.'" She grinned at Aunt Flossie and said, "I'm lookin' fo'ward to corruptin' y'all."

Aunt Flossie sniffed and glared at the girl. Ruth and Lynnie both rolled their eyes.

Ruth nodded to the top bunk. "You can have the top bunk. Last one here."

Liz grinned. "Suits me."

Aunt Flossie nodded to Lynnie. "Well, honey, it looks like you gals need to get settled in. How 'bout walkin' me to the car and make sure we didn't leave anything in the car."

Once out of earshot, Lynnie gave her opinion of Liz. "Oh, Aunt Flossie. I hope she isn't so ornery all the time. I doubt if she can make me worse than I already am. Don't worry, though. I think I can hold my own with her. I intend to give full attention to my studies, but with her around, I might have to spend most of my free time in Dodd Hall."

"Dodd Hall? Oh, yes. The library. Good idea."

When they arrived at Aunt Flossie's car, Lynnie gave a cursory look around the interior and in the trunk. She knew she hadn't left anything behind. She knew Aunt Flossie needed her as much as she needed her auntie. She hugged her aunt and wiped the tears of the older lady's cheek.

"Aunt Flossie, I wish you would sign into a hotel for the night. You'll be driving all night. The bakery can stay closed tomorrow."

"No, darlin', I'll be home by midnight at the latest if I leave now. I'll be thinkin' about you all way home. That'll keep me awake. Now don't you let that Liz corrupt your morals, honey."

"Don't worry about me, Auntie. I'm here to learn. As soon as I get my things in order, I will get on with the process of matriculation. There will be no Liz Watson nor anyone else to stand in my way of my education. I'm the only one who would stand in my way."

Flossie scrunched up her forehead. "And why would ya do that?"

Lynnie only shrugged. She hugged Aunt Flossie one more time. "Bye, sweet auntie."

Aunt Flossie pulled out a box of Flossie's Famous Molasses Cookies from beneath the driver's seat. "I'll be a-prayin' for ya day in and day out."

Lynnie grinned. "Thank you, darlin' Auntie. I'll share the cookies and be confident that you uphold me in your prayers."

Lynnie cried as she stood watching until the Packard was out of sight.

Lynnie dried her eyes and walked back into the room. She could see Liz had stashed her overstock of possessions everywhere—under both beds, in the closet, in the dresser drawers—while Ruth looked on with obvious concern.

Ruth attempted to halt the process of the wild child. "Whoa, girl. We need equal space. You may need to choose what you need to keep here and send the rest back to 'Kay-row.'"

Liz dropped the Southern charm. "I can't. My stepdad said, 'Don't bother to come back home,' so I brought everything I own with me. Mom brought me, helped me get it all out of the truck, and took off back to Georgia to His Royal Pain-in-the-Rump!"

"I'm sorry, Liz. I have an idea." Ruth offered a solution. "Let's go find the housemother and see if there is a storage room you can use. It doesn't look like Lynnie has a lot since her home's closer to campus. I have a good amount of stuff too. Maybe you and I could store some of our extra things."

Lynnie smiled at the possible solution. "Good idea. What do you say, Liz?"

"Sounds good, but then I'll have to decide what is important and what isn't."

As though on cue, a middle-aged lady with her light-brown hair pulled back in a severe bun and horned-rim glasses appeared—the housemother. "Good day, young ladies. I am Miss Jones, your dorm mother. Welcome to Florida State College for Women."

"Yes, ma'am. I'm Lynelle Van Sant—Lynnie."

"Hello, Miss Jones. I am Ruth Helton."

"Hey! I'm Liz Watson."

Miss Jones scanned the room. "My, you girls may have to live in the hallway from the looks of all your possessions. You will find you will acquire a lot more before the week is over."

"Funny you should mention that, Miss Jones. We wondered what we could do with all this stuff. Do y'all have a storage room where we could stash the extra?" Liz waved her hands toward her piles of luggage.

"Yes, Miss Watson, we do. There is an attic on the fourth floor of this building. Do you think you young ladies can carry it up the stairs? Let me know when you have what you wish to store, and I will bring the key. Why did you bring so much? I can understand Miss Helton's extra, but you are closer to home than most of our young ladies."

Liz shrugged. "I got kicked out of the house. I suppose this is my new home."

Miss Jones looked incredulous. "Kicked out? I can't believe anyone would kick you out!"

"Oh, yes. My stepdad. He said he'd be glad to get rid of me."

Miss Jones shook her head in disbelief and turned to Lynnie. "Do you need to store anything, Miss Van Sant?"

"No, ma'am. My needs are simple—a corner in the closet, a drawer or two in the dresser, and I can keep my books and music in my footlocker. It's all I need. I hope to go home whenever my aunt can come for me given the shortage of gasoline. I'll be fine until winter. I can help carry things to the attic."

"Of course. When you have things ready, I am in room 218. If I'm not there, leave me a note. And, Miss Van Sant, you will have a locker for your music in the Music Building. I'm sure it will be helpful for you."

Miss Jones turned to Liz. "Oh, by the way, Miss Watson, I see you have on shorts. You may wear them in the dormitory, but if you go out onto the campus or to town, you must wear a raincoat over them. Dresses are the dress code for classes."

Without further ado, she turned and left.

Liz cocked her head and looked cross-eyed at her roommates. "Well! Of all the junk I have, I don't have a raincoat! That figures."

Ruth and Lynnie laughed at their animated roommate.

Another lady appeared at the door with Ruth's telltale red hair.

"Oh, hello, Mother. You missed our housemother by a minute or two. But good news: I can store my extra things in the attic."

"Wonderful! These are your roommates?"

"Yes, ma'am." She introduced Lynnie and Liz to the older version of herself.

"Oh, I'm glad to meet you, dears. Would you girls care to join us for a light supper at the Sweet Shop after we get your things moved to the attic? You'll need a good meal after the work on your room. Once it is all fixed up, we cart the extra to the attic. I've noticed there is no elevator. I'll help." She looked at the pile of luggage and boxes in the room.

Liz looked a bit embarrassed. "Most of this stuff is mine because I brought all I own with me. Uh, long story."

"Well, no problem."

Lynnie looked with appreciation at Ruth's mother. She thought Mrs. Helton must be the kind of person who didn't let anything phase her.

Mrs. Helton reared back her shoulders and started to help her daughter sort her possessions. "We will have it sorted out in no time. We know all about this. We take everything we have with us, do we not, Ruth?"

Ruth grinned and nodded. "Right. We're Navy people. Right now, Father is on a ship in the Pacific, and my brother is stationed at Norfolk. We've packed and unpacked so many times that sometimes we never get to use what we've packed away before the next move."

Lynnie helped Liz choose what she needed to keep in the room. After half an hour, they had it well organized. Lynnie offered to go to the housemother and ask for the key to the attic.

Lynnie found the housemother in her room. The woman went with Lynnie to the dorm room and offered to help with the move. The five women made quick work of the transfer of Liz's and Ruth's things.

With the move-in accomplished, Mrs. Helton led the three young ladies to the Sweet Shop. Liz had sensibly changed into a skirt.

Mrs. Helton left as soon as they returned to campus. Ruth bade her mother a tender goodbye, and the three girls waved until she was out of sight.

After they returned from dinner and the girls got ready for bed, they talked for a short while. They discussed their majors. Ruth and Liz were both elementary education majors. When Lynnie said she would major in piano, Liz laughed and said, "I'm as musical as Bossy the cow."

Ruth laughed. "I'm not musical, but I do love good Chopin music."

As they talked, the three girls ate all of Aunt Flossie's cookies. Soon they were talked out. And before lights out, Lynnie started her new journal.

> Time to say so long to the last five years and begin on a new journey. I know I can't bring the distant past along. I want to prove to myself I can be a person who can stand alone. I love Aunt Flossie, but she won't live forever. I am my own person. Yet there is always this question in the back of my mind: Why bother?

As in high school, Lynnie excelled in college. As a piano performance major, she accompanied vocalists and instrumentalists in their presentations even while she was but a freshman. A girl's college had been good because she had no pressure to date. The rare occasions when men from other college campuses came for parties or dances, Lynnie avoided them. Ruth became her best friend, not only for the year but they were also able to room together throughout their college days. Liz too roomed with them each year.

Ruth liked to joke about their wild-child roomie. "We need Liz around to give us a taste of what we will be in for as teachers when we get out into the world."

Indeed, Liz had a wild streak, but they loved her anyway. The girls made a good trio. But part of Liz's wildness entailed sneaking out of the dorm and off campus to meet "guys," as she termed them. Most of the time she would crawl up the fire escape and through a window into the hallway. She often reeked of alcohol and acted tipsy—if not drunk. Her roommates never reported her, but they warned her over and over again.

Now and then, Joyce wrote to Lynnie to tell her of all the activities about Farmer's Corner and her love life. Aunt Flossie wrote every week and sent her articles from the Jasper newspaper and anything of interest—and cookies. Lynnie went home over the Christmas holidays, but with gas rationing, she couldn't go home again until summer break.

By the summer between her first and second year, Joyce and her boyfriend had decided to get married. Again, Lynnie played for the wedding.

Bobby Everett never came home at the same times Lynnie was home, but she talked with his brother, Jimmy. "Bobby's fine. He loves his stint in the Navy. I'm gonna join too soon as I'm outta here."

# CHAPTER 15

## *"Sonata in B Minor" for Piano by Franz Liszt*

*Florida State University*
*November 1947*

Lynelle Van Sant, now a senior at the newly named Florida State University, finally had to face male students for FSU had gone coed. Other than her music, she did not participate in campus life. Yet since the university had become a coed university, something positive put a new spark in Lynnie—not dances or parties but football games. She loved football games and never missed a home football game.

Football held no excitement for Ruth, but Liz and Lynnie loved it. It didn't matter to either girl if the FSU team won a game or not their first season. They both enjoyed the thrill of the game, although Lynnie didn't express her enthusiasm as boisterously as her spirited roommate.

Lynnie had a class, History of the French Revolution, with one of the football players, a senior transfer from a small college in Maine, John Clark. He had been in World War II and served in the Pacific. After his discharge, he decided he wanted a warmer climate to finish his education. A lot of the male students at FSU were older than Lynnie.

Lynnie caught the eye of the twenty-six-year-old, not only because of her attractiveness but also she appealed to him because she didn't flirt and she obviously studied. Her responses she offered in class discussions reflected her studies. He liked smart girls like Lynnie.

For a while, Lynnie ignored John's attention. By the time of the first football game, however, she had noticed him. She wrote in her journal:

> I won't ever date, but I do wish I could go out with him. He's handsome, smart, and the best I've seen around here. Reminds me of Bobby. Yes, I like John, but I made up my mind after what happened to me, I'll never marry. I'm not about to go out with anyone no matter how much I like him.

But Liz noticed John's apparent attraction to Lynnie and decided to take matters in her own hand. Liz reveled in the number of men at the university. "Wow! I feel like I've died and gone to heaven with all these eligible guys around." Every Friday and Saturday evening she had a date, a different one each time. Although she had no classes with John Clark, she had dated his roommate, Bill Thomas, also a football player. She had no real interest in Bill, but she told Ruth, "Yeah, I'll date him again if he can persuade John Clark to ask Lynnie out."

After class on Thursday prior to the game with Tennessee Tech, John stopped Lynnie after class as she gathered her books, ready to head for the music building.

"Good morning, Miss Van Sant. I hear you are a big supporter of our games. I'd like to get to know you better. Would you be able to go with Bob Thomas, his date, and me for a bite to eat after the game Saturday evening?"

Lynnie felt as though her face had turned beet red. She didn't know what to say.

She quivered inside and stumbled over her words in her lame excuse. "Uh…I thank you for asking. I…I have to prepare for a proficiency exam in piano. I'll be at the game to cheer you on, but…but

I will have to…have to say no. Maybe one of my roommates will be free."

She did not tell him her proficiency exam wouldn't be until the spring term, but she couldn't think of any other impromptu excuse.

"I don't want to go out with your roommates. Miss Watson has a date with Bob, and I thought we could make a foursome."

"Ah, yes. Miss Liz has dated Bob before, Mr. Clark. Thank you but no."

John scowled and scanned her body. He took in her feminine curves. "You like girls or something? Sheesh!"

Lynnie, her face burning, picked up her books and left, while the young veteran stood perplexed, his head cocked sideways and his hands out in disbelief.

On her way to the piano practice room, she still trembled inside. Her normal practice took all other thoughts from her head but not that day. She played like a grade school version of herself instead of a senior in college with a major in piano proficiency and a minor in music education. She stayed at her practice all evening, Friday evening, and the entire day Saturday except for the game. She drank only coffee, ate two bananas during the interim, and practiced.

When game time came, she went by herself and sat high up in the bleachers with some freshmen girls she didn't know. The team lost.

Liz blamed the loss on Lynnie. "Lynnie, I don't understand why you wouldn't go out with us. I'll bet if you had said yes to John, he would have won the game for us." Liz spit to the side.

Lynnie glared at Liz and went to the music practice room. Her practice did not improve. "What would Aunt Flossie say?" She wrote again:

> In class with John, I am so nervous. It is like I can feel his eyes on the back of my head. It makes me so nervous. I don't know if I can do this being in college with all these men. I don't want to go with John, yet I do want to go with him. I don't feel worthy, and I would feel like I'm

not true to how I feel about Bobby. I know my
notions are ridiculous for I'm certain I'll never see
Bobby again. This is so stupid. Why live? Why?

Each day in class made her more nervous than the day before. Lynnie's usual participation in class declined because she couldn't concentrate thinking of John's eyes boring into the back of her head. She still did well on the tests because she studied. The professor noticed her lack of participation and called her aside.

"You understand, Miss Van Sant, part of your grade in my class is dependent on your contribution to in-class discussion. You started out well. What has happened?"

Lynnie shrugged. "I…I don't feel well, Dr. Weiss. I think it's my monthly. I will attempt to concentrate more in class."

"Have you taken anything to relieve your symptoms? You could ask at the infirmary, you know. You are a good student—your quizzes show it. I'm here to help you."

"Thank you. I'll go to the infirmary."

Again, at bedtime, she added to her journal:

> I hated to lie to Dr. Weiss today about my monthly. It's really my three-times-weekly class with John Clark. But to save face, I went to the infirmary and got some Midol. Now if Weiss checks on me, I can say I got some medicine. I need to forget Mr. John Clark and Bobby Everett and get on with my life. But then why do I even need a life?

Her mind went back and forth with how to rise above the issue or whether she needed a life. Again, the next day, after a terrible practice day with one of her repertory pieces, her fingers were stiff. After another hour with little progress, she went back to the dorm, grabbed her bottle of Midol, stole Liz's little stash of gin, and downed the entire thing of pills and booze together.

She huddled with her pillow on her bunk, and before long, since she had eaten little for three days, she felt the effect of the booze. She lost consciousness and upchucked a large quantity of the pills and alcohol. A few minutes later, Ruth found her with the empty Midol container and empty gin bottle.

Ruth, supposedly on her student teaching assignment, had a cold and had been sent back to her room. Her roommate grabbed the empty bottle and screamed. She dropped the bottle and shook Lynnie. "No! Wake up! Wake up! Lynnie!"

She saw that Lynnie had shallow breathing, so she ran to the housemother's room. "Hope she's there." Ruth found her in her room.

Miss Jones had nearly fallen to sleep reading. Her eyes popped open, and she gasped. "I'll call the infirmary. You go back and try to arouse her."

Back in the room again, Ruth tried to rouse Lynnie. She couldn't arouse her, but she noted that Lynnie had slow, even breathing.

Within minutes, two premed students who worked as attendants in the infirmary arrived. "Men on board!" They raced up the stairs with a litter and carried her down the stairs and to the infirmary.

The nurse in the infirmary put a tube down through Lynnie's esophagus and washed out her stomach. It appeared most of the pills had not been digested. What alcohol and pills she did digest had only been enough to make her sleep.

But Lynnie would not be the only one in trouble.

The housemother questioned Ruth about where the alcohol had come from. "Do you know if Miss Van Sant had gotten the gin herself, or did someone give it to her?"

Ruth evaded the question. "Ma'am, I've never known her to drink before. I doubt if someone gave it to her. She doesn't drink."

Miss Jones's eyes sought the girl's, and Ruth could no longer avoid her. "But you have an idea where she got it, do you not?"

Ruth looked at her hands in her lap, avoiding Miss Jones's penetrating eyes. "I…I think the flask of gin belongs to our other roommate, Liz Watson."

She hesitated and then, straightening her shoulders, confessed. "I didn't report her because I did not want to get her in trouble. Of course, this incident changes things. Lynnie and I knew Liz had it, but we never saw her take a drink from it."

"You are culpable, Miss Helton. You didn't report what you knew. Is Miss Watson in class now?"

"No, ma'am. She should be in the library. She has a paper due tomorrow and always waits till the last minute to do it."

"I will stay with Miss Van Sant. I want you to go find Miss Watson."

Over the next hour, Lynnie came around, but she had consumed enough alcohol to make her drunk. She repeated over and over to the nurse, "Don' tell Aun' Floz…"

Once she sobered up enough to have an intelligent conversation, Miss Jones questioned her.

"Miss Van Sant, what were you thinking? Surely you had not planned to do away with yourself, had you?"

Lynnie made evasive comments. "I wanted to sleep. I had a couple of bad days, and I wanted to forget them. Please don't tell my aunt. She's been so kind to give me this opportunity, and my actions have been foolish."

"Bad days? Would you like to tell me about them? What bothers you? I know you are an exceptional student, and from what I hear, you are a talented musician. No day can be so bad you would endanger your life by such a stunt."

"Well, my piano practices are not going like I want them to, and I've been…uh…yes, I stay awake half the night. I played over the music in my head. Then I can't concentrate in some of my classes. I've had a couple of bad days. Please don't tell Aunt Flossie."

"I can't promise the Dean of Women will not contact your aunt, but I will ask her to wait, at least, until you have had a chance to talk to her."

"Thank you. May I go back to my room now? I feel strong enough. I beg your forgiveness."

"You don't need my forgiveness, my dear. You need to forgive yourself."

"Forgive myself?" *How can I forgive myself for letting that boy...?*

"Yes, forgive yourself and get back to what you have set out to accomplish here at Florida State University."

Lynnie shook her head as though to shake out the doubts and dark thoughts. "Yes, ma'am."

"Now get yourself back to your room and back to the young lady I know you are."

Miss Jones helped Lynnie get to her feet and into some clean clothes Ruth had brought for her.

Ruth went to the library to look for Liz, but after she searched the entire building, she had not found their absent roommate. She checked with a few of Liz's friends to see if they knew where to find her. No one had seen her. With no luck, she went back to the dorm. Liz was nowhere to be found. Ruth thought, *It's like she knows there will be trouble when she gets back to the dorm.* She hoped her elusive roommate had returned. But no, she hadn't come back.

Liz didn't return to the room until several minutes after curfew and, again, not by the front entrance.

Miss Jones waited for her. She positioned a chair right outside the girls' dorm room door and sat there awaiting the errant coed. As she suspected, Liz came up the fire escape, jiggled the window loose, and made a clandestine entrance.

"Good evening, Miss Watson. You will come with me to my room for a little discussion."

Lynnie, now awake, heard the exchange through the open transom above the door. She looked at Ruth.

Ruth, propped up in bed with a textbook, had heard and nodded to Lynnie. "Sounds like our Lizzie is headed for a bit of hot water."

"I did a stupid thing, but maybe this can be the motivation Liz needs to put her on a better path. I suppose she'll be mad at me for upsetting her fun and games."

Both girls were silent for a few minutes, but Lynnie spoke first. "Look, I know I did a stupid, wrong thing, but that aside, Liz has come in after curfew for two weeks, and I know she drinks on the sly—a lot. The bottle of gin had a good bit out of it. She would be headed for bigger trouble if I hadn't upset her little apple cart. I suppose she'll be furious with me, but I don't care."

Ruth got up from her bed and sat on the edge of Lynnie's bed. "Lynnie, this is all so strange. What made you do this? You told Miss Jones you wanted to sleep. Yes, I've been concerned about you while you have been awake. You have not been yourself. No matter what you say, I know you do sleep. Tell me what's going through your mind, sweet friend."

Lynnie hesitated. She never spoke of her troubles, but she counted Ruth as a friend. She took a deep breath. "I don't know, Ruth. What good is all this? Why study? Where will it get me? Where is my life headed? I can get a good education, get a job as a piano teacher, or maybe some minor performance opportunities. But I know I'll never marry, never have a family. I'll rot away to old age as a spinster, and no one will care."

"How do you know you'll never marry? You have all the right body parts. You're smart, pretty, and have a good personality. And gee whiz, I know you liked John Clark. But then you turned him down for a date. Why are you afraid to get involved?"

Lynnie shrugged. "I had him on my mind so much I loused up in both classroom work and my piano practice. I can't let it happen. Ruthie, there is a lot more to my story that I can't tell you. I can't tell anyone. Please know I appreciate your friendship, and let it go right there."

If Ruth had any clue Lynnie had experienced a sexual trauma, she never brought it up. She gave Lynnie a hug and pulled her face into her hands. "Lynnie, I am so sorry you've felt so bad, and I'm glad you are still here. I'm here for you. You can talk to me. You know it won't go any farther. Please tell me what I can do to help, okay?"

Lynnie didn't look at Ruth, but she nodded and wiped the tears from her eyes.

Just as Ruth slipped back under her own covers, Liz eased the door open into the room and crept in. Lynnie lay on her bed and turned her face away from her roommates. Liz minced around, getting ready for bed, but had nothing to say more than a few grunts to Ruth.

Tomorrow would be another day.

The next day, Lynnie got up before the others and left before Liz woke up. The two didn't cross paths until after nine at night. When Liz came in, Lynnie knew she had to face the situation.

"Liz, I'm sorry I got you in trouble. I didn't intend to interfere into your personal life to attempt to ease my own. Please forgive me. My own head's been messed up."

"Hey, no big deal. Yeah, I got more than a lot peeved when I found out you got into my booze, but I shouldn't have had it here in the first place. If I want to graduate, I've gotta start to act like an adult, huh? Miss Jones warned me, so I'm gonna behave. Well, sorta," she added with a giggle. "Yeah, she said something that kinda stuck with me: 'If you burn the candle at both ends, it will soon burn to the middle and self-destruct. You will burn out.' I do want to be worthwhile, so I can prove I can get an education and graduate. I want to prove it to my stepfather! So yeah, you're forgiven."

Lynnie gave a cynical laugh and mumbled, "Now I have to forgive myself."

She went about the next few days intent on a return to her previous reputation as a studious woman and talented pianist. But she thought about the need to forgive herself as Miss Jones had advised. Lynnie struggled for days with whether she could forgive herself. Not long after that, she wrote in her journal:

> It's easy to forgive someone who has done wrong
> unless you're the one who's to blame.
> It's easy to see why they erred or why they sinned,
> but it's hard to admit you're the same.
> So, God, if you hear—if you are real—
> once again, I implore, wash the stain
> from my soul and my mind.
> Help me walk step by step in the way I should go,
> toward an unburdened future to find. LVS

For the remainder of her college education, if suicide thoughts returned, they neither surfaced in her discussions with her roommates or in her classwork and piano, nor did she make another attempt. For some reason, the Dean of Women never talked to her about the incident. Nor did she contact Aunt Flossie. Lynnie's anxiety about John was short-lived. Bobby still remained in her fantasies, and if he surfaced, she would busy herself with other pursuits.

    Again, she excelled.

# Chapter 16

## *"Three Moods" for Piano by Aaron Copeland*

*Farmer's Corner, Florida*
*Summer 1953*

The three roommates had graduated in May of 1948. Liz did an about-face and finished with a 2.9 average. She got a job as an elementary school teacher in Miami, Florida. Ruth considered more college, but she decided to teach if she could find a school and save up for more education. She had also fallen in love her senior year with Ben Steyer, a premed student at FSU.

Ben had entered med school at Emory University in Atlanta. As soon as he graduated from medical school, the couple planned to get married. A little country school outside of Valdosta, Georgia, hired Ruth to teach seventh and eighth grades. Lynnie knew for the last two years what she would do. She had been told a position would be available at Hamilton County High School for her to teach music. Mrs. Landon, her old music teacher, would be retiring the year Lynnie would graduate from FSU and had recommended for Lynnie to take her place.

*Not sure if it's what I want, but it will make Aunt Flossie happy.* She had this thought often, but she had never voiced it. She jumped into the job with both feet, employed all the pedagogy she had learned, used standard music for high schools, and encouraged tone-deaf youngsters. She played for special concerts, played piano at the Farmer's Corner Chapel, and went about her life almost by rote. Faculty reviews were good. She did a good job.

It made Aunt Flossie happy to have her home, believing Lynnie had finally come to a point of satisfaction and contentment. *I used to wonder if Lynnie knew what bein' a Christian was all about, but I reckon the prayers and takin' her to church worked. She seems content goin' every Sunday and doesn't fuss a bit about playin' the piano. She even discussed something in Preacher Thomas's sermon she wasn't sure was in the Bible. We looked it up, and shore enough, she was right. Never used to like talkin' about it before. Praise you, Lord!*

*But,* Lynnie thought, *where's the joy in this? When I'm not in class or doing music in some other capacity or not busy with Aunt Flossie in the bakery, what kind of life do I have? And I am so bored in church. He preaches opinions—dogma. Why not end it all?*

She never followed through with that thought. She stayed by herself for the most part and played the piano for hours on end. The rare visits from Ruth were her sole social outlets. Joyce had moved to Jacksonville; Maudie and her husband had settled somewhere out west after the war. Bobby's parents had moved away, and neither he nor his brother ever returned to Farmer's Corner. Lynnie put Bobby as far back into her mind as she had tried to put Jay-Lee and her baby. She refused to think about them. As for John Clark, the crush on him passed, and she would laugh at her foolishness over him. She heard he had married and moved home to Maine.

Yes, there were days when she considered suicide, but she would go to her piano and play for hours and hours. Her music kept her out of her self-destructive mood. If she still thought about it, she would write in her journal.

> Is there a purpose to all of this?
> What if the life I've chosen is all amiss?
> Where will it lead?
> Is it greedy to want to succeed?
> There must be more
> to life than daily chore.

> Beyond this day by day
> a purpose on the way,
> and I don't have to pay
> for sins not of my own…
> for which I can't atone.
> LVS

Aunt Flossie frequently said, "Lynnie, you got the makings of a concert pianist. You ought go to Julliard. Why don't ya see if you could get in? Or how about Peabody in Baltimore?"

"Aunt Flossie, how could I leave? Live in some city away from you? You need me here. I don't think I could. You aren't young anymore."

"Pooh! You survived college without me. Anyway, I'll keep kickin' till I'm a hunnert years old. I've been thinkin' 'bout sellin' the bakery anyway. Here is what I've got in mind: You could go to a summer music program. This way, you can be here for the school year and then go away to learn each summer."

"Maybe. I might like the idea."

She scouted the music journals and found one that interested her, the Tanglewood Music Festival in Massachusetts, where Aaron Copeland taught on the faculty. In the spring of her first year at Jasper, she applied. They accepted her, and she spent the next four summers under the tutelage of the great pianists, including Copeland.

The first summer, she hated to leave and go so far away, but Aunt Flossie insisted. "Honey, like I said, I've thought about getting rid of the bakery, so I'll slow down—at least for the summer. I've got enough money saved so I never have to turn the ovens on again. I happen to like baking, so I keep doin' it. I ain't gonna live forever, so now's a good time to cut back."

Lynnie grinned at her aunt. "So a 'hunnert years' isn't forever, huh?"

Flossie made donkey ears at her.

Each summer, Aunt Flossie drove her to Jacksonville, put her on the train for Massachusetts, and returned to meet her at the end of the summer. They talked on the phone every week.

## JUNE TITUS

Before she went to Massachusetts in the summer of '52, Ruth asked Lynnie to be her maid of honor and play the pre-wedding music. She happily agreed and played all Chopin selections—Ruth's favorite. Ruth and Ben had a quiet wedding in Macon, Georgia, where he would intern. Both of their families came to the wedding, but they had few other guests. Lynnie and Aunt Flossie drove up to Macon. The old '29 Packard had been sold after World War II, and Flossie replaced it with a sleek black 1946 Packard.

After the wedding, Aunt Flossie drove Lynnie from Macon to Jacksonville again for her annual trip to Massachusetts.

At the end of the fourth year of Lynnie's stretch at Hamilton County, Aunt Flossie had an announcement. "I sold the bakery to a feller I know from Jasper, Hank Wickman. I'm gonna pack up and go to Massachusetts with you for the summer."

Lynnie's heart gave a leap, and then she let out an uncharacteristic whoop like a cowboy's yell at a herd of steers on a cattle drive! "Yippie ki-*yay!* Oh, Aunt Flossie. I couldn't be more delighted! Away from you, I'm incomplete—like I've lost my right arm." Then she thought of Jay-Lee and burst into tears.

They crammed all the clothes and other paraphernalia they thought they might want for a New England summer into the Packard and headed to Massachusetts.

The cottage Flossie rented was cute and cozy. "Oh, Aunt Flossie, this is adorable. You even have flowers to tend to. Despite my need for practice time and class time, I'll be able to come every day."

During the day, Flossie tended the flowers about the cottage, enjoyed the shops in the town of Lenox, or drove out to Wood's Pond to enjoy a day of fishing.

Lynnie had classes each day, one-on-one instruction in piano, and hours and hours of practice. During this time, Lynnie discovered Farmer's Corner may not be the end of the road for her.

Aaron Copeland had a suggestion. "Lynnie, I think you need to pursue a concert career."

Her heart flipped. In a way, it was what she thought she wanted. "You mean leave my high school job and pursue a masters in performance?"

He told her of an opportunity. "I know a man in Tampa, Florida, Dr. Foster at the University of Tampa, who arranges local concerts and wants a piano teacher for the university. He is head of the music department, and you are what he needs. Lynelle, you are tucked under a toadstool. You could be a far better than average talented performer. You could be extraordinary. You could eventually play in any concert hall in the world and have accolades equal to my own in no time at all. You are qualified. I know you have a bachelor's degree, but you could work on your masters and teach."

"I hate to leave my aunt." Her doubts went into high gear as she thought about it. *My life wouldn't be worth the space it takes up without Aunt Flossie. Ruth is so tied up with her life with Ben. I no longer have Jay-Lee—some days I don't even think about her. Aunt Flossie is all of life to me.*

Copeland went on. "I know you can't bear the thought of leaving her, but did you consider she might even be happy to move with you? She came up here for the summer, didn't she? At least look into the possibilities."

"Her leave the house she has lived in all her life? That won't happen."

"Have you ever asked her?"

"No."

"Do it. You may be surprised."

After her session with Copeland, she went straight to Aunt Flossie's cabin and skipped her afternoon practice session. Flossie sat on the porch to allow the sun to dry her long tresses that hung down about her shoulders. Lynnie could see her hair had become gray and thin, and Flossie's usual ruddy cheeks were pale. Lynnie frowned but didn't bring up the subject.

Lynnie didn't want to leave her aunt, but she knew she would have to tell her what Aaron Copeland said.

"Auntie, how would you like to move to Tampa, Florida?"

"Leave my place? Hmmm…" She pondered on the question, grinned, and rolled her eyes at Lynnie. "Well, maybe. I no longer have the bakery. We could sell the house too. I think Harry Wickman would love to have it. Ya got a job?"

"I might. Aaron Copeland has a friend, the head of the music department at the University of Tampa. He has asked Copeland to recommend a piano teacher. I wouldn't need to have my master's degree but would work toward it while I teach. This would be a masters in performance and prepare me to become a concert pianist. But…"

"Go on."

"I don't want to leave you, Aunt Flossie. I won't even consider it unless you are inclined to move with me."

"Go for it, babe. Papa took me to Tampa back in '27 or sometime before the stock market crash, and I loved it there. Tampa Bay is beautiful. Wait till you see the flowers and flowerin' trees down there. Yellows, pinks, all the rainbow colors. Beautiful! And then there is the water."

"Sounds luscious."

"Lynnie, you have another month and a half here, so go ahead and contact the man, and I'll call Hank. Let's get this show on the road."

Lynnie's mouth dropped open, and her eyes popped.

Within two days, Flossie had sold the house. In another week, Lynnie had the position in Tampa without a face-to-face interview, and by September first, they would be ready to move. Lynnie resigned from Hamilton County High School, and by the end of July, they packed up and headed the Packard back to Florida. Lynnie could see Flossie's excitement. Even some of the natural rosiness had returned to her cheeks enough that Lynnie's former concerns were shelved.

Before leaving Massachusetts, Lynnie called Ruth in Macon to give her the news. When they arrived in Farmer's Corner, Ruth came down for two days and helped them pack.

"I am so excited for you, Lynnie. I knew you could do this. You know, I can see into the future." Ruth giggled, grabbed a glass from the table, and pretended to look into a crystal ball. Lowering her voice to a sultry French-like accent, she gave her "reading." "I zee a name in neon lights: 'Mademoiselle Lynelle Van Sant in an all-Chopin piano concert.'"

"You and your Chopin. You know there are other composers such as Copeland, Coates, Cohan…"

Ruth had a smug look on her face.

Lynnie noticed. "What?"

"I think we might move to Tampa too. Ben has been interviewed by a doctor there who wants to sell his practice and retire. He thought about a cardiology residency someday, but he wants to do general practice first. We might be neighbors!"

Lynnie jumped over a packing box and hugged her friend. "Ruthie! What wonderful news!" Lynnie had an unfamiliar childlike excitement.

After a week of "sort through, pack up, toss, give away" Friday afternoon, after Ruth had gone back to Georgia, Flossie grabbed a cup of coffee and plopped down at the kitchen table. "Girl, we need to get us a place in Tampa. How about we drive down this weekend and look it over?"

"Aunt Flossie, you are full of surprises. No sense in this stuff all packed up without a place to go, huh?"

"Right. You've never been so far south. Now I'll warn you, if you think it's hot here, Tampa is hotter, even worse this time of year. It is humid in the extreme. Of course, you will have a decent Gulf breeze there if you are in the right part of the city. Lots of palm trees to stir up the breeze."

Lynnie called Dr. Foster at the University of Tampa and got an appointment to see him on Monday while she would be in Tampa.

Before dawn, the first Saturday in August, Lynnie and Flossie loaded up the Packard and headed south before the sun popped over the eastern horizon. Flossie, as excited as Lynnie, said, "Never even crossed my mind to leave Farmer's Corner, but I'm ready. Without the bakery, I feel lost, out of my element even in our own little village."

"Without you, I'd feel out of my element, Aunt Flossie."

Late Friday, they arrived in Tampa, registered for a room at the Hotel Floridian, ate dinner in the hotel dining room, grabbed a newspaper, and went to their room to comb through the real estate section of the paper. After a good night's sleep and breakfast, Flossie made calls. Several places listed in the paper sparked her interest. She wanted to see them.

"Honey, we may not be able to get a house right away. Would you be content to live here in the hotel until we do, or should we find an apartment?"

Lynnie, standing by the window looking at the traffic on the street, turned, raised her eyebrows, and looked over her nose down to Auntie. Flossie had a newspaper spread out on the bed where she was seated.

"Aunt Flossie, can we afford to live in a hotel?"

"Of course. Have I never explained to you much about my money? You've seen me go to the bank in Jasper, but I don't reckon you paid much attention. I am well fixed. You see, when the Great Depression hit, Daddy had been wise. He never put his money in the banks or stock market. While everyone else struggled, he had money. He bought up property for a little bit of nothin', and then as the economy improved, he sold it at a profit. He died in '35, but I kept up his model. Before you came to live with me, I owned the grocery store and five houses. I had sold them all off before the war. I didn't want the bother anymore. Then I invested the money I made. Daddy didn't believe in the stock market, but I have done well. It is a lot more stable now than back in '29. Yes, we can afford to live in a hotel. You're gonna inherit all I have when I go to meet my Maker."

"Oh, Aunt Flossie, don't even mention it! You have to live forever."

"Well, I will with Jesus, girl. I will."

Lynnie scowled at Aunt Flossie. "Wish you wouldn't say those things."

After they looked at several houses, they found a beautiful Craftsman-style house on North Ninth Street. They wouldn't be able to take possession until the first of October. It had five bedrooms and two baths, a luxury in Lynnie's estimation. Flossie didn't see luxury, only necessity. "Oh, Lynnie, I can see our furniture in this house, can't you? It's perfect."

Lynnie nodded with excitement. "I can see us here for the rest of our lives." She made a mental placement of her bedroom suite and the piano where she wanted them. She even envisioned a grand piano some day in one corner of a music room.

Early Monday, they went to the university, and Lynnie had a face-to-face interview with Dr. Foster. It went well. Dr. Foster convinced her that this would be a boost to a performing career. Up to this point, she had no real goals or purpose. She wanted to teach, but more, she wanted to get her master's degree and be a performing artist. "Aunt Flossie, I do like him. He is down to earth, yet a gentleman, and the kind of person you would think of as the department head. He said I would be able to live on campus until we move into the house."

With the interview over, a brief tour of the music department, and filling out paperwork, Lynnie wanted to get back to Farmer's Corner and wrap up her life there.

The Wickmans were not ready to live in Flossie's house yet. Hank's future idea would be to use the house as an investment. He would keep the bakery in the front and rent the rest. "Y'all can stay as long as you need, Miss Flossie. I ain't in no hurry."

In the end, Flossie decided to stay in Farmers Corner until they could move into the Tampa house, and Lynnie would stay on campus at the university. Flossie drove Lynnie and all her "stuff," as Flossie termed it, to Tampa the last weekend in August. They spent one night at the Hotel Floridian.

As Lynnie hugged Aunt Flossie goodbye, what she saw in her aunt's eyes made her shudder. *She's aging fast. I hope she can make the move without getting ill.*

Flossie hugged her and held both hands in her own. "I'll call ya when I get home. Hey, girl! Get yer mopin' mug turned up the other way. It's a month, not forever, till the movin' van will be pullin' up North Ninth Street to our pretty little nest."

Lynnie attempted a smile as her aunt crawled under the steering wheel and headed the Packard north to Farmer's Corner. She spoke to the exhaust as the Packard pulled away. "Will I ever see her again? Will she come back? Will she move here?" The rapid succession of events seemed bizarre to Lynnie.

## JUNE TITUS

Although the month went by at a crawl, Lynnie delved into teaching her students. At last, October arrived as a big Mayflower moving van lumbered up North Ninth Street with Flossie's Packard in the lead. Lynnie had taken the bus to the house and waited there for her. A rare excitement surged through her as she saw the Packard leading the van. *It's real. She's here!*

# Chapter 17

## *"Adeste Fideles," Latin Hymn*

*Tampa, Florida*
*1953*

By the time Flossie arrived and they moved in the house, Lynnie already had several freshman piano students at the University of Tampa. She told her aunt, "I have some great students, Aunt Flossie. So much different from the high school youngsters. These students are eager to learn."

Flossie laughed. "Better brains and not musical morons? What about your own classes?"

"I will wait until the spring semester to enroll in any classes toward my master's degree. Dr. Foster agrees and advised me on which courses to pick up next semester. He understands the move from Farmer's Corner to our new house with you should take precedence over my pursuit of another degree—at least till next semester."

Once they were settled and had the phone connected, she called Ruth. Aunt Flossie heard her squeal and rounded the corner from the kitchen. She saw Lynnie nearly jumping up and down in excitement.

Lynnie saw Aunt Flossie and cried out, "They're moving here! Be here in time for Christmas."

Ruthie said, "Ben will work with another doctor in Macon until we move, but we'll be in Tampa to look for a place to live over Thanksgiving."

"Great! You can stay here. We have a guest room. We bought a bed and dresser to put in it."

The Steyers found an apartment to live in until they would be able to buy their own home. They would move the first week of December. Delight filled Lynnie to know that her friend would be in the same city. They would become a part of the Tampa culture together.

Lynnie said to Aunt Flossie, "I know she'll look for a church right off the bat. Do you think she would like the one where you have visited? Shame on me! I haven't gone with you."

"Yes, missy, I've been wondering about that. I know it's a bit different from our little chapel at home, but least ways, they got a preacher each Sunday rather than our once-a-month preacher. I like the music, but the church is a mite big. I ain't got to know folks much. Come with me Sunday and see what ya think."

Lynnie made no promises. Some excuse always got in the way when Sunday arrived—a headache, a "needed" connection with a student, oversleeping, and so forth.

Aunt Flossie, however, didn't give up on her. "Someday, you will go to church." She thought, *I hope it won't be until I die and she has to go to my funeral!*

By and by, Aunt Flossie got to know some of the ladies her age when she went to the once-a-week women's circle. She would dress up in her second-best dress and hat and meet every Thursday with the ladies. "It ain't like back home, but I like these ladies. They have a lot of projects both here in Tampa and on the mission field."

"Auntie, I'm sorry I haven't been able to go with you. I always felt safe and homelike at the chapel. I knew everyone, and I played the piano there. Maybe someday, I will shove my stubbornness under the carpet and go along with you."

Flossie glared at her over her nose. "Good that you admit to being stubborn. That's half the battle."

Ruth and Ben, instead of Lynnie, went with Aunt Flossie the second Sunday after they moved, Advent season. They loved the church and went along with Flossie and encouraged Lynnie to go with them. At last, for the Christmas Eve service, Lynnie ran out of excuses and went with them.

In contrast to the lack of Christmas traditions or pageantry at the chapel in Farmer's Corner, where they only sang carols on the Sunday before Christmas, this city church had a beautiful candlelight service. It started with the choir procession down the center aisle with candles as they sang "O Come All Ye Faithful." This song set the tone for their singing of more familiar carols and a few unfamiliar ones.

Candlelight suited Lynnie. She could hide her feelings. In her mind, she went back to Crossnore so many years before with Jay-Lee as they listened to the Christmas story at the church in Crossnore. Tears ran down her cheeks, but she had dried her eyes by the time the service ended.

If either Ruth or Aunt Flossie noticed her emotion, they remained quiet. The four of them went back to the house on North Ninth and had refreshments.

Aunt Flossie came in from the kitchen with her Christmas specialty. "Can't have Christmas without my flamin' Christmas cake and some eggnog."

Flossie served up her celebrated cake, a yellow one with cherry filling, brandy poured over, set afire, and then topped with real whipped cream.

Ben laughed as he spooned the deliciousness into his mouth. "It might clog our arteries, but we can die happy!"

Ruth, ever ready with a comeback, said, "Spoken like a doctor who has worked for twenty-four hours with no time to eat. I'm glad you haven't given up the culinary arts, Aunt Flossie."

Flossie laughed. "Culinary arts, huh? They'll have to carry me out feet first before I'd give up bakin'!"

Ruth and Ben had a special Christmas announcement. Ben laughed as he looked at his wife. "She'd like to tell you about our Christmas present to each other."

Lynnie and Aunt Flossie looked at the couple. Questions lit up their faces.

"We are going to have a baby!" they announced together.

Aunt Flossie broke out in a "Whoopie!"

Lynnie looked stunned for a moment, as her stomach flipped. Then she caught herself. "Well! Congratulations. When?"

"Oh, we've known for a couple of weeks. Looks like early August."

Aunt Flossie hugged Ruth.

Lynnie shook Ben's hand and said, "Nice Christmas present."

The happy party broke up by the stroke of midnight, and Lynnie wanted some solitude. She wrote in her journal:

> I don't understand why I got so emotional tonight. I don't want to hurt Aunt Flossie and Ruth, but going to church is too hard. Church in Farmer's Corner meant community more than church. We had Sunday school every week, I played piano, and then the preacher came once a month. Tonight, I thought of my baby after Ruth told me about their baby. My little girl would be fourteen and a half now.

Early Christmas day, Lynnie and Aunt Flossie exchanged gifts. Aunt Flossie gave Lynnie a soft V-neck cashmere sweater, and Lynnie gave her aunt the newest rage in board games, "Scrabble." She liked words, and Lynnie thought it would be a good pastime for the two of them during school break over the holidays.

After breakfast, Lynnie went for a walk at her aunt's insistence. "It is such a beautiful day, honey. Ya need to get out and get some fresh air. We never had Christmases this warm in north Florida. Git, girl!"

About ten minutes after Lynnie left for her walk, the doorbell rang, and a delivery truck pulled into the driveway. Flossie expected it. The delivery truck had a piano, a big surprise for Lynnie. Aunt Flossie had bought her a beautiful brand-new Steinway grand piano. She had them take the old upright piano out first and then move in the Steinway.

Flossie knew where Lynnie always walked. She would take a bus to the waterfront, walk for an hour, and then take the bus back.

The men set the piano up and checked the tuning before they left. "Ma'am, you will need to get a piano tuner here this week, but it isn't too bad."

When Lynnie returned from her walk, she alighted the bus just as the truck pulled away from the house. At that distance, she couldn't see the name on the truck or the house for the delivery.

"Hmmm…delivery truck out on Christmas day? Someone's last-minute present, I suppose."

She watched as the truck rounded the corner three blocks away.

"I'm home, Auntie. Did you see a delivery truck out front? It headed down the street as I got off the bus. Someone must have gotten a last-minute Christmas delivery."

"Could be. You have a nice walk?"

"Yes. I love to watch the birds. Today I saw herons, pelicans, and lots of gulls. The gulls fight each other for food. There are other birds I didn't recognize."

"Ya can get your bird book out and see if you can identify them, but not now, honey. I'd like to hear some Christmas music. Why don't ya go play some Christmas songs while I start Christmas dinner?"

"Good! Sounds like you are in the spirit today, Auntie." She went to her piano room. When they moved in, since there were five bedrooms, three downstairs, and two upstairs, what had been designed as the front bedroom became Lynnie's piano room. Flossie followed behind her as she went into the room.

The new piano gleamed in the sunlight. Lynnie let out a squeal! "Oh, Aunt Flossie! A grand piano. It's beautiful. You mean to tell me you got rid of Ol' Plunker? Your daddy's piano?"

"Why not? He ain't here to play it, and ya need a good piano, girl."

Lynnie hugged and kissed Aunt Flossie and cried until Flossie had to shoo her off. She sat down and played all the Christmas carols she knew while Flossie cooked.

They ate their Christmas dinner together, and Lynnie played her new piano the remainder of the day. This was no day for dark thoughts. Happiness radiated from her that day.

Now and then, however, incidents crept in to remind her of Jay-Lee, the baby, or Bobby. But now, whenever she thought about Ruth having a baby, her mind flitted back sounds of her baby's whimper fourteen years before in Lenoir, North Carolina. To forget, she played the piano in the evening hours and on past midnight.

Aunt Flossie noticed and avoided any mention of the late-night noises except to say, "I hope the neighbors don't mind piano music to sleep by."

Lynnie ignored the comment.

# Chapter 18

## *"If You Knew Susie" by Buddy DeSylva and Joseph Meyer*

Lynnie looked forward to teaching her freshman piano students and the continuation of her studies now that 1953 had moved on to 1954.

One of her courses for her graduate degree was piano composition. She had to compose a major musical piece to be played at her graduate concert as a part of her final grade. She began working on it every evening when she got home. Aunt Flossie, despite her lack of musical ear, sat with her and listened to her measure-by-measure composition.

"I love hearing you play. You should consider volunteering to play at church. I know you would enjoy it," Aunt Flossie said.

Lynnie didn't answer.

If Aunt Flossie hoped the Christmas Eve service would spur Lynnie back to church with her, it didn't happen. Again, Lynnie resisted, but Aunt Flossie and Ruth were tactful. They didn't ask her to go, but they would sneak in talk about the church: "Lynnie, you should have heard how nice the choir sounded this morning," or "The pastor had a wonderful sermon about King David, when he was wandering in the wilderness hiding from King Saul," or "Ruth, those women in your Sunday school class are so friendly."

Lynnie chose to ignore them.

After the new year, Lynnie took two graduate level classes in piano and continued with her freshmen piano students. She liked her job and school and adjusted to life in the city. She insisted on bus transportation everywhere unless Aunt Flossie drove her. "The bus is fine. I can spend a few minutes with my mind off studies."

But Flossie wondered. She called Ruth to talk about it. "I know she's busy, but it seems like Lynnie's pulled away from the close relationship we've always had. Do you see it too?"

"She does seem distant even when she is with us. Her mind is elsewhere." Ruth had been reluctant to address the incident from college when Lynnie overdosed on Midol and gin. But now she decided to talk about it with Aunt Flossie. "Miss Flossie, may I come by while Lynnie's at the university today?"

"You betcha! Come for lunch, honey."

The aroma of Flossie's good homemade vegetable soup greeted Ruth's nose as she came in the house. She hugged Flossie and said, "Smells wonderful! Hope you have some grilled cheese sandwiches to go with it."

"Of course!"

As usual, starvation beset Ruth at midday after a bout of morning of sickness. As she enjoyed the meal as they sat at the kitchen table after a good lunch, Ruth noticed Flossie had eaten little, and she commented, "You on a diet? I can see it works."

Flossie shrugged and redirected the conversation. "You came over 'cause you wanted to talk about Lynnie. What's on your mind?"

Ruth hesitated with how much she should say, but she went ahead and asked, "How much did you know about when Lynnie overdosed in college?"

"What?" Flossie exploded. Her cheeks paled behind her rouge, and she stood up and knocked the chair over. Ruth set the chair upright, and Flossie plopped down.

"Ruth! I never heard about this. She never told me, and if what you say is true, why didn't the dean of women contact me about it?"

Ruth shrugged. "It happened our senior year. I always thought her feelings about one of the football players who wanted to date her made her do it. Lynnie told me she did like him, but she would never marry. He had asked her out, but she refused. She faked cramps and went to the infirmary to get Midol pills, found Liz's stash of gin, and took a combination of the two. I had to come home sick that day from my student teaching, God's way to save her life. I found her passed out, but she still had shallow respirations. I think the alcohol had made her drunk, and it might have worn off if we had left her alone. I didn't want to take the chance. The housemother called the infirmary, and attendants took her to get her stomach pumped."

Ruth could see Lynnie's aunt's shoulders slump. "I'm sorry, Miss Flossie. I thought you knew. I shouldn't have told you."

Tears streamed down Flossie's face. "I'm glad ya did. And ya know, I think she tried to do it before. As I look back at it, I think she walked in front of a truck on purpose in Farmer's Corner the summer before college. Oh dear. Ruth, I'm not sure what you know about Lynnie's past, and I promised her I'd never tell it. I won't, but know she's got a lot of pain from before she came to live with me. Let's keep an eye on 'er and give 'er love."

"Love it is. I do love that sweet girl. She and I hit it off the first day of college. I think she sees me as a sister. I think of her the same way. I have a brother but no sisters."

Lynnie's aunt and her friend watched Lynnie like a hawk, but they were discreet. Ruth made it a point to call two or three times a week and stop by without Ben whenever she could.

On one visit, Ruth made it a point to ask about men. "Hey, girl, they got any cute guys at the university? I know you have suggested you aren't the marrying kind, but a date now and then would expand your horizons."

Lynnie, not unkind in her retort, said, "I don't need guys, cute or ugly. My love is my music. It courts me every day."

Ruth got the message.

Aunt Flossie's made all Lynnie's favorite meals, sat with her when she practiced, and bombarded heaven with prayers for her dear girl.

Flossie, on the other hand, had serious health problems. Oh, indeed, she managed to hide it from Lynnie. But one day toward end of March, Lynnie came home from the university early. Her last student had canceled out for the day, so she had free time. When she saw Aunt Flossie, the woman's appearance shocked her.

"Auntie, are you okay? You are so pale. Let me look at you."

Typically, Flossie waited until a few minutes before Lynnie's bus stopped at the corner, dressed in loose layers to disguise her lost weight, and put on some makeup to reproduce the healthy flush or former days.

"Oh, ya caught me without my makeup. I've been too busy to get gussied up this afternoon."

"Nonsense. You have lost weight, and you are as pale as a ghost. Have you been to the doctor?"

"It's age, honey. Menopause. We don't look twenty forever."

"I thought you were going to live to be a hunnert years old. You are only fifty-five." She repeated her question. "Have you been to see a doctor? Make an appointment with Ben Steyer right now!"

"I don't need a doctor. I'm fine. Now you get yourself ready for a good dinner and maybe a game of Scrabble before you get to your piano. Huh? After all, we need to use the Christmas present you gave me. Let's get at it."

They played Scrabble long into the night, enduring Aunt Flossie's attempt to create words the way she spoke. "Aunt Flossie, you know *gonna* isn't a word and neither is *y'all*."

Lynnie didn't bother to practice or work on her composition that evening.

The next night, she worked again on the composition. She had decided to compose a suite, and it would be a musical biographical work. She batted around several names, and after telling Aunt Flossie's her idea for the work, she picked her aunt's brain for a good title.

"You could call it 'The Beggar's Return,' but that don't sound too good. I like that you are putting music to describe what you went through. You ain't a beggar, though. You were a poor, frightened, starving child when you showed up on my doorstep."

"Well, yes, I was a beggar, but I think a better word could be found. Vagabond? Gypsy?"

After hashing over several options, the two of them eventually came up with a working title, "The Wayfarer's Return."

While Flossie watched Lynnie, concerned for her mental health, and Lynnie watched her aunt, concerned for her physical health. She realized she had been so wrapped up in memories as she struggled with her suite she had not noticed. She knew that had to change.

After she noticed Flossie's possible health issues, Lynnie purposely became more sociable and focused on more than herself. Both Flossie and Ruth could see the change.

Springtime in Tampa brought nice weather with blooming flowers in their tropical glory, and Lynnie seemed content with her life.

Lynnie said no more to Aunt Flossie about a doctor's visit, but she mentioned her aunt's condition to Ruth. "I'm worried about Aunt Flossie. She says it's menopause, but she has lost weight, and she's so pale under all her rouge. Have you seen the change? I told her to make an appointment with Ben, but I don't think she did."

"I see it, too. She had me over for lunch back after Christmas, and she ate very little. Should I tell Ben?"

"Humph, didn't know you had lunch with her. No, don't say anything to Ben. Not yet. I think I'd rather have you mention it to her. Be direct with her. Tell her you've noticed she's too pale and suggest an appointment with Ben."

# Chapter 19

## "O Death, Where Is Thy Sting?" from *Messiah* by George Frederick Handel

As Lynnie rode the bus home from the university the next day, she noticed dark clouds coming in from off Tampa Bay. It gave her an eerie feeling. *Don't know why I have that feeling today. We have lots of those storms… Bosh.*

Entering the house, silence surrounded her. No aromas of Flossie's cooking emanated from the kitchen.

"Aunt Flossie, are you here? I'm home. I'm…" She felt a chill, as though those dark clouds she saw surrounded her, and her heart dropped. She ran to Aunt Flossie's bedroom and found her slumped in her reading chair with the Bible in her lap. Flossie was dead.

Lynnie screamed and fell over her aunt's cold body. "No! No! Please no. Why, God, if you are there? Why?" She sobbed and sobbed until the tears had expended themselves.

She rose from her aunt's body and walked to the phone. She dialed Ruth. She spoke with a wooden voice. "She's dead."

"What? She's dead? Aunt Flossie? Oh no!" Ruth never had a chance to talk to Aunt Flossie about seeing Ben. "Ben is right now home from work. I'll send him over to you. He'll be there as soon as he can get there. She doesn't have another doctor, does she?"

Lynnie shook her head.

"Lynnie?"

She realized Ruth couldn't see her gesture over the telephone. She croaked out her reply. "No. I...I don't know what I'm supposed to do."

"Ben will know. Hold on a minute, let me tell Ben, and then I'll keep you on the phone till he gets to your place."

Ruth came back on the phone in less than half a minute and continued to talk to Lynnie until Ben could drive to the Van Sant's house. In ten minutes, Ben arrived at Lynnie's, and Ruth continued to talk to her friend amid sobs and sniffs on the other end of the line. Lynnie couldn't speak.

Ruth could hear Lynnie's doorbell ringing. "That would be Ben," she said to Lynnie. "Go answer the door, and I'll head your way on the next bus."

Lynnie forgot to hang up the phone as she went to the door to let Ben in. He noticed the dangling receiver, picked it up, and spoke to his wife. "I'm here. You come on over." He hung it up as Lynnie led him to Flossie's body.

As Lynnie stood by the chair, she wrung her hands. The tears streamed down her face. Ben went through the motions: He checked for breath sounds and heart sounds. Obviously, Flossie had been dead for several hours. Rigor mortis had already set her body, and the color had left her skin. Ben took the Bible resting in her lap and placed it on the table beside her. He covered her with the quilt he found on the foot of her bed.

"Lynnie, I will need to call the coroner. As far as I know, she hadn't been seen by a physician for a while, so it will be a coroner's case. I've been on call every other Sunday and haven't seen her for a bit and didn't realize her condition. A cursory glance at her suggests it may have been an invasive cancer of some sort. There will be an autopsy, so you will need to sign the papers."

Lynnie nodded, but Ben wasn't certain she comprehended anything.

"Ruth is on her way to stay with you, Lynnie, so you won't be alone. She'll catch the bus. We are here for you. Do you want to sit here with her or be in the other room?"

"I…I don't want to stay alone. Oh, Ben. I should have made her go see you. I didn't even notice how sick she had become until a week ago. It's all my fault I didn't get her to go see you right then. She always dressed in loose clothing and piled on the makeup."

Ben led her out to the living room and seated her on the sofa. "Look, Lynnie. It's obvious Flossie has been sick, I would guess, for over a year or even more. She knew how to hide it well. Even I didn't notice it at Christmas, and I'm a doctor who is used to these signs. She piled makeup on her face to disguise it and wore her clothes in a way to not call attention to her weight loss. You couldn't have known. It's nobody's fault Flossie died. Her time had come."

Ben brewed cups of tea for Lynnie and himself while they waited for Ruth. Lynnie sipped at hers little by little, and with the warmth of the tea, she relaxed a little. Ruth and the coroner arrived at the same time. Tears rimmed Ruth's eyes as she realized the impact this death would have on Lynnie.

Ben took Ruth aside. "Look, honey, she has no idea what she's supposed to do—can't think straight right now. She will need to sign papers for the autopsy, but as soon as she does, I want you to give her this sedative and put her to bed. Could you stay with her at least until tomorrow? I can get along fine at home."

"Of course. My morning sickness seems to have stopped, so I'll be in great shape from here on. One thing I want to do is to see if Flossie had any papers to indicate what she wanted done. From what I heard you tell the coroner, she has been sick a while, and it would have been like her to have written down her preferences. You go on home. I'll call you early in the morning."

They hugged, and Ben left.

After the coroner gave Lynnie the papers to sign, she looked at Ruth. "Oh, Ruthie, what will I do without her? I called her my right arm. I don't know what to do next."

"You don't need to do anything tonight except sleep. Ben left a sedative for you. Here, I want you to take this. I am here, and I'll stay with you as long as you need me. You need to get some sleep."

Ruth took Lynnie to her bedroom, helped her undress, and tucked her in. She closed the door and went to supervise the coroner's attendants as they loaded up the body.

As Lynnie faded into her sleep, she thought about Jay-Lee. She mumbled as she drifted off to sleep, "Need you, Jay-Lee... Can't come to you... Need you, my sweet twin."

Ruth had shut the door to Lynnie's room and joined the coroner in Aunt Flossie's room. He handed her a card with his number on it. "Ma'am, when you find out which funeral home Ms. Van Sant is to go to, call me."

"Thank you, I will. I will go through Miss Flossie's papers and see if she left instructions. I am sure she would have."

After the body had been removed, Ruth cleaned up Flossie's chair and set the room in order. Then she opened the desk to see if there were any papers. Indeed, there were, just what she needed. Aunt Flossie had been careful to put matters in order. She started at the top of the pile and found it all.

First, she had all the paperwork for Myrtle Hill Memorial Park as the funeral home and mausoleum where she wanted cremation and her ashes interred. Next, to call Pastor Miller, the pastor of the church where Flossie attended and where the Steyers were now members. An envelope with his name on it lay beneath a copy of her will and, at the bottom of the pile, a sealed letter for Lynnie.

Since she had the funeral home information, she called the coroner and then Pastor Miller.

"Pastor Miller, this is Ruth Steyer."

"Good evening, Ruth. What may we do for you?"

"Pastor, I'm at the Van Sants' home. Miss Flossie died sometime today. Lynnie found her when she came in from the university. Were you aware of her illness?"

"Yes. She called me to the house two days ago and told me her death would be very soon. I couldn't believe it. She seemed so alive. I stopped in to see her that afternoon. I didn't realize it would be this soon. I urged her to tell Lynnie, but she said she couldn't. Is Lynnie okay?"

"Of course not." Ruth knew her tone was irritable. *Who would be okay in a situation like this when she didn't even know Flossie was dying?*

She swallowed and continued, "We've sedated her, and she is asleep now. She told me she noticed a couple of weeks ago her aunt had lost weight. She had caught her without her makeup, and the pallor surprised her. At the time, she urged her to make an appointment with my husband, but she didn't pursue it. Of course, she blames herself for her aunt's death. Do pray for her."

"I will, of course. My wife and I will come over and be there when she wakes up."

"Of course. I will stay with her for as long as she needs me here. Ben is fine at home without me."

Within an hour, the Millers had arrived with some homemade chicken soup. There would be food for Lynnie when she got up. Meanwhile, the three sat together and chatted about Flossie and prayed together for Lynnie.

Lynnie woke up around midnight and came out through her fog to find Ruth and the Millers in the living room.

Pastor Miller stood, went to her, and led her to the empty chair. "Lynnie, we are so sorry you found her gone—without...without knowing she was so ill. I'm here for you."

Lynnie, wordless, could only shake her head.

Pastor Miller continued. "Your aunt called me two days ago and asked me to stop by. She told me she was dying. I urged her to tell you. I'm so sorry...so sorry."

Lynnie shook her head again as though to dislodge the web of disbelief encasing her brain. "She...she was like that. She didn't want to tell me—couldn't, I guess. It's okay. Well, not okay, but we'll..."

Her mind went back to the death of her parents. *In a way, it's the same. Suddenly they were gone without any notice. Now she's gone.*

"What about funeral arrangements, Reverend Miller? It would have been like her to make preparations beforehand with you."

He nodded. "Yes, she made a few arrangements with me. She knew she couldn't last—she thought maybe a few weeks. I can handle it for you. We will plan on the funeral at the chapel at Myrtle Hill on Friday."

Although overwhelmed, Lynnie tried to take it all in. She stood up again in front of the pastor like a cigar-store Indian. "Why? Why didn't she tell me? If I had known…"

"I asked her why she hadn't told you yet. She said she didn't want to slow your progress down at the university. We can't change what is, Lynnie. Miss Flossie had a strong personality, and I could have goaded her like a mule, but it would not have changed the inevitable. She did not want to tell you beforehand for fear that you would quit school and give up. She thought when she died, you would have no choice but to go on. I wasn't so sure about that and voiced my opinion. I had prayed about the situation and decided to contact you Saturday. Obviously too late. I knew you had classes and students all week. I didn't expect her to go this fast."

"I'm glad she at least confided in you. I can't pretend to understand why she thought that way, but like you said, she had a strong personality."

Bonnie Miller slipped up to Lynnie and led her back to her chair. "Lynnie, you haven't eaten a bite. I brought some homemade chicken soup. I always keep some on hand in the freezer. Would you like a little bowl and some tea?"

Lynnie nodded as she sat down. "Call me Lynnie."

The Millers stayed for another half hour. "Look, Lynnie," the pastor said, "you need to get some rest. The next few days are going to be difficult. I'm as close as the telephone day or night. Ruth will be here with you, but when she goes home, if you need my wife to come and stay with you, call us." He turned to Bonnie. "Right, my dear?"

"Of course, Lynnie. No question about it."

The next few hours were all a blur to Lynnie. Ruth planned to stay with her for several days and help Lynnie go through the papers Aunt Flossie had put in order. As well, the days leading up to the funeral, although busy with details, Lynnie did by rote with Ruth leading the way.

Lynnie put off opening the sealed letter, but Ruth coaxed her to read it the day of the funeral. Lynnie could see that Flossie's hand had shaken, distorting her usual neat script, but the clarity of the message sounded like her dear aunt.

> My dear, sweet Lynnie,
>
> Yes, young 'un, I'm dead. I didn't tell you I got sick for a good reason. You would have insisted upon hanging 'round in Farmer's Corner and vegetating. I couldn't let you do that. I knew back last summer before we went up north I had cancer. That's why I sold the bakery. I'd seen my doctor in Jasper, and he said it had gone too far for surgery. He did suggest radium or something like them treatments, but I said no. If I'm to die, I need to get on with it so you can get on with the life you deserve. I'm all healed up now and sitting with my Jesus.
>
> Do not waste yer time in the blame game. Glad ya didn't see how sick I had gotten. I reckon I done a good job hiding it. I could live above my pain most of the time, and I really didn't suffer so bad. There were days, but God loved me and gave me strength. I've done lived a good life and ain't sorry, except for leaving you.
>
> By this time, you should have seen what I want. Wait till after my funeral, and then contact my lawyer. His name is on the front of the envelope with my will. All I got is yours to keep. He'll see to it. You'll be well fixed to finish your master's degree and to live well in the future.
>
> You've done well to get over yer past, and I reckon you can conquer the future. You were such a blessing, and to help you become Lynelle Van Sant turned out to be my greatest joy. Just recollect the things I taught you for your own future. It's more important for you to make sure God's part of your life. I'll be a-watching from

heaven as you go on with your life. One day, we'll see each other again. I pray you'll find peace that comes from Jesus.

I love you more than life.

Aunt Flossie

Lynnie tucked the letter into her own desk and determined to rise above her pain, and her anger too. The funeral would be limited to the few people whom Flossie had gotten to know at the church, the pastor and his wife, the Steyers, and Lynnie. Lynnie called Flossie's friend, Sarah Heller, in Farmer's Corner to let her friends there know about her death and the funeral at Flossie's church. Sarah and Burt Heller were the only ones to come. Flowers were sent from Flossie's Farmer's Corner Sunday school class.

Flossie was gone. How would Lynelle Van Sant get on with her life without her dear Aunt Flossie?

One way to get beyond Flossie's death would be to go to the lawyer and see about the will. *How can I do this? It seems so unreal to me.*

Three days after the funeral, Lynnie planned to call the lawyer's office. She had no need to do so. The lawyer called her.

Lawyer Farnham's deep, resonating voice sent a chill over Lynnie. "Miss Van Sant, all I need for you to do is come in and sign papers. I have taken care of all the details. Her bank account is now in your name. You have complete access to her account."

The amount of assets was a complete surprise to Lynnie in spite of the fact that Flossie had told her she would be "well fixed."

# Chapter 20

## *"Happy Birthday" by Mildred J. Hill*

*Tampa, Florida*
*Summer, 1954*

Three months had passed since Aunt Flossie died, and Lynnie slogged through her life—the master's classes and her freshmen students. She liked to teach these young people because they were talented and liked music. She would have a new flock of freshmen students in the fall. She wanted to prepare them for decisions whether to go into music education or piano proficiency. By the time of the term's end, she seemed upbeat, and on the face of it, her mourning had slid into the background. From all appearances, she had gotten past her aunt's death. But a lonely summer faced her.

The term had finished, and although she needed two more courses to complete her master's degree, they were not offered in the summer. "I guess I should get back to the suite."

After Aunt Flossie died, she set it aside and hadn't looked at it at all. Now at the end of the term, the composition seemed too overwhelming with no Aunt Flossie to urge her on and listen to her play it measure by measure. "I have a concert to give and prepare for in five months. It's just too much!"

On June tenth, the birthday celebration day Aunt Flossie had created for her, she cried all day. She yelled at herself in the bathroom mirror, "How can you have a birthday without Aunt Flossie?"

She could have—should have—called Ruth, but she didn't. Ruth's baby's due date loomed ahead at the end of the summer, and Lynnie couldn't stand to think of Ruth with a baby. She had always avoided babies because they reminded her so much of her own. Ruth usually called Lynnie every day, but she had not called yet, which suited her.

A cynical laugh escaped her throat. "Like Garbo in *Grand Hotel*, 'I vant to be alone.'"

She went to the piano and started to work on the suite, but she quickly shut the manuscript book and left her piano room, slamming the door behind her. Then she tried to read, but books didn't satisfy her. She threw a book against the wall. She decided to go for a walk and took the bus to the bay side. She walked for two hours. Again, like the low times back in high school and college and then her senior year at Florida State, with each step, she considered how to end her life.

Lynnie continued to struggle with the beggar image of herself with nowhere to go. "Wayfarer, my eye! I'm just a beggar!"

Aunt Flossie had been the glue of her life, her proxy right arm. As she walked by Tampa Bay near the Gandy Bridge, an idea entered her head. This bridge, unlike the one over the river near Lenoir, meant deeper water and a quicker death. She headed toward the bridge.

However, before she reached it, she ran into a strange woman in a pair of men's overalls with a worn lacy blouse over top of it. The woman wore a pair of plastic galoshes on her feet without socks. Lynnie could see the woman's toenails. A feathered hat covered her head with a long braid of brown hair down her back. All her property sat beside her in a collapsible grocery cart.

"That's scary." She watched her for a while. The woman, an obvious vagabond, stirred up overwhelming thoughts. *If it hadn't been for Aunt Flossie, it might have been me. She's gone now, and rather than become like this woman and wander about aimlessly, I'd rather be dead. Do it, Lynnie, or whoever you are.*

The synapses didn't seem to connect in her brain to tell her she had so much to live for. She, a woman of wealth and the promise of a fulfilling career ahead, could think only about how to end it all.

# JUNE TITUS

Lynnie turned away from the woman and walked onto the Gandy Bridge. Traffic ran light on the bridge. More negative thoughts nagged in the back of her head and beat with fury. By the time she had gone ten feet onto the bridge, she saw traffic had increased.

"Not now."

Oddly, she wondered what Jay-Lee would think. She retreated.

The vagabond watched her. Even from a distance, Lynnie knew the woman looked straight into her eyes.

Lynnie saw the bus approach the nearby stop. She turned her back on the woman and waited for it. When it stopped, she boarded and went home.

Birthday or not, she didn't feel like food. At suppertime, she thought she had made her decision. *I know I don't have a driver's license, but I will drive the Packard. Maybe I'll drive it into the bay. I watched Aunt Flossie drive it almost every day. I know how.* She grabbed the keys from the hook where Aunt Flossie had kept them, went to the garage, and cranked up the engine. She forgot to open the garage door first, but another thought struck her: *Why not? I'll go to sleep and not wake up.*

Her life as far back to early childhood on the mountain filtered through her mind.

*Jay-Lee, my twin... brothers, Jeb and Tommy... parents... around the table... corn bread and soup beans... Pa's banjo... boys clogging hard against the wood floor... dogs howling underneath... Jay-Lee and me jumping up and down, clapping our hands together... Ma sings:*

> *Chickens crowin' on Sourwood Mountain,*
> *Hey, ho, diddle-um, diddle-um day.*
> *So many pretty girls I can't count 'em,*
> *Hey ho, diddle-um day.*

The song faded, and she envisaged the woman down by the bay. The woman looked in the windshield and beat on it. She called her name.

"Lynnie, Lynnie. Turn off the engine."

A sound of shattered glass filtered into her ears.

"Lynnie, can you hear me?" A familiar voice.

Then a man's voice, also familiar. "I got the glass broken enough to get it unlocked. We'll get her out."

Lynnie felt someone pull her into the fresh air and lay her down. Someone put a cold object on her face. Cold and wet.

Ben had pulled her free from the car. He took her out into the backyard and laid her on the grass. Ruth had gone into the house and got a dish towel and a pitcher of water. She bathed Lynnie's face.

Lynnie couldn't articulate her words. "You shoulda…shou…le' me go."

"No, darlin'. 'Letting you go' won't happen. You have value. You are loved. Even if Ben and I weren't part of your life, God sees your value. God loves you, and we do too. Come on now, take some deep breaths. We have a birthday to celebrate."

Once she was alert enough to swallow, Ben carried her into the kitchen, turned the fan on high, and got her to drink water. Lots of it.

"Birthday." She gave a cynical laugh. "Some birthday."

Ruth put her hands on her pregnant hips. "Not 'some' birthday, Lynnie. It is your birthday, and we are here to celebrate. We have black forest cake, vanilla ice cream, and gourmet coffee. So get yourself in the house and let's party."

"Yes, Flossie!" she growled. "You sound like Aunt Flossie."

Ben had only kindness and compassion in his tone. "Lynnie, you will be all right. A couple more glasses of water to flush your system. Maybe a five-minute shower."

"No. I'm okay. I'll take a shower before I go to bed."

Ben nodded. "All right. Have you eaten today?"

She shook her head.

Ruth got the ice cream and started to dish up some for Lynnie.

Ben took the ice cream from her and put it in the freezer compartment of the refrigerator. "Ruth, get her a bowl of cereal or some toast. We don't want to throw cake and ice cream into an empty, fume-ridden stomach."

Neither Ruth nor Ben asked Lynnie why; instead, they showed their concern and love for her.

While she munched on her toast with peanut butter and jelly that Ruth fixed for her and sipped from a glass of iced tea, Lynnie brought up the subject. "How did you know?"

Ruthie looked at Ben. He rolled his eyes and sighed. "Lynnie, the last thing I wanted to do would be partying after I spent all afternoon trying to get febrile seizures under control and a temperature of 104 degrees down on a two-year-old. Ruth tried to call you but no answer. She insisted her pregnancy made it too hard to drive, so I had to tote her over here. When we pulled in the driveway, we could see exhaust fumes from the garage."

Ruth held Lynnie's hand in hers. "I didn't feel up to a visit, but the mother of the little girl Ben had worked with this afternoon, grateful for him to have her child back, gave us the cake she had made for a party they would not attend. I knew the cake would be perfect for your party. I would have brought it over with or without Ben, but I have a kind husband."

Ben smiled. "I love being manipulated—not at all." He winked at his round wife. "When we saw what happened, we both jumped out of the car. Well, jumped relatively speaking for Ruth. I opened the garage door and grabbed a cinder block propped against the next-door neighbor's fence. It had been there ever since the first time we came here to visit. I used it to crash in the back window on the passenger side. I did the opposite back window from you so the glass wouldn't hit you."

"Thank you. Ruth banged on the windshield, huh? I thought the tramp lady I saw on my walk this afternoon pounded on it."

Lynnie said nothing else for a moment, and her companions allowed her to gather her thoughts.

Then she spoke with her voice speaking barely above a whisper. "I'm glad you haven't asked why. I suppose I have been so dependent on Aunt Flossie. You know, I feel like her death has been mine too. There is a lot more to it. Always has been, but it's my story. I'm just glad you were here."

If Ruth or Ben were interested in her story, they never asked. Rather, they proceeded with the festivity.

After Lynnie finished the snack, she got up and helped Ruth and Ben set the table for refreshments. She made the coffee. "Glad it isn't Sanka. I need caffeine!"

Ruth drank water.

After they finished the cake and ice cream, Ben spied the Scrabble game on the shelf beside the table. "Hey, how about a game of Scrabble? I haven't played it yet, but I thought I might buy one for us."

Patting Lynnie on the back, Ruth laughed. "You had better be good because Lynnie is already an expert. I haven't won a game yet, and we've played—what? I think five or six times already since Christmas."

Lynnie sighed. *How can I play games when I almost finished my game?*

She said nothing, however, about her thoughts and took a deep breath. *Get on with life, loser!*

Then almost like her usual demeanor, she nodded. "You are better than Aunt Flossie, Ruthie. She liked to spell the way she talked—*y'all, uster, gonna*. Let's do it. Sounds like a good party game. But, Ben, no medical words."

"Rats!"

They had played several turns when the words on the board lined up for Lynnie to use all of her letters to spell the word *vagabond*. She cried.

"Lynnie, you are tired. We should let you rest."

"No, it's okay. I thought about the tramp lady I saw down by the bay. I know I'm foolish. We have to give Ben a chance to show he knows words other than medical terminology."

"Hear! Hear!" the physician commented.

The game lasted another twenty minutes, but Ben suggested they should not play another one.

Ruth agreed. "I am tired. Kickapoodle, your son or daughter, Benjamin Steyer, has been so active the last three nights, I haven't had too much shuteye. But how about if I sleep here tonight? I can stay awake here as well as home if the baby keeps me awake. I can sleep in my petticoat. Okay with you, Lynnie?"

"Why not? But you shouldn't go home by bus in your condition. Why not wait for Ben to come for you tomorrow after he finishes his patients?"

Ben looked out toward the garage. "Uh, Lynnie, how about if I take the Packard tonight, and Ruth can drive our car home when she's ready to come home? Would you mind? Since I broke the window, I will need to take it to the body shop and get a new one. I can drop it off first thing tomorrow on my way to the office. There is a good body shop in the next block from our house."

Lynnie shrugged. "I don't have any business behind the wheel since I never bothered to get a license. If you need a second car, I'll sign it over to you."

"We can talk about it later. I'll see to the window replacement."

The couple hugged as much as Ruth's oversized girth would allow.

Lynnie had no memories of hugs from a loving father of her baby during her pregnancy. Tears formed in her eyes, and she turned away from her friends, grabbed the keys to the Packard, and handed them to Ben.

# Chapter 21

## *"Cry Me a River" by Arthur Hamilton*

*Tampa, Florida*
*July 1954*

After Lynnie's suicide attempt, Ruth stayed all night and part of the next day. She awakened to the aroma of fresh coffee.

Rather than broach the subject of the "why" for the madness, she planned to steer the conversation to the "what" of the future. But Lynnie opened the subject before her friend had a chance to delve into why she would have done it. "Ruth, I appreciate your attention. I'm glad you've stayed. I do need you. I know it's foolish to want to kill myself, I suppose, but the urge has trailed me since—since age twelve. Without Aunt Flossie, I suppose I have thought my life isn't worth the space it takes up."

"I'm sorry, Lynnie. I can't imagine what you may have dealt with before Aunt Flossie, and I'd never ask. It's over, honey. We live not only for today, but we also live for tomorrow. Let's look at your tomorrows."

"Okay, but don't cajole me to go back to church! Going to the church for the funeral was enough for my blood right now."

Ruth scrunched one eyebrow and focused on Lynnie. "What did I say about church? Church doesn't make you a Christian any more than a barn makes you a cow. If your spiritual life is what bothers you, perhaps you need to consider what you believe and then live like it."

Lynnie looked puzzled. She shrugged. "I assume I'm a Christian. I had been in Sunday school as a child. They baptized me in the icy creek. And when I lived with Aunt Flossie, I suppose I took going to church for granted. I think one reason I don't want to go to church is it isn't same as our little country church. I feel no connection. So if I live in a barn and I'm not a cow, I am out of place, huh? I always feel like an outsider when I've ventured into churches other than Farmer's Corner."

Ruth studied her friend for what seemed an uncomfortable moment for Lynnie, who fidgeted her fingers on a pillow in her lap as though she were playing the piano.

"Do you know," Ruth asked, "what a real Christian is? How would you describe a Christian?"

Lynnie shrugged one shoulder and ran an arpeggio across the pillow. "I suppose a Christian is someone who isn't some other religion or an atheist, someone who believes in Christmas and Easter and obeys the Ten Commandments and has been baptized. I guess people who don't get drunk or cheat on their spouse or things like that may be considered Christians. But, Ruth, I think people obey the commandments even when they are part of other religions, and I know atheists who go by the rules too. So why be a Christian rather than one of these other religions unless it is your tradition and to enjoy the holidays?"

"Yes, many of the Ten Commandments are followed by most religions, and societies are made on the premises found in them. But, Lynnie, that's only religion and not a relationship. A true Christian—in other words, a follower of Christ—comes to the cross and dies with the Lord Jesus Christ. They die to their struggles to keep rules they can't keep."

Lynnie frowned and repeated, "Die to their struggles to keep the rules…"

"Right. No one but Jesus lived the Law with perfection, and because He died for our sin and conquered death, we are not only forgiven, but we are also free from the penalty of the Law. Jesus is our

Savior, and just as important, Jesus is our Brother. He had to be one of us to be able to take our place for the punishment for our sinfulness. As well, He had to be God in order to be the perfect sacrificial Lamb of God. Our worth is in Him when we turn away from our own struggle to do good. Is this helpful?"

Lynnie frowned as though she had just heard brand-new information. "I'll have to ponder on what you have said. It's a bit much to chew on. I know the stories, I have sung the hymns, and I've heard the sermons, but I never thought about it like you explained it."

Ruth didn't respond, but she took Lynnie's hand in hers. She nodded and encouraged her to go on.

"But, Ruth, I have known people all my life who call themselves Christian, and they lie, cheat, cuss, commit adultery, get angry, and act as though they are fine. I have known so-called Christians who are so tight they could rub Abe Lincoln's face off their pennies. There are church people who let their neighbors starve while they send their money to Africa. I don't see their Christianity works the way you describe it."

"Perhaps they are hypocrites, actors, or frauds, Lynnie. In some respects, they are wanderers, and they have wandered into the church without true belief. They have remained wanderers. The results are neither good for the church or for themselves. They need to have a relationship with Jesus. Yeah, they are in the church. I've even known leaders who live a double standard. A hypocrite is not a true Christian but a performer."

Lynnie's eyes shot wide open. "Aha! Like me performing the music of Bach or Chopin. I am not the composer."

"Eh…not necessarily a good analogy, but someone has to play what those dead composers wrote. Jesus, on the other hand, is alive. As for the performers, Jesus condemned them as imposters. The Bible tells us to follow Jesus, not a church leader, Sunday school teacher, or even a piano player. The real question you need to ask is not if there are frauds in the church but rather, Is Jesus a fraud? You can get to know Him in the Bible. The entire Bible is a book about Him, but if you read the Gospels, you will get to know Him. I challenge you to read them. Start with John's Gospel."

"Jesus a fraud? Such a concept never occurred to me. To think such a thing is, well, even to think it is a sacrilege, isn't it?"

"Like I said, Lynnie: Going to church doesn't make you a Christian. In other words, if I claim Christianity, it doesn't prove that I am one. If someone who isn't a Christian is baptized, it makes her wet. Period. To live for Christ—to follow Him—is the proof."

"Touché. No argument. Ruth, I will consider what you have said."

"One other thing, Lynnie. I think you should call a psychiatrist and get an appointment. Ben knows these doctors, and he can recommend a good one who won't load you up on pills."

"You may be right." Lynnie shook her head and wondered if Ruth thought she had lost her mind. "I'll think about it while I'm thinking about your explanation of Christianity."

The young women sat in comfortable silence for some time, and then Ruth started to giggle and patted her abdomen where Kickapoodle thumped against her abdomen. "I can see I'm in for another noteworthy night if I can't quiet this little one down. Do you think it's safe for us to walk outside up and down the sidewalk so this small person can settle down before I go home? You want to feel it?"

Lynnie almost shuddered. "No. I'll take your word for it. And yes, it's safe around here. No one out but neighbors. I could do with a stroll."

The warm and balmy afternoon with a good breeze blew in from the bay made the walk pleasant. The young women chatted about anything but what had been on their minds the last eighteen hours.

Lynnie wondered aloud, "Ever think about Liz? Wonder what our old roomie is up to these days?"

"I heard she taught in Miami for a while and then went into the Army, but I haven't heard a word from her."

Lynnie laughed. "The Army won't know what hit them, will they?"

So went the conversation, and after about half an hour, the idle conversation lagged, and young Steyer had settled down to a few nudges. They went back to the house, and Ruth got ready to go home.

"Lynnie, would it be an imposition for me to ask for Aunt Flossie's Bible before I go? I'd like to show you some passages to read that might help you. If you read her Bible with some of the notes she scribbled in there, it may help you."

"Of course. I know I should read it too. Might find out you are wrong!"

Lynnie brought the well-worn Bible out, and Ruth put markers in several places where it emphasized the points she had made earlier.

Assured Lynnie would not harm herself, Ruth went on home. "Lynnie, I know I can't see into your head. But know this, my dearest friend, I am here for you. I know we can't live together like you and Aunt Flossie did, but you will branch out soon. You will finish your master's degree this fall and be in a position of a possible professorship. I have no doubt your department head will hire you. Then you will soon be a performer. Mark my word. You are good enough."

"What? In front of audiences? You sound more like Ol' Flossie every time you talk to me."

"Well, I hope a little bit of Ol' Flossie's wisdom has rubbed off on both of us."

Ruth grabbed her purse and headed to the Ford in the driveway. "Got to get on home. My husband will expect a decent dinner tonight. He child is acting up again too. I think he wants his mama to eat a cookie."

Lynnie grabbed a molasses cookie from the kitchen and handed it to Ruth. "Here. Feed Kickapoo."

Lynnie watched as her friend pulled out of the driveway. She longed for the stable life her friend enjoyed. She thought about Ruth's statement, that living in the barn doesn't make one a cow.

*So if I live in a barn and I'm not a cow…*

She scratched out a little verse about it.

> If I live in the barn, do I moo and eat hay?
> If I sleep with the beasts, do I cluck, oink, and bray?

## JUNE TITUS

Does the place where I live reflect the person I am?
Or am I out of my group—adrift—on the lam?
Do I write my story? Do I choose my route?
Or is there a God who loves without doubt?

# CHAPTER 22

## *"The Lord's My Shepherd, I'll Not Want," Scottish Psalter, 1650*

The next morning, Lynnie awakened anything but fresh and rested. She had wrestled with the conversation about Christianity from the afternoon before into the wee hours before she fell asleep. Then she thought about the vagabond woman. *It could have been me. If I had not been so hungry the morning I got left behind by the watermelon truck, I may have traipsed for days. Where did I want to go? Key West,* she recalled.

It occurred to her she would like to see the vagabond woman again. She talked to herself in the mirror as she brushed her hair. "I can go to the bayside again, not to jump in or walk but to look for her, even talk to her, find out her 'why.' Ruth never asked me why I tried, and I can't tell her the reasons—not now—not yet. I think when I went down there yesterday, I had only a half the intention to jump, but when I saw her, I saw myself like her, a wanderer. So why live? But when I think about what Ruth said, maybe I don't have to wander anymore."

By evening, she had not resolved her query. She picked up Aunt Flossie's Bible and sat in the "Bible-reading" rocking chair. She read the passages Ruth had marked, but she wanted more. She turned to the book of John. She read about John the Baptist and realized he had wandered.

"But John's wandering had a purpose, to declare that Jesus had been sent from God."

She read the entire book of John in one session. It seemed as new to her as though she had never heard it before. She loved the image of Jesus, the Good Shepherd. Aunt Flossie had made a note in the margin by this passage: "The Good Shepherd goes out to find each and every wandering lost sheep. Look at Luke 15:3–7."

Lynnie turned to the passage and read the parable of the lost sheep. "Yes, I'm a wandering lost sheep."

She turned back to the book of John and read passages she recalled from Sunday school, but they seemed to have a new sense than the simple Sunday school stories. "Let not your heart be troubled…" and "It is finished…"

"I don't know. I do not know." She laid the Bible down and went to her piano. She knew she had to work on her suite. She wrote a section of the composition that repeated the beat of her question, "I don't know—I don't know," until she couldn't keep her eyes focused on the music. On her bed, she repeated over and over, "I don't know; I don't know." As she fell asleep, the phrase "I don't know" became part of her suite.

The next day she awakened as the sun filtered into her bedroom through the curtains she had neglected to pull before she went to bed. The pattern the sun made on the opposite wall was in the shape of a crucifix. It frightened her at first, but then she saw what had looked like a body on the cross came from the hanging planter outside her window. With the window dividers, the pattern made by the hanging planter resembled a crucifix. She shivered.

She sank to her knees beside the bed. "Lord, show me. I simply do not know."

Lynnie decided to put feet to her reflections and take the bus to the bay in hopes to see the beggar woman again. Midafternoon, about the same time she had seen the woman two days before, she got off the bus at the corner of Gandy Boulevard and West Shore Boulevard. She had seen the woman near this bus stop. As she walked along Gandy Boulevard toward the park where she had seen her two days before, she saw the woman seated on a bench.

The woman had on the same overalls and lace blouse, but today she had on flip-flops instead of galoshes, and she had exchanged her feathered hat for a pink hat covered in flowers.

Lynnie's skin felt jittery like the first time she played piano in a recital, but she approached the woman. "May I join you on the bench?"

The woman shrugged. "Suit yourself." She eyed Lynnie with suspicion. "What do you want? You come here to get me to go to the hospital and get help? Forget it! I like traipsing about."

"Not at all. I saw you two days ago and thought, well, I thought I could have been where you are if I hadn't been starved and walked into a bakery asking for bread at age twelve. Even with a stable home from then on, I have always felt like an unhappy wanderer—a vagabond."

The woman glared at her.

Lynnie, undeterred, continued, "I wanted to talk to you. Two days ago, I intended to walk out onto the bridge and jump in. Instead, I went home and attempted to finish the job. I let the motor run inside the closed garage and tried to die. Friends rescued me from my foolishness. I'm an emotional vagabond. I wanted to talk to you about a wanderer's mind."

The woman cocked her eye at Lynnie. "Hey, lady, I'm the crazy one here. What's with you? You frighten me. Yeah, I tried it a couple of times when I first went off my rocker, but someone always disrupted me. Someone told me if I killed myself, I'd kill God because we are made in His image. Don't know if I believe that or not, but I don't wanna take a chance."

Lynnie shuddered. "Kill God?"

"Yeah. That'd be bad. I suppose you want to know how come I live wherever I can find a place to sleep and get food to eat. I'm not telling you because it is none of your business."

Lynnie stayed seated but remained silent. She sat and sat. Half an hour later, the woman looked at her. "You still here?"

"Yes. I've thought about my life and about if there is a God. If there is a God, how can I know Him?"

"There's a God, okay? But you won't find Him here. I think you'll find Him if you help people who need help, if you love women and children who aren't loved at home, if you show someone you care, and if you feed a hungry person like you said you were at age twelve. I stop at missions or churches now and then as I gad about for a good meal and a change of clothes. I see God there."

The woman stayed quiet for a moment or two as though she gathered her thoughts. Then she looked directly into Lynnie's eyes. "Me? I like to wander. I've got schizophrenia, so I don't function too well in society. I try to stay one step ahead of them that'd throw me in the looney bin. I hate how the pills make me feel. I'm okay with being a wanderer, but I suppose I'm a wanderer of the soul."

*Wanderer of the soul. That's me.*

Again, the woman seemed to retreat into her own reverie. Then she smiled at Lynnie. "Someday, I'll find God too. Someday."

Tears rolled down Lynnie's cheeks. The woman's "sermon" touched her heart. Through her tears, she reached for the woman's hand. "Thank you. My name is Lynnie Van Sant. What is your name? I want to remember you."

"Me? I don't have a name anymore. I used to go by Grace Jones."

Lynnie stood and kept Grace's hand in hers. "Thank you, Grace Jones. I hope I'll see you again."

"Not likely. I'm about to head north. Too hot here."

"Do you need money to travel? For food?"

Grace hunched one shoulder in a shrug. "I'm not asking or anything."

Lynnie reached into her purse and pulled out two twenty-dollar bills and handed them to Grace. "Goodbye. Maybe we will meet again one day."

"So long. Don't say goodbye. Goodbye's forever. So long is a maybe."

"So long, then."

Lynnie walked for a while in the park until the next bus came. Glad she had talked to Grace Jones, she determined she would pursue a different life than the wanderer of the soul.

# Chapter 23

## *"I Am a Poor Wayfaring Stranger," American Folk Hymn*

*August 1954*

It had been a strange summer for Lynnie. She struggled with the idea of Christianity as Ruth had described it. Each night, she picked up Aunt Flossie's Bible and read it. At this point, Jesus had become real person in her mind—yes, as far as it went—a real historical person. She couldn't get her head around a relationship with the risen Christ she could not see, but she knew Aunt Flossie believed in the real presence of Jesus as well.

Each day, she missed Aunt Flossie, but then each day, she became more of her own person. It had been almost two months since her attempt to end her life, but she thought about it less and less. When the notion cropped up, she would go to the piano and play something other than her composition or write in her journal.

One day, when she went to the piano, instead of her classical repertoire, she opened Aunt Flossie's hymnal and started to play through. Up to this point, any hymns she played were the music itself and improvisations on the melody.

A title caught her eye: "I Am a Poor Wayfaring Stranger." She had never played the song, but the song brought up a vague childhood recollection. In her mind, her mother sang out back of the house as she stirred Pa's overalls with a long stick in a big iron kettle. Lynnie had forgotten the song until now.

*Ma has sweat streaming down her face, her brown curls hang down her back—barefoot—calico dress to her ankles. She humors the melody with a sob in her voice or some curlicues.*

> *I'm just a poor wayfaring stranger,*
> *Traveling through this world below.*
> *I know dark clouds will gather 'round me,*
> *I know my way is hard and steep.*
> *I'm going there to see my Mother...*

Lynnie broke down and cried and cried. "Oh, Ma! Are you with Jesus? I know you are. I know you went over Jordan. I know you believed. I want to believe. I really do."

She picked up Aunt Flossie's Bible and turned a passage she had read before. "It is finished!"

Now the passage made sense to her. "It means Jesus went through the punishment for me. Yes, I understand."

After her tears were expended, she called Ruth. Her friend, now in her final days before baby Steyer would make his or her debut, refused to drive the car. Lynnie, in order to see her, took the bus to visit twice in the last week. Ruth had said no more to Lynnie about Christianity, but she and Ben had both prayed for the skeptic daily.

Ruth answered the phone with a groan. "No. I haven't had the baby yet. I feel as big as Tampa Bay! Come on over."

"Maybe, but I wanted to talk to you some more about our conversation on Christianity. I believe! I know it is real. I want to have what you and Ben have, peace of mind. I want to have what Aunt Flossie had, the joy of life. I want to have what my mother had, a faith even in the harshest of life's circumstances."

"I'm not going anywhere."

An hour later, the two young women were seated side by side on the glider in the Florida room. A huge fan stirred the air in lazy circular swipes.

Ruth had her Bible next to her, but she didn't open it. "Lynnie, we are all sinners. You, me, Ben, Aunt Flossie, the mother you referred to on the phone. But Jesus took our place on the cross, suffered for our sins, and—"

Lynnie interrupted, "He said 'It is finished!' I figured it out and had to tell you. He went through the punishment for me. I understand. I believe. I get it! Ruth, I get it."

Ruth grasped her hand. "Hallelujah!"

Lynnie closed her eyes and prayed, "Lord, I believe. Help me understand. Help me become a real Christian, not nominal. Please redeem this poor beggar, this wayfarer, this vagabond."

The two friends hugged each other with tears flowing down their cheeks. They sat quietly on the glider for a few minutes. Then if the friends thought they had started an old-time revival, their plans were diverted without ceremony. Ruth had gone into labor.

"Uh...guess what?" Ruth had her hands on her abdomen.

"Little Kickapoodle is at it again?"

"Little Kickapoodle wants out."

"Oh, dear. You want me to call Ben's office? Does he plan to deliver the baby?"

"Yes and yes. But he will want to deliver it at the hospital, not here. I will need to have my contractions a lot closer and a lot harder before I go to the hospital. You ever see a baby born?"

Lynnie paled. Ruth might be her best friend, but she didn't want to tell her about the baby she left behind in North Carolina. *How can I? Never? Ever?*

Lynnie ignored the question and took a deep breath. She dialed Ben's office.

The nurse answered. "He's with a patient right now. May I have him call you back?"

"Yes. I'm his wife's friend. Ruth has started into labor. He doesn't need to come right now, but have him call, please."

"Oh boy!" The nurse laughed into the phone. "He has one more patient to see this afternoon unless someone else comes in. You think we can wait until he sees his last appointment? He might get too excited to treat the guy."

"I'm sure. Please ask him to call home."

Ben's call came in half an hour. Ruth answered. "What is it? Are you okay? Are you in labor?"

"Yes, I'm okay, and yes, Kickapoodle wants out."

"How close are your contractions?"

"Ten minutes and not too strong. Lynnie is here with me. You finish up and come on home if you will please."

Ben arrived in another thirty minutes. He examined her. "Looks like you'll go fast, honey. Are you all packed for the hospital?"

She cocked her head, glared at him with half-closed eyes, and punctuated it with a groan. "I've been packed for a week!"

Lynnie fixed a light supper, and the three talked on into the early evening, while the pains closed in. By eight forty-five, they were ready to head to the hospital.

Lynnie shared her news with Ben. "I have come to terms, Ben, with my need for Christ."

Ben offered a prayer of thanksgiving.

Ruth suggested, "Hey, maybe we need to name our baby after you if it's a girl. We might call her Flora Lynn for both you and Aunt Flossie. If it is born tonight, it will be the day of your spiritual birth."

Lynnie knew they wanted her to go with them, but she didn't want to. Her skin crawled with the idea of seeing the newborn, but she remembered: "Yea, though I walk through the valley of death, I will fear no evil for Thou art with me." *I am with Jesus. I can face this.*

Ruth's water broke the moment she arrived in labor and delivery. Within ten minutes, the nurse took her to delivery, setting Lynnie on pins and needles until fifteen minutes later, when Ben emerged with a bundle wrapped in blue. "It's a boy. Made it under the wire at 11:55. Couldn't call him Flora Lynn, but we've done you proud, Miss Van Sant."

Lynnie couldn't think of anything to say except "Is his name 'Kickapoodle'?"

Ben pulled back the corner of the blanket and revealed a little red-faced baby with a crown of red hair like his mother's. "I doubt if his mother would approve of Kickapoodle, so we have decided on Benjamin Van Steyer. Van for Van Sant?"

"Oh, good. Will we call him Van?"

"Such is our intent. I'm glad you were with her today. Thank you."

Tears streamed down Lynnie's face. "When can I see Ruth?"

"She is still in the labor room, and we will sedate her before we transfer her to her room. Here's my suggestion: I'll take you home, and you can come back tomorrow. Will that work for you?"

*Yes! Yes! Get me out of this place.* Lynnie smiled and nodded. "Good. Let's go."

The next day, Lynnie took the bus to see Ruth, walked with the new mother to the nursery window to take the obligatory view of baby Van, and sat with her friend all through the afternoon visiting hours. Lynnie wondered how she could ever get excited about this baby—*any baby. I don't want to hurt Ruth, but if she asks me to hold him, I might cry. God help me! Change this in me. If I belong to you, this has to change. I can't do it myself.*

Ruth remained in the hospital three days and then came home. Both mother and baby were fine. Over the next week or so, Lynnie did have the opportunity to stay with Ruth and Van several times. She went to the house to help Ruth almost every day.

Lynnie could see that new care for the baby had exhausted her friend. Ruth's mother had planned to come when the baby arrived, but her dad's deployment to Korea sabotaged the plans.

"Mother will come here after he leaves. She has to close up the house before she comes."

"I can come each day until school starts. Will it help if I come and stay?"

"You know it! Thank you, dear friend."

By the end of the first week, Ruth had been home and Lynnie became a fixture at the Steyer home, but she had not picked up the baby one time. With Van asleep, she sent Ruth to bed for a nap. "You need to sleep when he sleeps. Hit the hay, girl."

"Okay. You don't have to twist my arm. He kept both of us up for three hours last night. Ben helped, but doctor or not, the baby rules around here."

Ruth had been down for a few minutes when Van started to cry. Lynnie ventured into the nursery to see if she could quiet him.

"Okay little fellow, let's check your diaper. Ugh! I'd cry too if I had such a mess in my britches. I haven't changed a diaper for many years, but I suppose I recall how." She did it.

"There you are little man." She picked him up and held him close to her bosom and sang to him softly, not a nursery song but "I Am a Poor Wayfaring Stranger." She did cry, a cry that cleansed her very depths.

"Thank you, Lord. I did it for my baby. I did it for Van. I did it for You."

After this episode, she picked him up often to cuddle him. Van had her hooked. She didn't tell Ruth why she had been so reluctant to even be around him, let alone pick him up. *Done. Over.*

The next day, Saturday, Ruth's mother arrived. Lynnie continued to visit daily and play with the baby when he was not sleeping or when someone else held him. She relaxed and exuded happiness when holding him.

Ruth cornered her in the kitchen one afternoon. "Lynnie, I don't know about you and the baby. At first, you acted like you didn't want to look at him. Now you can't seem to get enough of him. How come?"

Lynnie shrugged and gave an evasive answer. "I've not been around many babies in the past. I didn't know how to act around a baby. They are so fragile and vulnerable, but Van is so precious. You were asleep the day before your mother came, and he cried. He needed his diaper changed. I did it, and we became fast friends. End of story."

Ruth looked down her nose at her friend. "Okay, I'll buy your version, and I won't ask any more—for now."

*Maybe someday I will tell Ruth about me.*

Now time had arrived to get back to the university for the fall sessions. She had been working every evening on her suite, and it sounded good. Every section of the work fell into place. She missed having Aunt Flossie's ear to hear it, but she visualized her as she played each section. She planned to present a two-hour concert for her final performance examination. This concert would not only include her suite but also several other piano pieces. In conjunction with Dr. Foster, she developed the repertoire for the concert.

She had five new freshmen piano students, and she had taken two more master's classes to complete her degree.

Between preparations for her concert, classes, and her students, she didn't have a lot of time to visit the Steyer home. Ruth's mother stayed for a month, and by then, Van had settled down into a nice baby routine. Lynnie tried to go visit on Saturdays, and then she bit hard into the bullet and went to church. When she left to go to the bus stop from her Saturday visit with the Ruth and Ben the first Saturday in September, she said, "See you in church tomorrow."

"Good!" Ruth said, looking at Ben and her mother with wide eyes and a wide grin.

Ben and Ruth were now members at the historic edifice. No little country church familiar to Lynnie, but she didn't care what brand of church—she would go. *I'm ready to attend, but I've no intention of any involvement. I want to enjoy the music and hear the sermons. Period.*

When Ruth suggested Lynnie should get involved with the music program, she gave a nonchalant shrug and answered, "My life's too complicated to get wrapped up in all the programs in the church. I've got a concert to put together."

Lynnie took the bus the short ride to church each Sunday and back home. She sat with Ruth and Ben, sang the hymns with her above-average alto voice, listened to the sermons, went home to work on her concert preparations, and played with little Van whenever she could find time.

# Chapter 24

## *"The Cat and the Mouse" by Aaron Copeland*

*December 1954*

The day fast approached for Lynnie's graduate concert. She could invite anyone she chose, and the small auditorium would hold only a small audience. She invited students from both the current class and those from the previous year, others in the same program as herself, Ruth and Ben, some of her neighbors on North Ninth Street, the bus driver whose bus she took every day, Mr. Glenn, and his wife. The invitations were printed. The stage crew and sound recording were in order. The reception afterward, a catered affair, had been set up at Lynnie's expense. The two-hour concert with an intermission after the first hour had been decided.

The concert, slated for Tuesday night, arrived with thirty guests. The small concert hall buzzed with anticipation. Her professor and the head of the department, Dr. Foster, were there to assess her work. Unknown to her, Dr. Foster had invited concert promoters from Miami and Jacksonville.

She would lead off in the first hour with a composition by her early mentor, Aaron Copeland, "The Cat and the Mouse." It would be followed by a Brahms Piano Sonata and, before the intermission, three nocturnes by Sergei Rachmaninoff. After the break, she would play Franz Schubert's *Piano Sonata in D* and J. S. Bach's *Chromatic*

# REDEMPTION SUITE

*Fantasy and Fugue.* To complete the program, she debuted her own composition, a suite, *The Wayfarer Returns*. She had written a brief poem of the same title and had it printed in the program.

Although no specific tunes could be pulled from the suite, Lynnie had used the styles of music from her early life in the mountains with echoes of ballads, folk music, jazz, a trace of bebop of her college years, and classical elements were woven through the suite. It chronicled the escape to Florida, upbeat tones reflecting the easy years but hints in counterpoint of her suicide thoughts. Lyrical passages interwoven into chaotic and angry sections characterized the suite. Yet she limited the discordant sections to brief moments with an easy flow into peaceful sections. The suite ended on a calm but triumphant chorus and flowed into a rhythmic poem.

> The Wayfarer Returns
> Restless journey to find serenity,
> Trek into a hope for someday to be free.
> Footsteps pound, ever pound.
> Sound against echoes of the past,
> Cling to what can never last.
> Soul ignored, e'er ignored—
> 'Til one day another soul,
> Like peering into some reflected pool,
> To see oneself—naught but a fool
> Who grasps the wind
> (for such is our brief end),
> And think our hopes are met by clinging
> to a friend
> But finds, after all, God is always there,
> Ready, waiting for the homeward prayer.
> (Lynelle Van Sant)

At the top of the program notes, she had printed, "This concert is dedicated to the memory of the late Florence Van Sant, who encouraged me each step of the way. Perhaps she is listening."

Lynnie's full-length black satin dress with three-quarter-length loose sleeves gave her a graceful appearance. She wore black satin one-inch heels. She usually wore her brown curls at shoulder length, but she had them pulled back into a French roll. Tendrils escaped around her face. She wore no jewelry. Her audience would see an elegant, well-poised petite lady emerge onto the stage.

As she took the microphone, she explained the first piece. "I would not be here today if the composer of my first piece had not encouraged me to pursue my master's degree in performance here at Tampa University. For three summers, Aaron Copeland taught and mentored me at summer music camp and connected me with Dr. Foster. This piece by Mr. Copeland is whimsical and avant garde, but a delightful way to set the mood for the remainder of this concert. Watch as the 'Cat and the Mouse' play across the keys of the piano."

She had her audience in her hand. Then with each piece, she gave an appropriate introduction, and by intermission time, she longed for a rest. After twenty minutes, she returned to the stage, calm and ready to delight her audience for the other half. Her own composition drew loud and lingering applause. At the end, she had a standing ovation. As she played an encore of the familiar Chopin *Minute Waltz*, she caught Ruth's eye on the front row of the auditorium. *This one's for Ruth.*

At the reception after the concert, the promoters from Miami and Jacksonville approached her. The woman from Miami cornered her before she even greeted any of her invited guests. "Miss Van Sant, I am Margery Shapiro from Miami Performing Arts. We have our eye out for new talent all the time. We have big-name performers for six of our annual concerts, but we like to bring in new talent on a regular basis to present to the community and give them an opportunity to expand their own resumé. We have a slot open for a July venue—if you will be available."

"Thank you, Miss Shapiro. I am honored you have considered me. I do not have a schedule at this time, but I hope to remain here in the Tampa area as much as possible and plan to resume teaching in January. If you give me your contact information, I may get back to you once I have my schedule in order and decide what I will do."

Lynnie escaped Miss Shapiro to mingle with some of the guests. Five minutes later, the man from Jacksonville approached her. "Wonderful concert, Miss Van Sant. We would be honored to have you come to Jacksonville any time. I am Walt Miller with the Jacksonville Symphony. We are a new orchestra, now in our fifth year. Dr. Busch wants some new talent to bring in. Here is my card. When you have time, give me a call."

"Thank you, Mr. Miller." She wondered, *Do I want to play anywhere else but around Tampa?* "I appreciate your interest, and I will consider it. My hopes are to perform in the Tampa area, but I may venture out some day. I will be teaching piano for the present, so my time away will be limited. Again, thank you."

# Chapter 25

## *"Cotton-Eyed Joe," American Folk Song*

Sometimes, when someone has been wound up in preparations or anticipation of some great accomplishment of what they set out to do, and then it is all over with, they crash. Like her big graduation from high school, the morning after her concert, Lynnie felt lost. Dark thoughts intruded again. *Shouldn't my new faith take care of this? I don't know where to go from here. Yes, I have my music students, but what else?*

When the old wayfarer idea crept back into her mind, she thought of the words she had written:

> *Restless journey to find serenity,*
> *Trek into a hope for someday to be free.*

Seated on her back porch, oblivious to the beautiful bougainvillea, hibiscus, and other flowers painting her environs, she became aware of movement. A mockingbird skipped about on the lawn. She spoke to him. "I feel like a restless vagabond again. Maybe I'll take a bus trip on down to Key West like I thought I might do fifteen years ago. I could do it now, but what good would it do? Too bad I don't have wings like you and can fly away from my thoughts."

She started to sing an old folk song, "Where d'ya come from? Where d'ya go? Where d'ya come from, Cotton-Eyed Joe?"

As she jumped from her chair, she knocked it over. She went into the kitchen and slammed the door. She thought about how to commit suicide this time so Ruth would not intervene a third time.

"No! No! I can't go this way again. But why do I still have the notion?"

The telephone rang. Ruth.

Lynnie laughed, one of those unstoppable laughs. She sounded hysterical.

"What in the world is this frenzied laughter?"

"Oh, Ruthie, I'm a mess! I can't even believe my own poetry! Today, I thought life had ended and thought about how I could do it without you interrupting. What is wrong with me? Why can't I let my new faith change these dark thoughts? I'm a great big mess! I even consulted with the psychiatrist Ben recommended last week, and these thoughts are coming more than before. He wanted to put me on Thorazine. I told him, 'No!' I'm not going back."

"Okay, Van and I are on our way over right now. Don't do anything dumb."

"Okay, but please tell me how to stop this nonsense. I don't want to do this, but the thoughts pop up when I least expect it."

"I'm sorry you feel this way again. Now until I get there, how about if you go into the kitchen and whip up a batch of Flossie's Famous Molasses Cookies? I'll bring the cider."

Lynnie looked at the telephone before she hung it up. "Cookies? Well, why didn't I think of cookies?"

Lynnie had the cookies baked and on the rack to cool by the time Ruth pulled into the driveway. She drove up in Aunt Flossie's Packard, now her car, with the broken window repaired and a good tune up. Lynnie had deeded it over to Ruth for one dollar as a gift from Aunt Flossie.

At four months, Van had become a real wiggle worm. He already knew how to wiggle Aunt Lynnie around his little finger. But today, Lynnie's mind focused on herself and not baby Van. As the two women sat over their cookies and cider, Van cooed and played with his toes on the blanket his mother had spread for him on the floor.

"Lynnie, I can't get into your mind to understand why you feel this way, but I'm glad you called. All Christians have temptations. They don't disappear all of a sudden when we turn to Him. In fact, as soon as Satan puts these obstacles in our path, God uses such incidents to strengthen us. We can fight the temptation, and we can decide not to fall into it again, but none of these things seem to work. If we allow it, the presence of temptation can cause us to fall. We pray in the Lord's Prayer, 'Lead us not into temptation…' It is not God who tempts us but rather Satan."

"I know Satan is real. He sure chased me this afternoon!"

Ruth patted Lynnie on the arm. "The next phrase in the prayer is 'but deliver us from evil.' Evil is Satan himself. I think of it this way: God leads us along the path he wants us to go, but Satan likes to put snares along our pathway. God won't take the snare away, but He can give us the tools to either bypass them, rise above them, or destroy them. One of those tools is to change direction. You thought of suicide again. My phone call may seem coincidental, but I doubt it. I woke up today and thought about you and your wonderful concert and wanted to tell you how proud we are of what you have done. Confession is good. Solomon said, 'Two are better than one because if they fall, the one will lift up his fellow.'"

"I'm glad you called. You know, you should become a Bible teacher. You make a lot of practical sense."

The two friends sat together and watched Van attempt to move about on the blanket. He tried to get up on his knees to crawl but would tumble back down. He giggled at his thwarted attempt.

With a plate of cookies and glasses of cider on the table in front of them, they watched the baby and laughed at his efforts.

After several minutes, Lynnie took a deep breath and plunged in where she never dared since the day she came to Florence Van Sant's bakery. She had alluded to it before but never discussed it out and out. "I've told you I have an old burden. It has haunted me like a constant specter too long. I suppose I imagine if I don't talk about it, it will go away. So far, it hasn't. I don't even like to remind myself, yet it crops up when I least expect it to surface."

"This ghost is your persistent burden. I suppose everyone has burdens. I told you to bake the cookies to distract your thought processes. Always a good way to elude temptation when it hits." Ruth held up her half-eaten cookie.

As she chomped down on her own cookie, Lynnie said, "Sounds like an exchange of temptations if you ask me!"

"Maybe. But they are good and good for us! But, Lynnie, we all have temptations." She held out her second cookie in her hand. My constant temptation is sweets. Once I get started, I don't want to stop. It's like I've committed suicide to my willpower."

Lynnie shot Ruth a sarcastic look. "I should have such problems!"

Ruth giggled and shrugged. "Well, Lynnie, I think you can be a strong, mature Christian, but you have to resist the devil. Like I said, you don't fight the temptation itself, rather you fight the devil. Jesus fought the devil by quoting scripture to him. Satan tells you you'll be better off dead. But rather than an attempt to talk yourself out of it, talk back to him. Tell him you are made in God's image, and to destroy God's image is to say God shouldn't have created you."

"Maybe that is what Grace Jones, my vagabond friend, meant when she told me suicide would be like killing God."

"Interesting concept. We are fearfully and wonderfully made. God didn't make a mistake when he made you."

Lynnie wept quietly. Once she had control of herself, she unburdened her heart and told her story. "Ruth, I'm not who you think I am. I am who Florence Van Sant created for a little twelve-year-old girl who ran away from a horror story. Lynelle Jessamine Van Sant isn't even my real name. My real name is Jessie Lynn Vance, and I am from North Carolina. But here is my story and the circumstances."

For the next half hour, Lynnie held her friend both spellbound and in shock as she chronicled her life from childhood to the time she showed up at the bakery door in Farmer's Corner. Her story exhausted her own emotions and Ruth's as well. She told how her parents had died before she had started school, and she went to live with strangers and to a boarding school. She had tears in her eyes when she told of the horrors of her rape and finding out she would have a baby. When she told she had left her older brothers and her twin sister, however, Ruth burst out in outrage.

"Lynnie! You've never contacted your twin? Your brothers? Oh, how awful! Terrible. For you and for them as well. Oh, Lynnie."

"Ruth, I couldn't—I can't. I can't go back. I'd rather die than go back, so I let them think what they would. Hopefully, they thought I had died."

The two friends hugged each other and cried together until Lynnie calmed down enough to finish her story. She went on with her story from Lenoir to Farmer's Corner and her rescue by Aunt Flossie.

Tears streamed down Ruth's cheeks by the time Lynnie had barely started her story. In the end, Ruth had gone through an entire box of tissues. Baby Van stopped his antics on the floor and watched his mother cry.

"Oh dear, sweet Lynnie. I didn't have any idea. I can understand your suite now and the poem. But you see—you see how vulnerable you are. The fact is you know it, so you are at first base. When temptations hit, switch gears in your thought process, pray to God, talk back to Satan, and call me!"

"Ruth, it is so hard sometimes. I've completed my master's degree. I've had my graduate concert. I attend church, but I don't fit in. My future ahead is unknown. I can never go back and start over. I can never know my real family again. I can never hold my fifteen-year-old daughter and claim her as mine. When I think about what I have lost, I get down in the dumps so far that it sets me off, and then I think these suicidal thoughts."

"You know, Lynnie, I think God made you strong, stronger than I could ever be."

"How can you say I'm strong? Whenever I get to the end of a milestone, I want to kill myself! I see it as weakness."

"No, you are using your own strength instead of the spiritual strength He has given you. There is a verse my daddy taught me back in high school, the third different high school in two years, by the way, because we moved around so much. I was so angry because

I couldn't develop any good friendships, and when I did have a new friend, suddenly we had to move again."

Lynnie nodded, thinking of all the friends she didn't even have a chance to tell goodbye.

Ruth picked up Flossie's Bible on the table beside her. "Look here with me."

Ruth showed Lynnie a verse about all people having temptations. "Look Lynnie, when we are tempted, it is God's faithfulness that keeps us from being overwhelmed by the temptation. There will be an escape route, and we do not have to do wrong."

Lynnie wrote down the reference. She would read the verses for herself later. "So it's His faithfulness, not mine. You may be right, Ruthie. You may be right. It's like you said a while ago: God heads us in the direction we are to go, but the enemy puts stumbling blocks in the way. God won't remove these distractions, but He will show us how to get around them, transcend them, or end them. I get it, I think, at least until the next time."

Ruth smiled and reached for another cookie. "Sure are good!"

"I could use some coffee. How about you, Ruth?"

"No. I'm still breastfeeding. Maybe a glass of milk if you have some."

"I do." She poured milk for both of them and put aside the idea for coffee.

As they sat with their snacks, Ruth said, "Aldous Huxley said, 'Experience isn't what happens to you. It is what you do with what happens to you.' I believe you have gone through stuff so you can conquer it."

"You may be right. I'll think this one through."

Van had started to get fussy, so Lynnie picked him up and felt the diaper. "Dry. Think he's hungry?"

After his momma fed him, he fell asleep, and they went home.

Lynnie waved goodbye. "Thank you for coming over. I needed you."

# Third Movement

# CHAPTER 26

## *"The More We Are Together"*
## *by Irving King*

*Spring 1955*

Lynnie knew the time had come to get on with the rest of her life. After she passed the milestone of the concert and had earned her master's degree, she continued to teach at the university and made herself available for local concert venues.

Church attendance in and of itself did not satisfy for her. She had been there each Sunday for the last six months and enjoyed what she learned in the Bible class. And indeed, she had learned a lot in the short time she had gone to church, but she still felt like an outsider. She didn't want to get tied up with the choir even as a musician. Yes, she could get involved with the piano in some way, but Lynnie felt like church activity constituted a futile exercise in religion. She wanted to live what she had learned about her newfound faith. Yes, she continued to worship with her brothers and sisters in Christ, but she wanted more.

As Lynnie looked through the bulletin each week for some useful ministry, she told Ruth, "Bible studies are fine, but they seem like a sponge to soak in Christianity. I want to wring out the sponge."

Now with Flossie gone, sometimes the evening hours were long. She would practice the piano most of the day, take a walk, and visit with Ruth, but evenings were where she needed to fill her life with positivity.

One night, she picked up a book of quotations and found one from Albert Sweitzer. It struck her apropos to her current thought process: "The only ones among you who will be really happy people are those who will have sought and found how to serve."

"So how can I serve? I'm not a missionary or a Bible teacher. I have music, and I have time. Lord, show me how to serve."

Then one Sunday, the bulletin had a short plea for volunteers at a local women's shelter for the homeless and abused women and children. She noted the address. *I know the place. I go by there on the bus on my way home from the university. I think I'll stop there someday soon after I'm done at the university for the day and see what I can do. If anyone knows how homelessness feels, I do. Maybe I can give some encouragement to a woman or child who is in the same boat as me those many years ago. I see this could be one way I can wring out for the good of others what I've soaked up here in the pew.*

Excitement about this new possibility for service invigorated her. She had no idea what would be expected of her, but she thought of little else as she taught her students the next day. She made up her mind. *I am going to stop at the shelter's office on my way home today, and I'm not telling Ruth!*

Normally, she went home and practiced piano after her day at the university, but this day, she got off the bus close to the shelter. She knew she could get a later bus to take her to her normal stop or call a cab.

Mr. Glenn, the bus driver, familiar with her routine, voiced his surprise. "Miss Van Sant, you ain't lost, are ya?"

"Not at all. I need to make a short visit here, and I'll get the rest of my ride home later. I'll see you if you are still on the route."

The man shrugged as she stepped from the bus. "Don't be around here too much after dark, Miss Van Sant. My wife and I both like you too much for somethin' to happen to you."

"Thanks, Mr. Glenn. I hope you don't see me as a girl in the market for trouble!"

"Ho! Not you, ma'am. You are a lady. I'm on my last run now, but my friend, Mike, does the evening run. I'll tell him to look out for you."

The shelter, a large white two-story house, sat back a little way from the street. A fence surrounded the property, and a closed gate at the front entrance barred the entrance for the safety of women and children housed in the facility. *Looks foreboding!*

She rang the bell at the gate. It seemed to her like a long time before anyone came, although it had been no more than five minutes. As she had her hand poised to ring again, a slight white-haired woman came to the gate.

"Yes, ma'am. Can I help you? Do you need a safe place to stay?"

Her question socked Lynnie in the face. Her mind went back more than twenty years when she stood outside Aunt Flossie's bakery, indeed needing a safe place to stay.

"Oh, hello. My name is Lynnie Van Sant. I saw a plea in our church bulletin that you needed volunteers to help here. I should have called, but I didn't have the opportunity."

"Oh, yes, ma'am. I am Mrs. Smith, one of the staff. Please. Let me open the gate."

The hinges needed a bit of oil and squawked like a goose as the little lady pulled it open. "Please come inside."

"Yes. I apologize that I didn't call first, but I made up my mind to stop in today. I'm on my way home from the university." Lynnie followed the woman through the gate, up the steps, and into the broad hallway.

After they were inside, she could hear the chatter of children and smelled what promised to be a good supper. It suggested soup or stew. "Mrs. Smith, I am interested in volunteer work here. I don't know what I can do, but I would like to do more than sit in the pew and soak up my religion."

The lady laughed. "Well put. So many people act like caterpillars at church."

Lynnie scowled. "What?"

"I think of it like this: They are caterpillars. They crawl in and out of church, but they never emerge into the butterfly they were created for."

Lynnie giggled at the image.

"We are a family here, but our family comes and goes. Sometimes, they are here for several weeks and other times only as short as an overnight. We take women and their children through eighteen years of age. Let me show you around first."

Talking as she toured the facility, Mrs. Smith showed her a large room with a lot of chairs lined up in rows and an upright piano in the room. "We call this our assembly room, where we meet each morning for chapel service and special celebrations like Christmas. We have Sunday school for them here. No one is required to attend—however, we do encourage it."

As they walked into the dining room, Lynnie asked, "Do you ever have girls who come here—pregnant girls—with no family?"

Mrs. Smith sighed. "Oh yes, more times than we want. These are the girls who often stay until after the baby comes. If they do not want to keep the baby, we cooperate with a local adoption agency."

"Who is the youngest such girl?"

Mrs. Smith stopped, cocked her head, and looked into Lynnie's eyes. "You have a story, don't you?"

Lynnie nodded. "I was twelve. I…I came here because I thought I could help someone who was like me."

Mrs. Smith laid a thin blue-veined hand on Lynnie's. "I am certain you can. God has laid this ministry on your heart and sent you to us." She hesitated. "Miss Van Sant…"

"Lynnie, please."

"Lynnie, I assume this is not common knowledge, and it will go no further than you wish. I suggest you share it with our director, Mrs. Caulfield. She isn't here this afternoon, but she will be here all day tomorrow. All our volunteers must be interviewed by Mrs. Caulfield."

Lynnie nodded and looked about at the dining room. Although there were two small tables along one side of the dining room, a long table set up in family style was in the process of being set for the evening meal. A young woman was setting the table. She was neat in appearance, but her face and demeanor suggested that she was too familiar with physical abuse. Mrs. Smith introduced her.

"This is one of our family, Lee. She's been with us for a while and is a marvelous cook. Lee, this is Lynnie, who has offered to volunteer here. Are you feeling better today?"

"Yeah…headache's gone."

Lynnie commented, "It smells like beef stew. Perfect for today. It's making my stomach growl."

"Yes, ma'am. Thank you."

Mrs. Smith let Lynnie peep into the kitchen. "We won't bother them now. Would you like to stay and have supper with us? There is always room for one more."

"It would be better than going back to an empty house and eating the last of my molasses cookies, but I have piano to practice tonight to get ready for a concert coming up soon. Perhaps another evening."

Mrs. Smith laughed. "Surely you would have more than cookies!"

"I do, but I had a big meal at school today, so I plan to heat up soup for supper."

"You play piano! How wonderful. Most of the time, our piano lies dormant. I wonder if you could give lessons?"

"Why not? That would work for family members who stay but not for overnighters."

"True. Let's go see the rest of the house."

Taking Lynnie to the far end of the first floor, Mrs. Smith showed her an activity room where two women were chatting and doing needlework. One of them had an infant in a makeshift bassinet—a cardboard box padded with receiving blankets.

Lynnie made a mental note. *I think I'll buy some baby stuff for this place. I've got the funds. Why use it all on myself?*

Mrs. Smith made introductions before leading her to a room across the hallway where four children, aged from toddler to elementary age, played with well-used toys.

Another mental note: *Buy toys too.*

A volunteer kept watch on the children. She was reading to a little girl about four years of age. Mrs. Smith introduced her. "Lynnie, this is Mattie White, one of our regular volunteers. She comes every Monday."

Lynnie gave the lady a big smile. "Hello, Mattie."

From there, they walked up a set of stairs to the sleeping area. Six small bedrooms—three on each side of the hall—accommodated either two or three women or a family. A bathroom at one end and an infirmary at the other end completed the floor.

"Mrs. Smith, what happens when you have a large family including teenage boys? Where does everyone sleep?"

"Ahh, good question. Boys twelve and over, when we have them, sleep in a dorm-style room in the basement. It isn't ideal, and they do get into fracases down there. We have a man on the property, Jack, who does yard work and maintenance and listens to the boys. Most of these boys have not had a good father figure, and Jack's presence usually means a lot to them."

Lynnie laughed. "I understand that. I went to a boarding school till I was twelve. The boys were always scuffling."

When they went back downstairs, Mrs. Smith showed her the office and a small room on through where Mrs. Caufield counseled the women. "When you come tomorrow, I'll be waiting for you to ring the bell at the gate, and I'll bring you here to chat with her. I have no doubt she will be delighted to have you here. One thing she stresses is that she doesn't want volunteers who have an agenda, such as wanting to come in here and change everything. We do what we do with the resources we have. We are a ministry dependent on donations."

Lynnie nodded. "My only agenda is to serve in a semblance of the manner Aunt Flossie served me when she took me in at age twelve. I've hidden the story for the last sixteen years. Other than Aunt Flossie, who died last year, only one other person, my friend Ruth, knows about my life. I do not want my story to leave here. How much should I tell?"

"I understand. Mrs. Caufield and I both have our own stories, and many of our volunteers, as well, have been through traumas we can barely imagine. You will be safe, Lynnie. It is a safe place for our family of guests and for us as well."

"Thank you."

"Oh, speaking of safety, how about Jack taking you home? I need to send him out to the store for a few groceries, and he can take you home first."

"I won't argue with that. I do not drive, and I take the bus everywhere. My usual bus driver went off duty after he dropped me off here."

As she shook hands with Mrs. Smith, she said, "I teach my last student from one to two in the afternoon tomorrow. I will catch the two twenty bus, which should get me here by two forty-five. Will that be good for Mrs. Caufield?"

"You come on then. I will tell her you will be here. She is very flexible in her schedule. We look forward to seeing you tomorrow."

# CHAPTER 27

## *"Awake My Soul" by Phillip Doddridge*

Lynnie left the Women's Shelter filled with a new sense of purpose. Although she was a Christian now, she felt as though she had been sleeping. Her new sense of purpose made her feel awake and ready to serve God.

Jack made her short ride home amusing. One of those ageless people, who may have been forty or seventy, he told her all the funny stories about the teen boys' antics in the dorm in his South Florida black patois. Lynnie's sides ached from laughing by the time he dropped her off at her front door.

"Missy, I be glad to bring yo' home when yo' come. But I hopes yo' stay fo' chow next day yo' come."

"I will. Thank you, Mr. Jack. I plan to come and talk to Mrs. Caulfield tomorrow. I may, indeed, need a ride." She handed him a twenty-dollar bill. "This is to help with the groceries you have to buy."

"Yahoo!"

When she arrived home at almost dark, chills crept up her spine as she thought about what the bus driver said. She had never been afraid around her area of the city in the evening. Reasonable quiet characterized the part of Tampa where she lived, but crime had become a real problem in parts of the city. A few days before her venture to the Women's Shelter, the crime boss Charlie Wall had been murdered in his home. Gambling, prostitution, and gang activity were on the rise in the city.

*Glad Jack brought me home. I'll pay him to cart me each time. The bus is safe in daylight, but maybe I need to take more care at night.*

She walked into the house, locked the door behind her, and pulled all the shades down.

To volunteer would put a breath of fresh air in a Christian walk she felt had already become stagnant. She might be able to engage in the disrupted lives of women and children like she had been.

Tuesday, after her last student, she looked forward to her interview with Mrs. Caufield. It was raining, but she didn't have to wait for the bus. It pulled up to the stop as she arrived.

When she got off at the shelter again, Mr. Glenn grinned. "Hey, you gonna traipse about Tampa again this evening? At least it's early. My last stop here will be four fifty. You be careful now."

"Thanks, Mr. Glenn. I plan to do a bit of volunteer work, but anytime it's late, I have a ride home. Thank you for caring. See you later."

She no sooner rang the bell at the gate than Mrs. Smith appeared. "Just on time! Come on in. Mrs. Caufield is eager to meet you."

Mrs. Caufield, a portly matron, likely in her fifties, reminded Lynnie of Aunt Flossie. Her heart gave a leap. *A gift—a reminder of my sweet Aunt Flossie.*

If Flossie had only been a simple, uneducated country baker, she was a wise and perceptive woman. By the same token, although Mrs. Caufield spoke with a cultured tone and came across as refined and sophisticated, Lynnie could tell after ten minutes in her presence that she too was wise and perceptive.

The interview went well. Although Lynnie did not reveal much of her story, she told Mrs. Caufield about having a baby at age twelve. "I understand the fear, the worthless feelings, the self-loathing a girl has under similar circumstances. I don't know that I can counsel such a girl, but I can listen."

After a brief pause, Lynnie continued her story. "Because my baby would be taken away from me, I ran away. I was homeless. I can relate to women who have nowhere to go. Those few days, when I had no idea where I would end, were terrible, and I still have nightmares about them. I hope I can be of some use in your ministry here."

"You were brave to do as you did, Lynnie. Did you ever contemplate ending it all?"

Lynnie gave a cynical laugh and nodded. She looked at Mrs. Caufield and said, "You knew that, didn't you?"

The woman shrugged, and with a hint of a tear in her eye, she said, "Maybe. I've been there."

"Yes. I thought about it several times growing up. I tried it three times, but God intervened—stories in themselves. Since I have trusted Christ as my Savior, I haven't thought about it except for one time. Again, God intervened, a lesson learned. It seems I have to have something to do to counteract my notion of uselessness. I suppose that is one reason I am here. My main reason, however, rests on the idea of working out what I believe."

They discussed Lynnie's music career and her relationship with Christ.

Then the director quietly mulled over their interview for a few minutes. She smiled broadly. "Lynnie, I think you will be a good fit here. We need volunteers, but we need to be careful whom we let sign on. Some ladies come here with the idea that they can change the world. They want this or that social program to be instituted. They want to lecture the women on how they have brought their problems on themselves. Or they want to soothe their own consciences by putting in hours as a volunteer. Every volunteer we have here doesn't necessarily have a crisis history, but those of us who do tend to stick to it. When can you come?"

Lynnie grinned a toothy grin. "I am free any evening and Wednesday afternoons. I do have a concert coming up next month, so I need to practice at least four hours most days. Can you use me Wednesdays?"

"Indeed. We have a Wednesday morning volunteer, but no one wants to come Wednesday afternoon. They have services at their places of worship and believe they take precedence over outside activities, as well as they should. You do not go to Wednesday evening services?"

"I haven't really gotten involved at this point. I've gone with my friend Ruth a few times. Could I not serve Christ in this way instead of soaking up sermon after sermon? I go to Sunday school, church worship, and evening service on Sunday, and I'm learning a lot. Don't get me wrong. But I want to serve in a way God has prepared me."

"Good. Do you want to start tomorrow afternoon?"

Lynnie smiled and nodded. "I can be here by say one o'clock. That will give me time to grab some lunch, get my things together, and catch the bus."

"We do have our own Wednesday evening service. I lead a Bible study for the ladies, and Mrs. Smith has a Bible time with the children. Since you are a pianist, would you be willing to play some hymns for us to sing? I'd like these women and children to learn some hymns. Singing scripture and biblical concepts is Bible teaching too."

Understanding well the concept of learning through music, Lynnie nodded. "I would love to. Do you have any hymnals?"

Mrs. Caufield laughed. "We have four."

"No problem. I can work with what you have. You choose the hymns, I will look them over, and you all can share. I'll play it by memory."

Just as the interview was almost over, an irate young woman stormed into the office.

"Helen? What's the meaning of this? Can you not see I have someone with me?"

"Yeah...but you can't put her (emphasis on her) in my room—that...that n—"

"Don't say the word, Helen. We are all the same here."

"She ain't the same as me! She's colored."

"Helen, at the Women's Shelter, we are women. We are from the inside out, not the outside in. You came here because someone you trusted to love you and cherish you abused you. Justine, or Justie as she calls herself, trusted someone to love her too. He raped her, beat her when he found out she was carrying his baby, and he left her hurting and penniless. She is one of our family the same as you. We are too crowded here this week to provide separate rooms. If you are unwilling to share a room with someone who doesn't look like you, you are welcome to leave."

"It ain't right. Where I come from, they have to know their place."

"Mmmm, Jim Crow laws, huh? Well, Jim Crow is one fellow we don't let in the front gate here. We need to help each other, Helen. Think of how you can help Justie and not how you can condemn her for how God created her. Now what is your decision? Do you want to go back to your husband, or will you stay with us?"

By the time Mrs. Caufield finished speaking, tears flooded the woman's face. She sniffed a time or two. "I can't go back to him. Maybe I can go to my mom's in a few days. I'll stay. I'm sorry. Just the way I was brought up. I'll try to make it work."

"Good. You are old enough to be her mother, and hers died when she was a little girl. Think about ways you can be a momma to her if she was your girl."

Helen's eyes bugged out. "A momma to… Reckon I could. I got a daughter older 'n her."

"Good. Glad you made that decision."

Helen left, shaking her head and muttering, "Momma to a colored…momma…"

When Helen was gone, Mrs. Caufield turned to Lynnie. "That doesn't happen too often, but you can see the need for careful handling of these situations. I hope the conflicts don't scare you off."

"Not at all. I assume Justie is very young. What is the story here?"

"As I said to Helen, Justie's mother died when she was small. She grew up with an abusive father, who sold her to a man for a quart of whiskey. You heard me tell Helen what happened. The girl is only thirteen years old. She is twelve weeks pregnant. She went to the rescue mission, and they sent her here. I've only had a brief interview with her. I wanted her to get settled in first."

Lynnie's eyes teared up. "I want to help her if I can. I had my baby when I was only twelve. I know God has sent me here."

Mrs. Caufield nodded silently. She picked up Lynnie's hand and held it for several moments. "I know God sent you here at this time—His perfect time."

Lynnie frowned and looked at the door where Helen had just left. "What about prenatal care and delivery?"

"We have a retired doctor on our board of directors, Dr. Reich, who comes in and conducts a free clinic once a month. He is available too for emergencies. He can deliver babies right here if necessary."

Lynnie nodded and thought back to the midwife who had taken care of her and delivered her baby.

After a few more minutes of chatting, Lynnie looked at her watch. "It's twenty till five and about time for my bus. I'll be here tomorrow then. Looks like the rain has stopped."

Mrs. Caufield handed her a key. "This will get you in the gate and the door here by my office but not the front entrance. Please do not lose it or loan it to any of our guests because they are difficult and expensive to replace. As well, if it gets into the hands of someone one who is a threat to one of our family, it could mean real trouble not only for them but also for the rest of us."

"I will remember. I'm not one to lose things. Growing up as I did, we never took anything for granted." Lynnie put the key on her key ring and zipped it into her shoulder bag.

After a few more words, Lynnie went out the door by the office and awaited the bus. She didn't have long to wait. With a toot of the horn, the familiar face smiled at her from the open bus door.

"Miss Lynnie, you aren't thinking of moving over here, are you?"

"Not likely, Mr. Glenn. I am going to volunteer on Wednesday afternoons and evening. I'll have a ride home, so you won't have to worry about me."

"Good. I do worry about you being out and about in this town. Guess you heard about that big crime boss getting murdered. That was right around the corner from here."

"Thank you for caring." She winked as the driver. "With you on the bus route and God's Spirit in my heart, I am safe."

Mr. Glenn grinned and pulled away from the curb as she took her seat.

# CHAPTER 28

## *"Hoedown" from Rodeo by Aaron Copeland*

Lynnie may have shared with Mr. Glenn and the half-dozen other riders on the bus about her volunteering at the Women's Shelter, but oddly enough, she still did not tell Ruth. *If Ruth thinks it's strange for me to always be away from home on Wednesdays, she hasn't said anything.*

From the first day at the shelter, she was busy listening to the women, reading storybooks to preschoolers, and connecting with Justie, the now fourteen-year-old pregnant girl.

At first, Justie was reluctant to open up, but when Lynnie shared part of her own story with the girl, they found a point of bonding beyond anything Lynnie had ever had before. It was different from Aunt Flossie or Ruth because it was on the level of her own experience. It transcended the boundaries of age, education, or race. They became sisters.

For Justie, Lynnie was like that older sister she'd never had. She had little concept of a mother since hers had died before she had much memory. Her father had abused her mentally and physically. She told Lynnie, "Pa sold me to a white man for a quart of whiskey. When I got a baby, he threw me out. That's when I came here."

Lynnie, however, had another entire life beyond her volunteering. In the few months since she had started her volunteer work, she also gave three major concerts in the area, one as the sole artist and the other two in conjunction with other performers. The money boosted her bank account, but she didn't care about the money. She enjoyed performing for the enjoyment of others and the ability to provide it. Branching out beyond the area, she had a concert scheduled for Jacksonville in the near future, the first concert outside of Tampa. She had misgivings about how to get there. She had never flown in an airplane before and planned to take a train; however, the symphony insisted that they would pay her way and bought a round-trip airline ticket for her.

When she called Ruth to tell her about her plans, she said, "Sounds like I am to be treated like a celebrity! Guess I will do what Aunt Flossie would do: Accept it and say thank you."

"I told you, girl! See? You will be a celebrity."

"I don't want celebrity status. I want to play the piano."

Walt Miller, the man who had attended her concert at the university, met her at the airport. "Miss Van Sant, we are all excited about having you for this concert. Our first stop will be to meet with the director, Dr. Busch."

Dr Busch was all business, and confirmed that she would play Rachmaninoff's *Piano Concerto No. 2* with the full orchestra. He didn't waste any time with small talk and took her to the concert hall immediately to rehearse the piece one time with the orchestra. He seemed pleased with what he heard.

The concert was scheduled for eight o'clock; the orchestra performed some preliminary selections before she came on stage. Since Lynnie was a newcomer to Jacksonville, the applause was muted as she entered the stage prior to intermission. In sharp contrast, after her performance, she received a standing ovation. At intermission, she went into the music room and visited with some of the orchestra until someone tapped her on the shoulder.

"Miss Van Sant, there are some people in the hallway who would like to speak with you."

"Me? I don't know anyone here beside these people in the orchestra."

"The man insists he knows you, but he didn't give his name. He's dressed in his Navy uniform."

"Navy…Bobby," she whispered. Her heart leaped into her throat. "Thank you. I'll see him."

When she went to the hallway, indeed Bobby Everett stood before her resplendent in his dress whites—Bobby and a beautiful lady.

"Bobby Everett! What a surprise to see you."

Bobby grasped Lynnie's hand and brought it to join the lady's hand. "Lynnie, this is my wife, Jeanette. Jeanette, meet the world's greatest pianist, Miss Lynnie Van Sant."

"Oh, Bobby! This is wonderful. I never thought I'd see you again. This is the first I've ventured out of Tampa in three years since I moved there and look who I see. You look fabulous in your fancy uniform! How did this happen that you came here to see me tonight?"

"I'm stationed here for now when I'm not deployed elsewhere. Jeanette and I have a little house here."

They talked a bit in the hallway, but when Lynnie noticed the orchestra return to the stage after their intermission, she said, "Let's go inside the music room so we can sit and visit."

In the course of conversation, she found out Bobby and Jeanette had been married for two years and had a little girl. "She's at home with a babysitter," Jeanette told her. "When Bobby saw your name in the paper, he said we had to come and hear you. I'm so glad we did. You were wonderful!"

*A girl.* "Do you have a picture of your little girl?"

The proud daddy produced the picture of a little blond-headed toddler.

"She's a little sweetie. You are blessed." She held the picture in her hand and looked at Jeannette. "She looks like her momma."

Bobby grinned. "Spittin' image!"

"So, Bobby, do you still play violin?"

He looked at Jeanette, and they laughed. "You might not recognize the music, Lynnie. We have gotten into Celtic music. Jeanette plays the banjo and the Celtic harp, and we play with some other navy people who play a variety of Celtic instruments. We have a jam session any Saturday night we can get together. Lots of fun."

"I'm impressed." She laughed and shook her head. "You were good enough on the violin to do well, but I guess you had to unlearn things. Yet the transition from Copeland to Celtic might not be too difficult. Do you think you can still play the hoedown from *Rodeo*?"

"Haven't tried for a long time. I heard you studied piano under Copeland. Did you enjoy him as a teacher?"

"Yes, three summers. He was a wonderful teacher."

"So how long are you here, Lynnie?"

"Only tonight. I have to get back to Tampa to teach my students at the university. I teach new freshmen piano students. I have a few private piano students as well, so I don't know how long I'll continue at the university. My great enjoyment these days is volunteer work at a women's shelter."

"Good, good." Bobby hesitated a moment and then put his hand on her arm. "I heard Aunt Flossie is gone. I'm so sorry. I would have sent a sympathy card, but I didn't have your address. Joyce's mother wrote my mom about it."

Lynnie learned Jimmy, Bobby's brother, had been killed in Korea.

"Oh, Bobby. I didn't know. I haven't talked to anyone from Farmer's Corner since Aunt Flossie's funeral. Jimmy expressed what life should be for a young person. I can't believe he is gone. I'm sorry for your loss."

The three talked until the concert ended, and the orchestra members filtered back into the music room. Lynnie hugged Bobby goodbye and watched as he and Jeanette left hand in hand.

Lynnie took a deep breath. "It's over. I don't need Bobby anymore. I'm happy for him, and I'm happy for me. I really am. Thank you, Lord!"

After a brief reception for the orchestra and the Philharmonic dignitaries, when the orchestra honored her, Walt escorted her back to the hotel. She crawled into her hotel bed and slept well, content to know Bobby Everett had a good life and a good wife.

The next day, when she got out of her taxi at the airport, she had a bizarre experience. A man in the uniform of a naval officer ran up to her. At first, she wondered if Bobby had sent him. The man grabbed her and started to plant a kiss on her lips. Then he stopped in his tracks and said, "Oh, I am so sorry. I thought you were someone else."

Lynnie's heart beat double-time. She looked about for a security person, but the man left and disappeared. It took her several minutes to calm down.

She wondered about it the entire flight back to Tampa. "I wonder if he knew Jay-Lee and mistook me for her. That's the only thing I can think of. Strange. I still have the heebie-jeebies!"

# Chapter 29

## *"There Is Sunshine in My Soul Today" by E. E. Hewitt*

The thought of someone thinking she was Jay-Lee cast a shadow on her trip home, but thoughts of the shelter shed a bit of light in her mind. The Jacksonville Symphony paid her way and gave her a substantial honorarium. She accepted it with grace but then sent the money to the Crossnore School in the mountains of North Carolina as an anonymous gift.

All through this period, Lynnie came in demand for weddings and wedding receptions. Although she routinely went everywhere in the daytime on the bus, for her concerts or nighttime, she always took a taxicab.

She told Mr. Glenn, "Can't get on a bus all dressed up, and I don't ride the bus after dark."

Lynnie still had not told Ruth or even the church she had signed up as a volunteer at the shelter. She had been at the home every Wednesday for the last six months, and no one seemed to have missed her very badly.

After several months, Ruth questioned, "How come you never answer your phone on Wednesdays?"

*Think I'll still keep her in suspense.* She grinned. "I didn't get home until late." It was the truth or quasi-truth perhaps.

One afternoon, after her day at the university while on the way to visit with her new friends, as she liked to think of them, she chuckled about the lack of attempted contact. "Six months. I've not been available, and Ruth and I talk or see each other a couple of times a week as well as Sunday. Maybe God needed me to do this on my own without help from Ruth. Thank you, Lord."

She felt that the time she spent with Justie, including teaching her how to play the piano, was God's way of putting "sunshine in her soul."

Lynnie had discovered the girl had a natural musical ability when she came to the Wednesday evening Bible study for the first time. She went to the piano and picked out the melody of one of the hymns they had sung before the study time. The next week, when Lynnie came, she started piano lessons with the girl. Justie loved music, especially jazz.

Others too asked for lessons even if their time at the shelter was brief. Lynnie didn't believe it was a waste of time. They might never go on with piano, but they would have the joy of music in their hearts and heads if not their fingers. She offered free lessons Saturday afternoons for anyone who wanted to continue after they left the shelter.

Justie had decided to keep her baby and raise it; however, the dilemma was how would she support herself.

"Miss Lynnie, I reckon I could go on welfare, but I don't know if that is right—lettin' the government take care o' me. Mrs. Caufield say I can stay here so long as there is room. She'll let me work for my keep doin' laundry. What do ya think? Should I do that?"

"Justie, you can only take one step at a time. Once your baby is here, then you can decide about that. At least you have that option, and it is a secure place so long as there is room."

"Yeah…" She had an evil glint in her eye. "Helen's gone now, so I don't have her raggin' on me all the time!"

One gorgeous October Wednesday, when the sky was clear and blue, what Lynnie called Carolina Blue, she arrived at the shelter and nearly bumped into Dr. Reich and Mrs. Smith coming from the infirmary.

"Oh! Miss Lynnie!" Mrs. Smith's eyes snapped with excitement. "You will be pleased to know that Justie has a fine little girl. She weighed seven pounds and has bright-red hair. Perfect baby, isn't she, Dr. Reich?"

"Indeed. The delivery went well. She asked if you could come to see her when you arrived. Go on, Miss Van Sant." He nodded his head cynically. "Go look at the newest indigent added to society."

Lynnie wondered at the doctor's cynicism, but she was glad all had gone well with the birth. *Not time to think of how another indigent was added to the human race. Just another baby to love.*

Justie looked good for having just delivered a seven-pounder. She was sitting up in bed, all smiles as she cradled a bundle in her arms, the red hair peeping beyond the receiving blanket.

"Oh, Miss Lynnie! Looky at what God done give me. A little redhead. She gonna be light-skinned, but that's okay. I don't mind." She pulled back the little blanket to let Lynnie see the baby.

"She's going to be pretty, Justie, just like you. I'm glad it went well for you."

"She already been feeding. I hope I got good milk for her."

Lynnie remembered when her milk came in. *I showed up at Van Sant's Bakery with milk all over the front of my filthy dress. I was so afraid, so ashamed… How did I ever survive?*

Justie's chatter brought Lynnie back to the present. "Mrs. Caufield says I can stay here in the infirmary till I'm up and about real good. Me and my baby, we gonna move into the room back of the kitchen. Ain't no one stayin' there since the woman who used to be the cook here—you remember Lee—when she left. I'm gonna learn to cook and sew and do all sorts of stuff. She said I can still take piano lessons too if that's all right with you."

"You know it is. We will have your lesson the same time as always—2:30 every Wednesday afternoon. You will have to make time to practice if you are on a work schedule."

"Yessum. I will."

"What is your little girl's name?"

Justie grinned broadly. "Thought you'd never ask. She is Mazie Lynn. Amazing Mazie for my mother, and Lynn for you."

Lynnie's mouth dropped open. "Why, thank you, Justie. It is a privilege for you to name her for me. I know your mother would be honored if you named her Mazie. Will you call her Mazie?"

"I reckon she'll always be Mazie Lynn."

Justie tucked the covers around her precious baby and nodded up and down, repeating the name, "Mazie Lynn, Mazie Lynn, Mazie Lynn…"

Lynnie kissed the new mother on the forehead and slipped out of the infirmary with tears in her eyes.

*1956*

Although several women or women and their families came and went from the shelter, Lynnie offered piano lessons for them while they were there. Also, some of them continued with lessons, either coming to the shelter or to her home for private lessons. Justie was one of those she taught at the Women's Shelter. Justie, or Justine, the name she now preferred, proved to be exceptional. She remained at the shelter with baby Mazie Lynn in the back room by the kitchen, working in the kitchen for the most part. She became a good worker and an asset to the shelter in not only the kitchen but also entertaining the other residents with her piano music.

Lynnie decided it was time for a recital. She approached Mrs. Caufield. "How about a benefit concert and student recital for the Women's Shelter? Several of our former residents are advanced enough to play, and Justine is amazing. I could end the recital with some selections as well."

"Oh, yes! We will need to get the piano tuned, but yes. Although I will have to run this by the board of directors, you can start planning."

The board approved, the piano was tuned, and the students were selected and began working on their music. The concert was slated for May 12, the day before Mother's Day.

Lynnie had been a volunteer at the shelter for a year by this time, but she still had never told Ruth and Ben where she was on

Wednesdays. *I want to invite Ruth and Ben, so guess it's time I tell them, huh?*

April 1 was Easter. She met Ruth at Sunday school and pulled her aside before they went to the sanctuary for worship service. "Hey, girl, I'd like for you and Ben to set aside an evening for a special concert. In case you have been wondering where I've been on Wednesdays, I have been volunteering at the Women's Shelter since this time last year."

"So that's where you've been! And why have you not shared this important detail of your life with one who you claim to be your best friend?"

With a cheesy grin, Lynnie answered, "I have no idea why. I guess I wanted to prove that I could do something productive on my own besides piano. Anyway, now you know. I'm telling you now so you can plan to come to a special benefit recital and concert. It will be at the shelter, featuring the students I have been teaching. They have all been residents at the shelter, and all but one of them are gone. Justine, the girl who remains there working now, has a real talent. The concert will be the Saturday before Mother's Day. I'm counting on you and Ben."

"I'm amazed, Lynnie, yet I'm not. I knew you would do something like this, and it's perfect. You've been in their situation and can relate to their needs. Thank you for doing this. And yes, we will plan on it. I'll get a babysitter for Van, and we'll get gussied up for an evening gala."

"I think I told you I didn't want to be an oversaturated sponge, soaking up all the Bible lessons but not wringing it out for the benefit of others. I saw a plea in the bulletin last spring and showed up on their doorstep. I love what I do there. I've been there every Wednesday but two, when I had Wednesday concerts."

The recital, a highlight of the Mother's Day weekend, drew in board members, pastors, families of performers, and volunteers with their families. The assembly room was standing room only. The students did not disappoint; they performed beautifully. Some of them were able to play only the simplest of pieces, but they did so with near perfection. Justine played two pieces, Beethoven's "Fur Elise" at the beginning and then "Just the Way You Are," by Jerome Kern as the finale of the students' recital. The girl played both songs with great feeling, drawing loud applause from the audience.

Lynnie engaged a caterer to provide refreshment during the intermission.

Then after the intermission, she provided another twenty-minute recital of concert pieces by Chopin, Beethoven, and Copeland.

Proceeds from the recital and concert provided some much-needed funds for the general operation of the shelter, and it brought attention to the ongoing needs of the institution. It also made an impact on the call for new volunteers.

When Lynnie talked to Ruth after the concert, she indicated an interest, but she shook her head when Lynnie pressed her. "Lynnie, you know I can't leave Van to do this now. Wait till he's in school, and then I can think about it. By the way, Ben talked to Dr. Reich about sharing the load of his involvement at the shelter. He's made arrangements to take call once a week."

"That's great. I'm glad he did that. I am passionate about this place, and for my best friend's husband to be involved, is…well, it 'puts the icing on the cake,' as the saying goes."

Lynnie told Ruth about Justine. "When she came here, her story broke my heart. It was too much like my own. I think that is why I have continued to come week after week. If I can come alongside someone like me and give them courage and hope in Jesus, it is the place for me to be."

"It helps, I suppose, that she shows talent for the piano, but I hear what you are saying. I'm very happy for you and hope you don't give up on any of these women and their families."

## CHAPTER 30

## *"Que Sera, Sera" (Whatever Will Be, Will Be) by Jay Livingston and Ray Evans*

Indeed, Lynnie did not give up on any of the women, despite her other obligations. For three years, after she gained her master's degree, Lynnie continued to teach piano at the university, but she had gained several private students, including those she had started at the shelter. She believed a change needed to take place. She called Ruth.

"Hey, girl, what's on your mind?"

"I'm ready for a change. I am so busy with piano students and concerts. I am not putting my best effort into my position at the university. What do you think?"

"I think. Yes, you have to do what you think is right. I wondered how much you could pile on yourself."

Lynnie went on with her rationale. "I have not been at the university long enough for tenure, and my private students are more important at this point. I have concerts to prepare. I am needed at the Women's Shelter. To me, it's my primary ministry. I need to drop a thing or two."

"I concur, dear friend. Last night Ben and I talked about how too-busy you have become."

In 1957, she resigned from her teaching position at the university and concentrated on her private students and an increasing load of concerts as far away as Tallahassee, Jacksonville, Fort Lauderdale, and Miami. Her earnings were either sent anonymously to Crossnore

School or placed in a fund for improvements at the Woman's Shelter. Wednesday after Wednesday, she faithfully took the bus to the shelter and enjoyed Jack's ride back home.

Little Mazie Lynn was growing into a smart little girl and at age two could already match pitches with the little songs the children sang. Lynnie kept an eye on her and hoped she could start her on the piano by the time she was four years old or maybe teach her to read music and sing.

Justine had developed into a graceful, well-spoken young woman. Lynnie's influence, as well as Mrs. Caufield's, had shaped the girl's life.

*1964*

Lynnie's life settled down over the next few years. Van grew up way too fast. Ben and Ruth had enrolled him in a private school. They had bought a new home in the area, a good choice. Ruth also had a secret of her own, but rather than hiding it, she told Lynnie. "Uh…by the way, I am signed up to take Red Cross volunteer duties at the hospital."

"Oh, that is wonderful. It will give you something to do while Van is in school. Good for you."

Ruth shook her head back and forth. "Speaking of school, they don't have a piano teacher. Think you can teach Van?"

"I'll try."

This was not a good decision. Van had a tin ear. After a year of lessons, although he loved his aunt, Lynnie decided to discuss it with him before she told Ruth he wasn't a good piano candidate.

"Van, do you like to play the piano?"

"Uh…well…well…not much. I'd rather play football."

She stifled a laugh. "I thought so. I know you practice hard, but you don't seem to catch on to how to play, do you?"

"Nah. It all sounds the same to me."

When Ruth came to pick him up, Lynnie got honest with her. "Ruthie, much as I love you and love Van, he will never be a piano player. He has no ear for it, and his little hands would much rather catch a football."

"Oh! I am so relieved. It's torture to hear him practice. He wanted to do it to please you, so we have endured it. Maybe our next child will be a piano player, huh?"

No next child materialized. Ruth and Ben tried for years to provide a brother or sister for Van, but it didn't happen. Lynnie felt sorry for them.

Van did well in school and became their little star football player, and Aunt Lynnie went to watch him play whenever she could.

Another of Lynnie's little ones grew up enough to go to school as well. Mazie Lynn, now six years old, would start first grade in September. Justine had been teaching her at the shelter, but she needed to be in a real classroom. The area around the shelter was in a part of town that was deteriorating, and the school had a reputation for troublemakers and low achievement.

One Wednesday in the middle of July, Justine discussed her concerns with Lynnie. "Miss Lynnie, I know my Mazie Lynn needs to be in school, but I hate to send her to one that's even worse than where I went to school. There's stories of fights and bullying all the time. She's not quite black and she's not quite white, and she'd be ripe for bullying."

Lynnie thought about this conversation over the next week. When she returned, she had made a decision. She talked with Mrs. Caufield about it, and the director agreed it was the perfect decision for all concerned.

Lynnie could hardly wait until Justine's lesson. The girl excelled on the piano, and Lynnie had hopes that she would stick with it. She played with such feeling as well as precision. But Lynnie had an idea.

"Justine, I have a proposition for you. I have more and more concerts as well as my private students. I almost do not have enough hours in a day to take care of the mundane things in my life—like…"

Justine interrupted with a grin on her face, "Like cooking, laundry, and housework?"

Lynnie nodded. "You got it. How would you all like to come and live with me, take care of my house, and let Mazie Lynn go to school in my neighborhood? The elementary school is clean, has teachers who care, and a good reputation among the parents. What do you think?"

"Oh! Miss Lynnie, I'd love to do that. Do you have room for us?"

"Indeed, I do. My bedroom is on the first floor, but there are two upstairs for you and Mazie Lynn. And I want you to get your GED. That way, if you eventually want to go to college, you will have a high school diploma."

Justine frowned. "How am I gonna pay for that?"

Lynnie cocked her head and smiled. "You don't expect to work for me for nothing, do you? You save your money."

Justine, overwhelmed by the possibilities, silently shook her head.

"So what do you say?"

The girl broke out in a broad smile. "I say yessum! When?"

"Whenever you want. You can come home with me when Jack takes me home tonight, or you can wait till next Wednesday. I think school starts August 24, so you should be settled in before that."

"Next Wednesday."

On August 11, Justine Brown and her daughter, Mazie Lynn, went home with Lynnie to stay.

The timing was providential, or as Justine said, "God did it."

Lynnie agreed. At the end of the year, the Women's Shelter closed. The signs had been there that the end was in sight. In spite of Lynnie's efforts in her annual benefit concerts, encouraging volunteerism among women of the church, and her own weekly volunteering, both funds and volunteerism had declined. As well, fewer women sought the respite of the shelter but opted other routes of assistance. Rent of the facility had risen in contrast to the donations.

Safety issues too had increased in the neighborhood, and when the estranged husband of one of the residents broke in and attempted to kidnap his child while holding a knife to the child's mother, the attack was only foiled by the quick action of Mrs. Caufield and Jack.

Mrs. Caufield saw what the man intended and simply lifted her eyebrow to Jack, who was fixing a squeaky door in the next room.

Jack knew that signal and came up on the man from behind. He grabbed the man's wrists in a viselike hold so that he dropped the knife. Mrs. Caufield grabbed the knife and escorted the man from the premises.

Then Thanksgiving day, Mrs. Smith had a stroke and passed away suddenly. Mrs. Caufield felt she had no recourse but to close the shelter. The advisory board agreed. The lease of the building would run out on December 31, 1964. The first of December, Mrs. Caufield, along with volunteers, began packing up and disposing of everything. With deep sadness, she packed up her own belongings, years of accumulation, and collected keys from the volunteers. Lynnie and Ruth went with her when she handed them over to the president of the board.

Within a week, Mrs. Caufield left Tampa for good.

Lynnie's volunteer days and bus rides to the shelter every Wednesday were over. She discussed the future with Ruth.

"Ruthie, what am I going to do with myself? My piano career is very rewarding, and I have chances every day and with every concert to impact the lives of others. My students are making progress, and I think I'm helping them with other life skills. Yet I have this itch to do more, to be involved in the lives of those who are hurting from deep hurts like the ones God has brought me through. Justine is an example of what can be done with a life so messed up redemption seems impossible. She is a wonder."

"What about joining me as a volunteer at the hospital? You could join the Red Cross Gray Ladies. I go in once a month, but you can go as often as you want to."

"That's right. Interesting idea. Where better to find hurting people? I can still be a servant of God but in a different capacity."

With this idea in mind, she looked into joining the Gray Lady volunteers at Tampa General Hospital. Again, every Wednesday she donned her gray uniform and pinned on the gray-and-white cap with its red cross on the front. For the next four years, she rode the bus, this time to and from the hospital, to be a Gray Lady. Her duties as a volunteer centered on the children's ward. She read to them and in doing so developed a new burden. She told Ruth, "I believe God has given me a new burden for children I would never have known if I had not gone through what I did. When I suggested to Aunt Flossie I would have been a better person if I hadn't had to go through it, she said, 'God doesn't have a suggestion box.' What He allowed in my life is for the good of others. Thank you, Lord!"

In the late sixties, she gave a benefit concert for the hospital for the plans for their expansion.

Ruth had been volunteering on a different day from Lynnie's, but she decided to change her day and increase to weekly instead of monthly. They would meet for lunch in the hospital cafeteria and catch up on things.

Lynnie voiced her concern for her wards. "I need to concentrate of what's going on with Justine and Mazie Lynn. Justine finished her GED, and she was accepted at Bethune Cookman College in Daytona Beach. She wants to major in music education. She saved up her money from working for me. I'm so proud of her. But what to do about Mazie Lynn? She is only thirteen years old. She needs to be with her mother or in another stable home environment. I am delighted to have her here, but what about when I go out of town for a concert? What about during the school holidays when her mother doesn't have a break from college? I feel so responsible for her."

Ruth pondered a bit on this. "Lynnie, why wouldn't she go to Daytona Beach with Justine?"

"Justine wants to live in the dorm. She can't have Mazie Lynn with her. I'd like to continue too with her voice lessons. She is really good and beyond my expertise. I can get good voice lessons for her here at the university."

"Good grief, Lynnie. When you are out of town, she can always stay at our place. I need a girl in my life. She and Van get along like brother and sister, including arguments and competition. She is a good kid, polite and respectful."

Thus, it was, when September arrived and Justine left for college, Justine made Lynnie Mazie Lynn's legal guardian. Lynnie thought, *It's almost like when Aunt Flossie adopted me. What a privilege to have a daughter.*

To make it even more like mother and daughter, Mazie Lynn started calling her Mom. "Mom, I know my real mother is Justine, but it's kinda weird. She's so young—only fourteen years older than me. She's more like a sister. I've never even called her Mom or anything like that. She's Justine. I hope it's okay for me to call you Mom 'specially since I'm close to being white. Lots of people don't even know my mother is black. She said my father had red hair and had real pale skin, a white guy. She didn't even know his last name—just Joe somebody. I'm as much your kid as I am his, huh?"

Lynnie laughed and hugged the teenager, amazed at the rationale for being "Mom."

When Justine left for college, it was just the two of them: Mazie and Mom.

Mazie had dropped the "Lynn" as soon as her mother was out of earshot. "Too much baggage there, Mom. You just call me Mazie—and particularly when you've made some of Aunt Flossie's Famous Molasses Cookies."

Being a mother figure was new for Lynnie, but she moved right into it as though she had always been a mother. Mazie's world was far different from the world she had grown up in back in the 1930s. The so-called sexual revolution, availability of mind-altering drugs, rock 'n' roll, lack of formality…so many differences. Mazie educated her as much as she educated Mazie. She was proud of the girl and how she was emerging into a beautiful, talented young lady.

Lynnie and Mazie went to church together, and Lynnie saw to it she went to youth meetings at church. She encouraged her to get involved in the activities at both the church and at school. She sang in the adult choir, led the singing in youth group, and was a soloist for both the church's Christmas program and the one at school. Lynnie cried tears of joy to hear "her girl" sing.

Justine was home for Christmas, and both the real mother and the legal guardian mother rejoiced in the grace and beauty of their girl's voice.

# Chapter 31

## *"Can't Find My Way Home"*
## *by Steve Winwood*

Although proud of her two protégés, Justine and Mazie, at the same time, Lynnie's mind went to the shadows. This was not the deep shadows of suicidal thoughts but doubts and fears over Justine's future. *Justine is different. I can't put a finger on it, but I feel like we are losing her. Is it an attitude? Is she not doing well in school? She seems distracted.*

Lynnie was concerned. Reluctant to probe, she still asked, "Is everything good at Bethune Cookman? Tell me about it."

Justine shrugged and seemed to evade the question. She gave generic answers like a ten-year-old school boy. "Classes keep me busy—music theory, English 101, History of Europe... I'm making good grades."

"What about friends? Do you have time to do anything fun with your friends?"

Justine was even more evasive. "Sometimes I go to games and concerts. You know, all the stuff they have on campus, but most of the kids there are younger than me."

Lynnie let it go and talked Justine and Mazie into a game of Scrabble. Justine seemed to be a million miles away and lost by one hundred points.

Mazie picked up on it. "Hey, Justine, you got a boyfriend over in Daytona Beach? You're pretty enough."

She shrugged. "Thanks. I've seen a few guys. I'm a bit older than most of them. Not really interested."

Mazie and Lynnie looked at each other, and Lynnie nodded sidewise. Mazie got the hint to let it go.

It was almost a relief when Justine went back to Bethune Cookman.

May of 1969, Justine called. Mazie answered. "Hey, sweetie, I won't be coming home this summer. I'll be taking summer classes, and I'm playing piano in a jazz band. We have several gigs set up for the summer."

"No!" Mazie screeched into the phone. "We were counting you to be here all summer. Justine! I can't believe you'd do this to us without even a note or call."

Lynnie heard Mazie yell into the phone. Alarmed, she came to see what happened.

Without another word, Mazie handed the phone to Lynnie.

"Justine? Is that you? What did you say that upset your daughter so much?"

"Okay, I'll tell you too. I thought she'd be okay with it. First, I'm staying here and taking summer classes. Then I got a job playing piano for a jazz band. We have several gigs lined up for the summer."

Lynnie heart dropped, but she managed to maintain her composure and said nothing to oppose Justine. "Justine, do try to come home before the fall semester. We love you."

One Tuesday evening at the beginning of August, the hottest day in the year, when the temperature at eight in the evening was still hovering in the mid-nineties, Justine and another girl showed up.

Mazie was upstairs in her room doing vocal scales. The window air-conditioner ran at high tilt along with the ceiling fan. She was facing her mirror to watch her mouth as she did the scales like her voice teacher had suggested. Although she didn't hear Justine come into her room, suddenly two faces joined her in the mirror, Justine's and another girl's. But Justine didn't look like herself. She had her face all painted up, her hair was in a wild "afro" hairdo, and she had on a low-cut, long-sleeved sequin dress hiked up to mid-thigh. She was skinny as a rail.

# JUNE TITUS

Mazie tried not to laugh, but she couldn't help it. Giggling, she turned around and asked, "Where's the Halloween party? Did you bring me a costume too?"

"Hello to you too, Mazie Lynn. I want you to meet my friend, Sabrina Carvey. We're in the band together."

"Yes, ma'am. How do you do, ma'am."

Sabrina grinned. "Juss, you didn't tell me your kid was white. I don't know about that. It isn't natural. Nice voice if she'd sing jazz or rock 'n' roll."

Sabrina's comments got Mazie and Justine's friend off on the wrong foot. But Mazie was cordial "How long are you staying?"

"Just tonight. Have a gig every night from here on till school starts again."

"Justine, you've lost too much weight. Are you eating right? Are you healthy? Don't make me worry about you."

Justine didn't answer. She merely lifted her shoulder.

Mazie looked at Sabrina. "And yes, Ms. Carvey, I am white. I go to a white school. I go to a white church. I have white friends. I sing white music. And I am black too. It may cause me a lot of racial difficulties in the future, but I am leaving that to God."

Sabrina's jaw dropped. She didn't know how to respond, and so she didn't. Justine nodded to her friend to leave Mazie alone. They went back downstairs to join Lynnie.

When the door closed, Mazie sat on her bed and cried.

Lynnie too felt like crying. *Where is the Justine who left here a year ago? Lord, I thought we guided her the right way. I fear for her. Her friends—are they good or bad for her?*

Now that Justine was there in front of her, she felt awkward. *I don't know how to talk to Justine. Help me, Lord.*

"So, Justine, tell me about the concerts—your 'gigs.' Where do you have them? Do they pay well? I know you are a good pianist, classical and jazz."

"I don't suppose you'd like it, Lynnie. We play a lot of rock 'n' roll too. Rock is what the kids like." Justine had dropped the "miss" from addressing the woman who had been more than a mother to her. "It's loud. Since we play in bars and on the beach, it has to be loud because the kids dance and make a lot of racket. That's the excitement of it. We really crank up the decibels. I play the piano when we are in a place that has one, but then I play a synthesizer—great instrument. You can get all sorts of sounds from it by playing it as a piano."

Sabrina chipped into the conversation. "Money isn't bad. It's enough to pay the rent and buy books and stuff."

Lynnie nodded. "It doesn't look like you make enough to put food in your mouth. You don't eat enough to feed a bird, Justine."

Lynnie noted that Justine turned away as though she wanted the conversation about her weight to go away. Lynnie had a notion there was more to the story. *Prayer, Lynnie, but keep your mouth shut.*

Joining them, Mazie brought in a plate of cookies and some lemonade she'd made earlier in the afternoon.

Justine's eyes brightened. "Oh! Flossie's Famous Molasses Cookies. It's not a trip to Tampa without these. You'll love them, Sabrina."

Conversation was stilted but cordial enough. Refreshments done, they all went off to bed.

Justine's room had twin beds, so Sabrina slept in there with her. Being next to Mazie's room, Mazie heard the murmurs from the next room and the tears. She prayed for the woman who had birthed her even if she couldn't call her Mother.

The next morning, after a light breakfast, which Justine barely ate, the duo was ready to leave for Daytona Beach. Classes would begin in a week. Mazie, however, wanted to talk to Justine alone.

"Justine, come on out to the kitchen, and I'll load you up with some cookies to take with you."

Once she had her alone, Mazie asked what was bothering her mind. "Justine, you aren't doing dope, are you?"

"Why would you ask such a question?"

Mazie noted that she didn't deny it. "You are nervous and so thin. Those could be signs. I worry about you. You're my mother, although we have always been more like sisters. I'm concerned for how you look right now."

"Well, Miss Know-It-All, don't worry about it. I'm fine. My schedule is grueling, and I don't have time to eat half the time."

Mazie knew she had to let her worries over Justine go, and a few minutes later, Justine and Sabrina left.

When they were gone, Mazie told Lynnie what she thought. "Mom, I think she's on drugs. I don't know anything about drugs, but I've heard about how nervous people are when the drugs wear off and that they get skinny because they don't eat."

"Oh, honey, I hope not, but I am afraid you may be right. We will pray, and we will encourage her in the Lord."

The two got on their knees and prayed for their beloved Justine right then and every day thereafter.

Justine visited no more. In the spring of the year, Justine Brown was dead from a drug overdose.

The Dean of Women called one Thursday morning. Justine was in the hospital. Lynnie was preparing for a concert in St. Petersburg when the phone rang, and Mazie answered. She heard Mazie scream and then call out for her.

Lynnie jumped up from the piano and ran to the phone. "What is it? Is it Justine?"

"It's Justine's school."

Lynnie picked up the phone. "Hello, this is Miss Van Sant. What is it?"

"Justine has been taken to Halifax Hospital. She evidently has overdosed on heroin. The doctor at the hospital doesn't think he can pull her out of it."

"We will get there as soon as we can."

Lynnie hung up the phone. Tears dripped down her cheeks as she hugged Mazie.

"You will not be going to school, and as soon as I make some calls—some cancellations—we will take a cab to Daytona Beach. Justine has to be our priority."

So it was that the two people who meant the most to Justine hired a cab to take them to Daytona Beach. They arrived shortly before she breathed her last.

Friends? Sabrina? Nowhere to be found.

Justine died on Friday, October 8, 1970, with Lynnie and Mazie holding her hands as she slipped away. Lynnie had her body taken back to Tampa. She called Pastor Craig, a different pastor from when Aunt Flossie died. He officiated at a graveside ceremony for Justine at Myrtle Hill, and she was buried next to Aunt Flossie. Ben, Ruth, Van, and a few friends still around from her years at the shelter attended. No friends from Bethune Cookman or the jazz band came.

Mazie held her head high and vowed to get on with her life. On the way back to the house after Justine was buried, she said, "Mom, she was never my mother, but I loved her. I know I need to be on my guard in so many ways. I'm only fifteen years old, but I think I know where I want to go with my life. I want to sing, but I know that going professional has its pitfalls. I can't judge her, Mom, but I hope I can learn a lesson from her life."

# Intermezzo

# CHAPTER 32

## *"Piano Concerto in A, Opus 16" by Edvard Grieg*

*1970–2003*

Over the next thirty-some years, Lynnie's life changed very little from year to year. Her role as a concert pianist and teacher took up much of her time, and she became a familiar fixture as a Gray Lady in the children's ward where she read to little children and made little rag dolls for the girls and bears for the boys. She became a happy and well-loved fixture in the community. The old thoughts of suicide sometimes cropped up, but she turned the notion around and did something for someone else. She never mentioned it again to Ruth. Such low times were fewer and fewer, and the joy of her work superseded the darkness of the past.

Mazie graduated from high school and then the University of Tampa with a degree in music education and a minor in voice. She taught music in a school in Miami for several years and was a paid soloist in the large church where she attended. In time, she met a doctor who, after establishing a practice in Miami, went to seminary and became a minister. John Arnett wooed the young singer, and after they married, he took the pastorate of a church. After a few years as pastor, they felt the call to the mission field and went to Papua, New Guinea, to plant churches and meet the medical needs of the tribal Matbat people. Mazie's beautiful voice would now teach the Matbat people in South West New Guinea, using their unique music style to create hymnody for their worship.

*It's like every time I have a "right arm," it leaves me! Just like I left Jay Lee.* Rather than grovel in missing her sweet girl, before the Arnetts left for the mission field, Lynnie told them her story.

Mazie tearfully hugged her mom. "Now I know why you could love Justine and me. You had been there. Thank you for telling me. I have no doubt that I will run into similar stories wherever God leads us. You are a beautiful example of compassion, humility, and faith. I'm going to miss you so much."

When Mazie talked to Lynnie after she had been there a year and had learned enough of the language to understand them, she said, "Mom, I have found where God truly wants me to be. I've come home."

But anytime Mazie returned home to the United States, she and John stayed in Tampa and made their headquarters with Lynnie.

Van grew up and followed his father as a physician. He also followed Ben's dream of being a cardiologist. He built a good cardiology practice in Orlando. Part of each trip home to see Ruth and Ben, he also spent some time with Aunt Lynnie.

Lynnie kept tabs on all her piano students from the home and followed their careers, whether they became musicians, doctors, butchers, bakers, or candlestick makers. One girl, a sweet girl named Glory from the shelter, did make a career out of producing scented candles.

By this time, demand for her in concert venues not only in the Tampa Bay area but throughout Florida continued to be frequent. Because she didn't drive, she flew to these locations and hired a cab to take her wherever she needed to go.

Lynnie remained healthy and became even more wealthy than when Aunt Flossie died. Lynnie inherited a healthy bank account of more than half a million dollars. As well, she had stock in General Electric, General Motor, and IBM that paid dividends far beyond what they were worth when Flossie died. She had served the Tampa community well. Many charitable organizations had her name in their brochures as a donor. With the Women's Shelter no longer in existence, she found other local outlets for her generosity. She served on the board of directors for the hospital until she was seventy-years old, when they offered her emeritus status, which meant she no longer had a vote.

# Fourth Movement

# Chapter 33

## *"The September of My Years" by Jimmy Van Heusen and Sammy Cahn*

By the turn of the century, all the traveling affected her health. Ben Steyer noticed. After a few years of observation, although not her regular physician, he addressed the issue with her. She had just turned eighty years old.

"Lynnie, we are both considered elderly. You are eighty, and I'm pushing eighty-five. My eyesight is beyond repair, so I have had a drastic slowdown in my practice. No new patients and I am in the process of turning over old ones to other physicians. I'm done."

"No surprise, Ben. It's the right thing to do."

"I am going to advise you to limit your concerts to the Tampa Bay area. You have lost weight, and I can't find any medical reason for it. I think you have spread yourself too thin. Do you still volunteer at the hospital?"

"Not as much anymore, but I still have my hand in it, or maybe I should say my mouth, reading to the children. I still have twenty piano pupils too. You may be right. Five of these youngsters will graduate from high school this year. That leaves fifteen. I may lose some more of them too because either their interest has flagged, or they have no real ear for music. I like going to Miami and Jacksonville, but I noticed they don't invite me like they used to. I know I've gotten old."

"Eighty isn't old, but it is a time to slow down and enjoy life. It's been weeks since you have been over to our place. You've become a stranger. I think you and Ruth need to take a vacation together."

"And leave you home to fend for yourself?"

"Here's the deal. Van is signed up to go to Los Angeles next month for a cardiology conference and wants me to go along. He is paying my way. His wife and the children are headed off to Charleston to visit her mother, so it leaves Ruth alone. If you two could go somewhere for the week, it would mean a lot to her. She needs to get away and have some diversion and rest. I think it would do both of you good. There, you have my prescription."

So in February of 2006, Lynnie and Ruth packed up Ruth's ancient 1946 Packard and drove to Key West. The trip would be a nice getaway for Lynnie and Ruth.

"Here we are—two old ladies in an antique Packard car celebrating our more-than-sixty-year friendship," Ruth said.

When Ruth mentioned that they were old ladies, Lynnie could see that Ruth had aged a lot in a short time. She thought, *Do I look that old?*

As they drove over the seven-mile bridge, Lynnie told Ruth about her twelve-year-old notion to go to Key West. "I heard the people in the watermelon truck say the road we were on went all the way to Key West. I decided I wanted to go there because I figured no one would ever find me there. I had only a vague idea of the whereabouts of Key West. Now we can find out! Let's have some fun."

"Yeah—fun to visit, but I'd never want to live there again. Seventh grade we lived there when Dad had duty here. Too crowded even then."

Crowded might be an understatement. Driving through the streets to their hotel, they noticed that parking places were not to be found. When Ruth pulled into the parking garage of the hotel, she created a sensation with the antique car. The attendant drooled with the idea of driving it. He parked the Packard at the hotel like he owned it.

The two friends took the bus everywhere. They rode the conch train. They had their pictures taken at the southernmost point of the United States. They watched the crazy chickens everywhere; they toured Hemingway's house and saw the six-toed cats. Then they took a boat ride out on the ocean side one afternoon. Their hotel accommodations were comfortable with the garden courtyard area right outside their door, where a rooster gave them a wake-up call each dawn. They went to the sunset celebration at Mallory Square with all the jugglers, clowns, and musicians. One of the musicians was a banjo player who reminded her of growing up in North Carolina—a banjo picker she'd heard play as a young girl.

Despite all the activity, Lynnie could see Ruth didn't seem to be herself. She had a terrible color, a yellow not suggestive of a healthy glow. "Ruth, you don't seem to have much of an appetite for this wonderful cuisine. All you want to do is sit around. Are you okay?"

Ruth brushed off the question.

Lynnie didn't think her friend had lost a lot of weight, but she looked drawn and, yes, yellow. Her vibrant red hair had gone sandy and had lost its vibrancy. Lynnie couldn't stand to see her friend out of whack. On the way back to Tampa, she had to ask her friend, "Okay, Ruth, you're sick, aren't you?"

"I am. I've known it for a while. I have hepatic cancer—cancer of the liver. It has already metastasized into the common duct and beyond."

Lynnie shuddered, and her heart sank. Flashes of Aunt Flossie's and Justine's death clouded her mind. *Why must those closest to me die with no cure available? Here…love…gone, here…love…gone.*

Lynnie looked at her friend, incredulous she had not confided in her. "And you waited till now to tell me? Will you have chemo? Radiation? Surgery?"

"No. It had already gone too far before I even had any real symptoms. The vague symptoms I did have made me think I had indigestion, so I watched what I ate. Ben's eyesight is so bad he never noticed. And Van hasn't been able to get away from his practice for the last six months. Six months! He would have noticed."

"Oh Ruthie! I didn't realize he hadn't been to see you." Lynnie scowled. "That isn't like Van."

"I understand. Doctors have commitments to their patients." Ruth seemed to take it all as a matter of fact.

"Anyway, when Ben recognized the implications of my symptoms, he suspected gallbladder disease at first. We did diet and watched for a day or so. It didn't take him more than a day or two more to realize it wasn't my gallbladder. He expedited tests. They showed hepatic cancer. I will die, Lynnie. I know that, and I have accepted it. I'm eighty years old, and I'm ready to go. I don't want any intervention. Palliative care and then hospice."

Lynnie took a slow, deep breath. She wanted to cry, but her best friend needed her support. "I'm sorry you must go through this. We will walk this road together. You, Ben, me, and Van."

"I agree with what my dad said before he died, 'I might be ready to die, but I dread the process.' That's how I feel, Lynnie."

When they got back to Tampa, Ruth pulled into her driveway. "Ben can take you home. When I talked to him last night, he said he was already home. I'm exhausted and need to get to bed."

When Ben saw Lynnie, he knew Ruth had told her. He carried his wife's bags into the house and then offered to drive Lynnie to her place. He wanted to talk to their friend.

Lynnie hugged Ruth. "I will come and stay with you as soon as I get some details ironed out. I'm with you and for you, sweet friend." She turned and followed Ben to the Packard.

He drove through his own tears. "Lynnie, why didn't I pay more attention to her? I'm a doctor. Have I let my career come before my bride? I should have seen it. I can't blame this on my loss of vision. I neglected her, Lynnie."

"Ben, I don't know what to say. I know Ruth is ready to face it in her own way. She doesn't blame you. She chose to ignore it until nothing could be done. She knew how to hide her symptoms. She even denied them—it's like Aunt Flossie all over again—like Justine." Her words made her shudder.

She sniffed in a deep breath and went on. "Her faith is her strength, Ben. She is able to stand up to life because of her faith in Christ. We need to come along beside her and help her stand up to her death."

"I'm glad you know. I had to tell Van this week rather than focus on the newest treatments for congestive heart failure and pulmonary edema. Now he is beating himself up. He feels guilty because he didn't come to visit her for the last six months."

"It's not like Van. I'm not sure I understand."

"Another subject, Lynnie. He and I have already addressed it. But you know, it put a real damper on the trip. I don't think he got anything out of the conference, and I didn't care about it. It turned out, however, not a waste of money, though. We bonded in a way we never had before, sorry to say, over his mother's illness."

"You know I am here for all of you, Ben. You, Ruth, and Van, and his family."

Van came to see his mother the next day after they got home. He rescheduled his patients so he could take an extra day with Ruth. After his dad had told him the news in Los Angeles, he knew he would have to come to see her as soon and as often as possible. That night, he went to see Lynnie.

"Aunt Lynnie, Mom will die from this. It is beyond medical intervention at this point. I know more than I want to about this diagnosis, and it's pretty scary. I'm glad she doesn't want a bunch of radiation and chemo. But it means the inevitable. Death and soon. What do you think?"

"Van, I don't know what to think. I want to keep her, but I don't want her to suffer. When I think back to Aunt Flossie's death, I wonder if she didn't choose the best way, to go when it's time. She never told anyone about her illness, and one day, she died. I came home from the university and found her. She had finished her course. I hurt for a long time, and I wished she had at least told me. I think I would want to go just as she did when it's time, but I'm not your mother. At least we are here to come around her to help bear the burden."

"I know she is grateful for you, Aunt Lynnie. So am I. Dad says she might last weeks to months. We will make her comfortable. It's all we can do. I really hate death although I am used to it. I lose patients, and it saddens me, but then I get over it and get on with my life. But this is my mother!"

He didn't say anything for a few long moments. Lynnie knew something was bothering him that he was having a difficult time saying.

"Aunt Lynnie, it's my fault she is dying. I got so wrapped up in my life as a doctor. I wanted to get ahead. I lived for me. I neglected Mom, neglected both of them. I didn't come to see them. I didn't know Dad's eyes had gotten so bad he had to give up his practice. I didn't know Mom had gotten sick. All I cared about centered around Benjamin Van Steyer. My wife and the boys kept at me about my lack of attention to them, but I ignored them."

The humbled doctor cried as Lynnie took him in her arms. They held each other for several minutes until the man had control of his emotions.

"Van, what is done is done. We need to focus on her comfort, on how to show her love. I know how terrible it is to see someone you love die. Aside from Aunt Flossie's death, I'd never been around much death until I started to volunteer at the hospital children's ward. Then Justine died—the same as Aunt Flossie. She hid her addiction from us."

"That's terrible."

Lynnie nodded. "Now at the hospital, I get attached to a child, and then they're gone. It hurts so much. Van, I will be with all of you in this. I plan to go and stay with her. I'll stay in your old bedroom. I need to make some personal changes, cancel or reschedule some things, and then I will go and stay with her. It will free your dad to wind up his practice until he needs to stay with her too. It won't be easy for her or for all of you."

"Thank you, Aunt Lynnie. I love you."

"Back at you, Van."

Ruth herself made the decision not to have treatment. She said, "I don't want to linger and be miserable with side effects. The results of the cancer and the dying process will be enough misery without the prolonged agony of failed treatment. Let's party till we can't party anymore."

The party ended by the first of August of 2006. Ruth had terrible pain, and opiates only lasted a short while. But if she couldn't party, at least she maintained an unparalleled serenity. The radiance about her defied comprehension. The woman's attitude testified to her faith, courage, and love. A day in her presence made others feel God's presence. Lynnie moved into the spare room and stayed with her day in and day out. She canceled a concert, furloughed her piano students, and stayed with Ruth to the end. Indeed, the stay lasted only a few weeks.

Van and his wife, Brenda, came each weekend, so long as Van didn't need to be on call. The final weekend, they brought their teenage sons to say goodbye to their grandmother. Ruth's brother flew in from California.

By the time her brother arrived, Ruth had lapsed into a medication-induced sleep most of the time, but she rallied enough to recognize him. All the family was with her. Ruth's face beamed with a smile shortly after her brother arrived. "All is well. See you in the Tomorrow." She slipped back into her sleep and stopped breathing within ten minutes.

Ruth was gone, and Lynnie knew another arm had been detached.

Despite Ruth's waking hours filled with pain dulled but not relieved by heavy doses of opioids, her death had been peaceful in the end. The funeral was three days later at the church with a filled sanctuary. Ruth had been a beloved friend, Bible teacher, volunteer at the hospital, wife, and mother.

# Chapter 34

## *"The Best Is Yet to Come" by Cy Coleman and Carolyn Leigh*

After Ruth's death, Lynnie processed her grief by a headlong dive into her students and preparations for another concert. She rescheduled one she had cancelled for September.

On the other hand, life had slowed down for Lynnie. Her private piano pupils had dwindled, and although she believed one of them would be headed for a music career, most of them took lessons because affluent young ladies and some young men were supposed to play the piano. They did well enough, but their hopes and dreams didn't include being great pianists.

One student, however, Ernie Capitoli, would prove to be the best she had ever taught, even better than Justine had been. He would graduate from high school in the spring and had already been accepted at Florida State University to study piano proficiency. She envisioned him as accepted at Eastman, Julliard, or Peabody after graduation.

Concerts too had been reduced to a rare benefit or someone who needed a piano player for an event—a reception, banquet, or reunion perhaps. By the end of the 2008, her career had all but dried up.

One day, close to Christmas, Ben called. "I have some news for you. How about if I pick you up for lunch? Ever eat at the Samaria Café? Great Greek food."

"I never ate there, but it sounds great. But you are still behind the wheel with your vision?"

"Yeah. I'll drive, and you can be my navigator. See you in an hour."

She laughed when he showed up in the Packard. The sixty-two-year-old car still ran like a top.

"So what's your news? Good, I hope."

"Yes. I have put the house on the market, and I bought one in The Villages. It will be close to Van. His boys are almost grown and will soon leave the nest. Benji started at UF, and Joseph plans to go to FSU next year. Van is one of the best cardiologists in Orlando, and he isn't going anywhere. I'll be close to them. I wanted you to know."

"I'm glad you told me. I'll miss you."

"Well, I thought maybe you would be interested. Maybe you could do it too, Lynnie. You've told me your career has dwindled down, and you don't need your big old house. Sell it and move to The Villages."

"I don't think I want to live in a place where there are miles and miles of senior citizens, Ben. Thanks but no thanks."

Ben guffawed. "What? Turn down the opportunity to play golf, join any kind of club you can imagine, shuffleboard, run about in your own golf cart, and—oh yes, hang out with miles and miles of senior citizens."

"Well, I have contemplated the idea that I should sell the house. I could go into a retirement home—it's yards and yards instead of miles and miles of seniors. I have my eye on Legacy at Highwoods Preserve. It is nice out there. I did a benefit concert there a few years ago and liked what I saw. It is still close to civilization. It's expensive, but with the sale of North Ninth, I can afford to move into a retirement facility."

"Have you put your name on the waiting list?"

She shrugged. "No. I suppose I should. But what if they have a place for me, and the house hasn't been sold? Or the other way around, I sell the house, and they aren't ready?"

"Did you ever hear of trusting God?"

"Touché!"

# JUNE TITUS

Samaria Café, a delightful change for Lynnie, included not so much the food as Ben's emergence from his grief over Ruth's death. He enthusiasm to keep going forward cheered her.

As soon as they ate their lunch, Ben did not head back to Lynnie's house. He drove her out I-75.

"You lost?"

"No. You'll see."

When he pulled into the Highwoods neighborhood, Lynnie had no doubt what he had in mind.

She rolled her eyes at him. "Oh?"

"Go on and check it out. Call me on your cell phone when you are ready to go home. I'll come back and get you."

"You're serious! Okay. I will ask for a tour, get the paperwork, and I'll call you."

As she got out of the car, she turned and looked back at Ben. He gave her a thumbs-up and drove on around the circle as she went into the facility. *Okay, Ben Steyer, I concede.* She shrugged and rang the doorbell. She stood with her shoulders straight and her head high until someone came to let her in.

She asked to be directed to the office. In the office, a nice young lady greeted her. "Good afternoon. May I help you? Miss Van Sant, isn't it?"

*Dear me! Someone recognizes me?* "I don't know if it's good or bad, but yes, I am."

The lady laughed a musical lilt to her voice. "Yes, I've heard you many times in concert, once in the benefit concert you gave here soon after I first came to work here. My name is Calista Owens. How can I help you today?"

"Calista. Yes, Calista, I may sell my house and put my name in here. As you mentioned, I did play a benefit concert here, and the facility impressed me. I am in no great rush, but if I can get my name on your list, perhaps Providence with let me sell my house and be able to move in at the same time."

"Wonderful. I will get the paperwork together for you. Would you like a tour meanwhile?"

"Of course. I'd like to see what options might be available."

"Great. Let me page Molly. She is our lifestyle director. She will be happy to show you some rooms. We have two empty apartments at this time, but they are already taken. One of our other residents will be happy to show her rooms to you. Then you can see a different model as well."

While Lynnie waited for Molly, she gazed about what she could see. Fine artwork along with amateur paintings lined the walls, comfortable-looking furniture had been strategically located, and the floors gleamed. It seemed like an invitation. A few residents chatted with each other in a room across the foyer.

"I see you admire the artwork. Many of these have been painted by residents and are 'on loan' to us to display. We offer art classes among other activities."

Molly arrived. "Oh, Miss Van Sant. I don't know if you remember me, but we met when you were here for your benefit concert. I would be delighted to show you around. I don't know if Calista told you or not, but we have two empty apartments we can show you. One is the Deluxe model, our largest apartment. The other is the Classic. As well, I can show you an occupied unit. Millie, our Scrabble Queen, loves to show off her Grande apartment."

Lynnie smiled and nodded.

An old dog rounded the corner as they walked toward the elevator. "Oh, here's your chance to meet our family pooch." Molly held out her hand to an old and grizzled Irish Setter. "Mrs. Murphy, meet Miss Lynnie. She might be part of our family soon."

Lynnie scratched the dog behind her ears and allowed her to lick her hand. "Oh, what a dear lassie you are."

Lynnie looked at Molly with moist eyes. "I had an Irish Setter as a girl. We called him O'Hara. Mrs. Murphy will make me feel like a girl again."

"Indeed she will. She adds a lot of comfort around here to some of the folks, in particular those who can't get around anymore."

Molly indicated for Lynnie to follow her. "The first apartment is on the upper floor."

Lynnie looked around as she followed to the elevator. *Everything looks spotless.*

"Here we go. This is the classic model. A new occupant will be here tomorrow, so this is a great time to see it. All cleaned up and fresh."

"Dear me! How will I ever live in such a tiny space?" She snapped a couple of pictures on her cell phone to show Ben the limitations.

"Yes, I understand. But, Miss Van Sant, this is our smallest unit. Let's go down the hall and see our largest model."

"You may call me Lynnie. I might think you are one of my piano students when you call me Miss Van Sant."

Molly laughed as they made the short walk down the hall to the larger apartment.

"Well, it's still smaller than my five-bedroom house, but then who needs five bedrooms?" She snapped several pictures. "I want to visualize where I can put what furniture and what I should get rid of before I move."

The unit had a little kitchenette, a separate living area from the bedroom, and a walk-in closet. "I think I would like to put my name in for one of these. I could do it. I could bring my own furniture, but oh dear, I'll have an awful lot to dispose before I move. But let's do it. Now I pray God will orchestrate a smooth transition in His perfect time."

"We will trust it to happen. Okay, back down the elevator to Miss Millie's room. She will ask you if you play Scrabble, of course."

"I do. I haven't played for a bit, so I'm rusty. I used to play with my friend, Ruth, but since she died, I haven't played. It would be good to get back to it."

Molly rapped at the opened door.

"Who you got with ya, Miss Molly?"

"Good afternoon to you too, Miss Millie. This is Miss Lynnie Van Sant. She has put her name in for an apartment when God orchestrates it, she tells me. Lynnie, this is the one and only Millie Revell."

Millie stood and took hold of her walker. "Well, I swannie! You know He will. Miss Lynnie, you look to me like a good Scrabble player. You know the game?"

"I do, Millie. I look forward to the challenge of a new partner in crime."

Millie laughed. "Well, praise the Lord, and pass the ammunition! Y'all look around my grand estate. It's all I got, but it's home. Let me show you about."

Aside from a set-up Scrabble game and a few books on the table beside her chair, she kept the apartment neat and clean. Lynnie thanked Millie for her hospitality and followed Molly back to the office.

"Millie is larger than life around here. She loves to sing and has a beautiful voice. She was the lead gospel singer in her church choir. When she had a stroke, she almost gave up, but with physical therapy and a lot of encouragement over the last couple of years, she has reemerged as a wonderful example of aging well."

Lynnie laughed and nodded in appreciation of Millie's history. "I like her. I hope I can give her a run for her money with Scrabble."

Lynnie looked for Mrs. Murphy again, but the dog had disappeared.

Back at the office, Lynnie picked up the paperwork from Calista and punched in Ben's number.

He sat in the car under the shade trees out front. He had gone nowhere.

# CHAPTER 35

## "Where Could I Go" by James B. Coates

*Spring and summer 2009*

Back in her own house, she put the paperwork onto her desk and walked about her house. She looked at all the life she would need to relinquish if and when she were to go into the retirement facility.

"How can I do this? I know…I know. I can't take it with me. I don't even have anyone to leave it to in a will. Mazie certainly doesn't want it in New Guinea. Well, I'll call her and ask. Some can be donated, sell a lot of stuff, but my piano? How can I ever give up my piano? Oh, Aunt Flossie, how could you ever leave Farmer's Corner and give up your life there? How can I do this?"

She laughed. "Good grief, Lynnie Van Sant. When you arrived in Farmer's Corner, you only had a filthy homemade dress and a filthier pair of used shoes."

She sat on Flossie's rocking chair and rocked back and forth for a long time with her mind in a deep valley of thoughts. Those thoughts never climbed out of the depths. Then she took a deep breath and went to the desk. She filled out the paperwork and called Calista at Legacy to let her know she would have the documents hand delivered before the office would close. Then she called a cab and had it hand delivered to the residence before Calista had a chance to leave for the day.

As soon as the cab took her fare, she called Irv Watson, a realtor friend, and made arrangement to have him list her house on the market. Irv showed up the next day and had the house listed on MLS by the end of the day.

Next, she needed to decide what furnishings she would take with her. *Easy. Bedroom suite, kept from my beautiful room in Farmer's Corner. I can't use it all but should have room for the bed, dresser, and dressing table and chair. I'll take the sofa, easy chair, one end table, coffee table, and Aunt Flossie's rocker. I'll need my desk and bookcases, the kitchen table and chairs, and a few other small pieces.*

"But what do I do with my beloved piano?" She laughed. She thought about her most terrible piano student: Van. "Ought to give it to him to remind him. No. It gets donated to the church." She called Pastor Craig, soon to retire himself, and told him her plans.

"I won't let you have it until my move is official. I have put my name in at Legacy at Highwoods Preserve, and I have my house on the market. It may be months or even years, but if the church will use it, I want to donate my piano when the time comes."

"No doubt about it, Lynnie. We can use it somewhere. What I will do is pass this on to the music director for the best use. We have the concert grand in the sanctuary, but I think there are other places where we would need it. This is more than generous of you."

"Not at all. I will have no room for it. I saw several pianos at the facility. If they don't mind if I play, I will have a piano. I'll let the church know when it is available."

Over the next several weeks, she sorted, packed, and made piles: "keep," "toss," "sell," and "donate." Potential buyers came and went. No word from Legacy. Still, she sorted, packed, made piles, and called Salvation Army to come for donations.

All in time, six months of time, the call from Calista came the middle of July. "We have the Deluxe apartment for you. It will be ready the first of August. How is progress on your house sale?"

"Oh boy. I've had a lot of lookers and some interested, but no firm commitment. I don't know whether to go out on a limb and say yes or not. How long will you give me to answer?"

"I have several people on the list after you, so I can't give you more than a week."

"Thank you. I will get back to you within a week. So now to my knees for God's will in this."

She hung up the phone and sank to her knees and prayed. "Lord, I'm praying a Miss Flossie prayer. She knew how to pray and trusted you would perform Your will. She never knew the day when I would do the same, but her example has instructed me. If you want me to leave here and live at a retirement facility, send the right person to buy my house before the end of the week. I trust you. Because of Jesus, Amen."

But when she went to bed, she had the first nightmare she had experienced in years: the same one as always. *Osama Ben Laden after me...demon face...breathe hot with fire...knife fire surging up through me...ton of bricks...unwashed...reeking...speaking words from hell... Help me, Jay-Lee...hel...ll...p...got to reach Jay-Lee. The closer she gets, the farther she goes...baby cries...endless horror...O'Hara lying dead under the Scrabble board...* She woke up screaming for Jay-Lee. Saturated by a cold sweat, her entire body trembled. Her night clothes were too wet for comfort. She thought she had become ill.

Lynnie changed into dry clothes, went to the medicine cabinet, and grabbed a bottle of Acetaminophen. She poured two caplets into her hand and started to put them in her mouth. Then she looked at the bottle, poured the entire bottle of pills into her hand, and stared at them.

"No!" she screamed. "No, no! A thousand times, no! Life is good. God is good. Never again!" She spit out the two unswallowed caplets and dumped the entire contents of the bottle into the outside trash can.

Unable to sleep the remainder of the night, she took Aunt Flossie's well-worn Bible and went to the rocking chair. First Corinthians 10:13, she read it over and over.

> No temptation has overtaken you except what is common to mankind. And God is faithful; he will not let you be tempted beyond what

you can bear. But when you are tempted, he will also provide a way out so that you can endure it.

"God can do this. I can't." She read through several of the Psalms until the sun broke over the east and flooded in the window. After breakfast and an hour at the piano, she had calmed down. She submitted to whatever would occur.

At nine in the morning, the phone rang—Irv. "Got a buyer. These folks are from Memphis, Tennessee. He has a new job here. They would like to move in the second week of August. It will be a cash transaction, no loan. They will meet your price. They want to close as soon as you can do it."

"Oh! Thank you, God!"

"Well, I'm not God, but you're welcome. I take it then you are ready. Will it work out for you with the retirement home?"

"Yes. They called yesterday. I can move in after August first."

"Perfect. We will have your closing on August first. They will take possession August—let's see, take possession the eighth. Both Saturdays. You can get moved in by the end of the week."

Lynnie, weak from excitement, anxiety, and overwhelmed with God's answer to her prayers, looked heavenward. "What do you think of this Florence Van Sant?"

It was official. She picked up her cell phone and made that international call that she'd been putting off. Since it was only twelve thirty in the morning in Papua, New Guinea, she put the phone back down and waited until suppertime.

"Hello…"

"Hi, Mazie! I finally did it!"

"Oh, Mom! I was just thinking about you. What 'finally did it' did you do?"

"I have sold the house and will be moving into Legacy at Highwoods the eighth of August."

"Oh wonderful! I have been so concerned with you in that big house. We have actually talked about bringing you here to live with us, but the time hasn't been right. I am so glad."

"Question, Mazie: Do you want me to put anything from the house into storage for you?"

"Good grief, no. We have more than we need now. Sell, donate, or trash what you don't need to take with you."

Lynnie said, "I'll send you pictures of my new place once I get settled."

They chatted a few minutes and then…

"Love you, Mazie."

"Love you back, Mom."

The house on North Ninth became a frenzy of activity over the next two weeks. More boxes packed, more things tossed she didn't want, and more items of furniture sold. She had listed items for sale on Craigslist, somewhat leery about scammers, but Irv encouraged her. Friends from church piled in with food and muscles to help pack and carted home items Lynnie shared with them.

"When Aunt Flossie and I moved here, we had little help. I am overwhelmed, grateful, and not a little embarrassed I'm so needy. Thank you all."

A good friend from the Sunday school class, Jeannie Gibbs, had organized the help and came each day. Friday night before moving day, Jeannie said, "Look, I know you will be a greater distance from the church. How about I come and pick you up so you don't have to take the bus?"

"I will think about it, Jeannie. I do appreciate it. It won't be this week, though."

"I thought you'd say no. Don't blame you. But I will be here bright and early tomorrow morning for your move. How about eight?"

"The truck to move my stuff to Legacy will be here at seven and should have everything on the way by then. So eight it is. Don't eat breakfast before you come, and we will stop at Cracker Barrel."

"Sounds good."

# REDEMPTION SUITE

When she went to her room to sleep her final sleep at North Ninth, she pulled out her journal and wrote:

> I don't know what lies ahead, but I refuse to be afraid. I refuse to miss this place, charming as it is. I refuse to grieve. I will not be afraid.
>
> Fear no evil?
> Fear not the fearsome?
> How can I know that harms
> won't dog my way?
> All's well until
> I walk beyond this place
> of simple charms,
> and sunshine turns to gray.
> Rather fear God…
> Then nothing left to fear…
> No cause to be afraid,
> for He is in control.
> Fear is sheer fraud…
> A foolish trust in self…
> A lie—a flawed charade
> that leaves a god-less hole. LVS

The next morning before the sun was up, Lynnie awakened early with excitement. A mocking bird greeted her as she sat on the back steps in the predawn drinking her coffee. She tweeted back to the bird and silently gave thanks to God.

*Thank you, Lord for allowing me to live in this beautiful place for these fifty-five years. Will I miss it? I will miss the lives that I've shared here—Aunt Flossie, Ruth, Ben, Van, Justine, Mazie, and my many students. Each have given me a different joy. They are all still in my heart—like Jay Lee. Thank you, Lord…*

# Chapter 36

## "Make New Friends" by Joseph Parry

*Legacy at Highwoods Preserve*
*August 9, 2009*

Before Lynnie went to bed in her new home, she took out her current journal and wrote a final entry before she went to sleep:

> This is it. My life is now on a different trajectory. I will discover who I am all over again. I believe I have made a good decision. Why? God worked out the details. I trust the Lord to lead me through the details. Life is good. I am ready for the next venture in my redemption suite.

Lynnie woke up a bit disoriented the day after her move into her new home at Legacy. Once she realized she had embarked on her new life, she laughed at herself. She had read some of her old journals the night before, and one of them remained on her bed.

"I guess it is time to put away those past songs and write an entire new song of my life."

She shelved the journal and looked about her new place. Sunday and under normal circumstances, she would be up and off to church. She had always taken the bus to church, with only a short ride. While Ruth lived, she would either pick Lynnie up or take her home from church. Now twice as far away, would she continue to attend there? "Maybe there are other churches near here. I'll have to check them out."

She made herself some breakfast in her kitchenette, dressed for the day, and then watched a TV church service. "I'd rather get out there and play the piano in the lobby all day, but I don't know if I should presume I'm free to do it unless I check with Molly or Calista."

After lunch, she went into the grand piano room and sat down near a window. Jeannie had given her a crossword puzzle book, so she worked on it. It didn't take long before the resident dog paid her a visit.

"Well, hello, Mrs. Murphy. I'm glad you can join me?" Lynnie petted her and let her lick her hand as she had the first time they met. "I think you and I will be best of friends." The dog sat down by Lynnie's feet.

"Well, I see our Mrs. Murphy has befriended you."

Startled by the voice, Lynnie jerked her head up and looked into the blue eyes of a handsome white-haired man who had silently slipped into the seat across from her.

"Yes, I met Mrs. Murphy when I toured here six months ago. I had one like her as a girl."

"She's our resident dog. Belongs to us all, the Legacy family. We actually call her Murph. She's pretty deaf, but she smells who will be her friends. When Murph accepts someone new, they are an official part of the Legacy family. Welcome to our home."

The man studied her for a brief moment and then said, "Although you are new here, I'm sure we've met before, haven't we?"

Then he raised his eyebrows, he asked, "I saw you at supper yesterday, and you seemed familiar. Aren't you the lady who came and played banjo with me a while back—last fall, I think?"

She scowled and then laughed. "Who me? Play the banjo. No, I play piano. My name is Lynelle Van Sant—Lynnie. I heard a fellow play banjo in Key West few years back who resembles you." She hesitated a bit and then said in a whisper, "My pa used to play banjo."

"I am sorry, Miss Van Sant. I mistook you for someone else. I forget her name. I have a slight issue with my memory, with names in particular. I'll have to ask Harry. He's my son. But you could be twins with the banjo picker lady."

The comparison to a twin made Lynnie's heart drop. *Jay Lee? Could she have been here? No, that's ridiculous.*

The man kept up the conversation. My memory is lots better now since I'm off all those high-powered blood pressure pills my old doctor had me taking. Still, your face is familiar." He scrutinized her as though some thought cogitated in the back of his mind. Then he nodded. "Ah, yes. Now I remember. Stella and I heard you play in concert. Stella loved classical music. May I introduce myself? I'm Ju…" He grinned. "Luke Harvey. Why don't you join me for a donut and a cup of coffee or tea, and then you can tickle the ivories on our grand piano over there?"

The strange sensation she had about Jay-Lee disappeared. Lynnie shot Luke a wide grin. "Yes, I'd love to play, but I wasn't sure if I needed permission. I had to get rid of my beautiful piano. I gave it to the church."

"Of course, you can play. That's why it's here."

She took a deep breath and smiled. "Good to meet a friend. I moved in here yesterday. It's all new to me."

Luke bowed and led the way to the refreshments with Murph on their heels. "Murph will beg for a piece of donut, but don't give her anything with sugar on it."

After perhaps half an hour, they were finished with the donuts and coffee. Then Luke had a visitor, a younger version of himself. He introduced the man as his son, Harry Harvey.

Lynnie thought, *He looks familiar…Key West, I think it might be the same man.*

After a polite exchange, she went to the piano and played. Her new friend, Luke, sat with his son and listened. Luke appeared mesmerized by her music. Others came in and gathered around in the nearby chairs. She played for half an hour. She played a mix of classical pieces and her arrangements of familiar hymns. The dog crawled beneath the piano and went to sleep.

Meanwhile, Luke and his son slipped away. From the corner of her eye, she saw them walking down the hallway.

Lynnie thought, *Luke seems nice.* He reminded Lynnie of Carrie Willson's daddy—the girl her brother, Jeb, wanted to marry. That man had played both the fiddle and the banjo. She shook the image from her head and played for a few more minutes.

The evening before, soon after she had moved in, she had gone to supper in the dining room. There she saw Millie, the Scrabble Queen, at a table and joined her. Millie had invited her once again to join her Scrabble group. When Lynnie got up from the piano, she saw the Scrabble Queen heading her way.

"Oh, Miss Lynnie. I'm so glad to see you at the piano. I heard you once before at a concert. I liked this better. Up close and sort of personal. You in for a game of Scrabble before dinner?"

"Why not. Your place or mine?"

"Come on over to my place. It's all set up and ready to go. Our Scrabble group meets Tuesdays and Thursdays in the activity room, but we play anytime we want in our rooms. I hope you can join us Tuesday."

Lynnie walked along side of Millie. It took a long time due to Millie's weak leg from a stroke, but she moved along well with her walker. "Someday, I'll get rid of this ol' walker. Maybe not this side of glory but someday." Her rich laugh resounded down the hallway.

In the Scrabble game, the two ladies battled against each other with vigorous minds. The game belied their aging bodies. First, Millie moved ahead with "Quiz," a triple letter score for the *Q*. Then Lynnie volleyed back with a double coup as she connected with three different high-scoring words and her own triple letter with an *X*. Back and forth for an hour they played, and in the end, Millie won by one point.

"Millie, I have enjoyed this game more than any I've played since Aunt Flossie died fifty-four years ago. Even more so because she would try to cheat and make up words. Thank you. I look forward to Tuesdays and Thursdays."

As she walked back to her room, she thought about her new life, how it could be a new ministry. She already liked Legacy. The man, Luke, had encouraged her to play the piano, and Murph, a dog like O'Hara in Farmer's Corner, had befriended her. *Life is good*, she thought.

She grinned when she thought about the man who introduced himself as Luke. *I've been diagnosed as a lonesome old lady, if I am to believe Dr. Ben Steyer! If some old bird gives this chickadee some attention, I will accept it as a remedy for my 'condition.'* She laughed. *I can't believe Lynnie Van Sant is thinking such thoughts!*

When Lynnie came to dinner, she looked for Millie and Luke, but they had not arrived yet. She sat with a man and his wife, Hack and Joanne Loudon, and Dr. Marshall, a retired physician she recognized from when she had volunteered at the hospital. Hack and Joanne were big into jigsaw puzzles, and Joanne attempted to perk Lynnie's interest.

"We average four of them together every week. Hack likes those crazy 2,000- to 2,500-piece puzzles, but I like smaller ones with animals. You'll have to join us. There are hundreds of puzzles in the activity room."

"Thank you, Joanne. I played Scrabble with Millie Revell and plan to join her group on Tuesdays and Thursdays. But I may have to stop by your puzzles and take a look."

Dr. Marshall snickered. "What you need to do is distract Joanne while she is puzzling and snitch one of her pieces. It'll puzzle her!"

Hack liked that idea. "Yeah, drive her nuts. Glad you suggested it."

Lynnie laughed at the men's teasing. "So what do you like to do, Doctor, other than performing surgery on people's mental integrity and driving them nuts?"

"I read. I'm into mysteries. Not gory murders but more like international intrigue. I like John Grisham. And you, Miss Van Sant, what beside Scrabble floats your boat?"

"I play the piano. I read too about current issues. I've volunteered, first at the Women's Shelter until it closed and then at the hospital. I'm retired from my piano students and concert tours now. I recognized you from the hospital. These volunteer activities have been somewhat of a ministry for me. My career, however, has been the piano."

"Yes, I recall going to several of your concerts with my wife—she's gone now. We always enjoyed the concerts. You will play for us here, won't you?"

Lynnie shrugged. "You won't have to ask twice."

Lynnie often played the piano in the afternoons before dinner. Murph would end up under the piano. Because she couldn't hear, Lynnie assumed she enjoyed the vibrations of the instrument. She laughed and thought back to O'Hara and how he would always set up a howl when she started to play, but he'd settle down after a few notes. "It's good to have a dog around again."

After a few times of her afternoon concerts, Luke approached her. He had a puppy dog plea written across his face. "Would I be too forward to ask if I could play my fiddle with you sometime?"

"I'd love it. Do you play classical or fiddle music?"

"Believe it or not, both. I am self-taught for the most part, but I did study the classical violin in high school. Mom, my sister, taught me fiddle music. My technique may not be up to snuff, but I enjoy it. Try me."

"Good. Let's do it tomorrow afternoon."

He wiggled his bushy brows. "It's a date!"

Lynnie's face turned red.

Between the Scrabble group, the piano, and an occasional foray into the outside world, which included a shopping trip or visit to a nearby church, Lynnie kept busy and the lonesomeness faded into the past. "What did I say to Ben about not wanting to live around miles of old people?"

In addition to her own interests, she talked with some of the residents who were discouraged or lacked mobility. She had a happy new life, not at all lonesome. "Best decision I have made in years."

She sat with a lady named Evelyn one day at lunch. The woman's face wore the marks of discontent. She sat alone at the table.

Lynnie countered the crabby face with a cheery "May I join you?"

"Suit yourself. I'm told it's a free country."

*That phrase. I've heard it before from the vagabond lady so many years ago... Grace Jones.*

Lynnie smiled at the unhappy lady. "Yes, and thank God it is. You sound as though you have doubts."

"Why shouldn't I? My daughter! My daughter who I raised all by myself and gave her every advantage her deadbeat father refused to give her took my freedom away."

The woman went on to tell how her daughter had insisted she must sign over her house to her. "She conned me into using all my hard-earned money to pay for this prison."

"I'm sorry you must go through this. How long have you been here?"

"She threw me in here six months ago. Then she comes in all smiles and cheer like it's the best thing for me. Humbug!"

"I imagine, though, you have been able to make some new friends and get involved in some of the activities."

"Why? My life is over."

"I had the same notion too before I came here. I have been a concert pianist and teacher, but it all seemed to disappear when I turned eighty. I had a nice home I'd lived in for fifty-five years. I had a gorgeous grand piano. I had memories with each piece of furniture, book, pot, or pan. But my doctor friend wisely encouraged me to sell my home and move here. Good thing too. I am as happy as I have ever been."

"Well, it might be okay for you, but I don't buy it. I've heard you play the piano. At least you have some ability you brought with you."

"What did you do for your life work to provide you with your hard-earned money?"

"I worked as an executive secretary in one of the largest business firms in Sarasota. I made good money. As I said, I raised my daughter as a single mother after my rascal of a husband ran off with some floozy. I made it good. Now she has it all, while I sit here getting indigestion talking about it."

"Oh, dear. Forgive me for the reminder."

Lynnie changed gears and attempted to give Evelyn a solution to diffuse her anger. "By the way, do you like to play Scrabble? Three of us play together on Tuesday and Thursday afternoons. We need another player if you are interested."

"Maybe. I'll think about it."

The next day, a Scrabble day, Evelyn did show up. Each time she came after that, she seemed to enjoy it more, and she became quite a challenge to the Scrabble Queen.

# Chapter 37

## *"Love Can Build a Bridge" by Naomi Judd, Paul Overstreet, and John Barlow Jarvis*

Scrabble, communication with other residents, and activities were good, but Lynnie's most enjoyment came when she played duets with Luke. From August through September and into early October, the sounds of Luke's fiddle and Lynnie's piano entertained the staff and residents at Legacy. Often, she and Luke chatted together about their lives.

One afternoon after they had played together, they sat in the lobby to chat and relax. Luke told her about his new knowledge of a family he had never met.

"Seems like my Papa already had a wife and family in North Carolina, but when he met my mother, he decided to marry her too."

"Oh dear! A bigamist! How scandalous. Well…outrageous, perhaps. You do not seem to have allowed it to keep you from a good life. Do you know any of your family in North Carolina?"

"No, but I think I need to go to North Carolina and meet them. I have learned I have a half-sister who lives in North Carolina. She is six months older than me. It's awful, but it's rather nice to know I have family. Whether they would acknowledge me or not is the question."

Lynnie said nothing for a few moments as she thought about her own family. *Jay-Lee, Jeb, Tommy, wonder if they're still alive, and would they welcome me back after all these years? I wonder about my baby, now seventy years old.*

She shook herself from her reverie. "Luke, it will be noteworthy to see how it all pans out. Sounds like a good story in the making."

For the next few days, Lynnie needed to prepare for a concert she had been invited to give, a soiree sponsored by the DeSoto DAR society. She practiced on another piano in a meeting room, so she wouldn't bother anyone. She took her meals in her room and concentrated on the concert.

A few days before her concert, she thought she had prepared well enough to take her meals in the dining room. She looked for Luke, but she didn't see him. She hadn't missed him up to this point. Luke hadn't mentioned that he would be away, but when he didn't show up for a few days, she wondered if he might be ill.

*Never thought I would miss some man! Well, since Bobby.*

Friday, the day before her concert, she asked Molly, the lifestyle director, about Luke.

"Luke Harvey isn't sick, is he?"

"Junior? Oh, no. His son came a couple of days ago, and they left. I don't know where they went, but he's fine. I know you've been busy with preparations for your concert tomorrow, so you two weren't playing together."

"Junior. You all call him Junior, don't you? Thank you. I shouldn't worry about him. He's a big boy, isn't he?"

"Oh yes. He is a big character. Did you know he started to call himself Luke after you came here?" She cocked her head and eyed Lynnie. "Hmmm…"

Lynnie didn't bite.

"Miss Lynnie, Junior's not only a character, but he's also a talented musician. I'd like to get him to play a hoedown for a square dance. What do you think?"

"Great idea. I see several of the residents who sit all day with little to engage their minds. They can at least tap their toes to some good hoedown music, even if they can't dance. I'm all for it."

"By the way, I know it's two months away, but I'd like to put together a program for Christmas Eve. Some of our more mobile residents will be out with families, and for those who stay, I want to have a special program. I'd like you to help me if you will. Those who stay here for the holiday will be welcome to invite guests. Would you like to do this?"

"Of course. I'll get with you next week after my concert."

As she left Molly's office, she wondered about Luke's sudden name change. *Why would he change it when he met me? I can't see that he would have changed it for me, especially since we had only met.*

Luke, gone for almost two weeks, came home on a Thursday, the day of the Scrabble group. The girls had played in Lynnie's room rather than the activity room and didn't have dinner in the dining room. Friday, the day after he came home, Lynnie walked outside and saw Luke on his little patio in an attempt to resurrect an almost-dead plant.

He spoke to his geranium. "Sorry I have neglected you. You look so sad. What can I do to cheer you up?"

Lynnie giggled to herself and answered as though she was the plant. "Yes! I have felt neglected, Luke! Where have you been?"

He screwed up his jaw and looked at the plant sidewise as though it had spoken to him. "Well, I'm glad to have been missed, but I had some human plants to cultivate in North Carolina." He then turned around to see Lynnie on the sidewalk laughing.

"I wonder. Do you think your plant will answer you? What is the plant? Looks like maybe a former geranium."

"Ah, Lynnie! Here, look. It is still definitely a geranium. It had big red flowers when I left, but for almost two weeks, it had to fend for itself. How are you, Miss Lynnie? Come on up and sit with me for a spell."

"Did you say you've been in North Carolina?"

"Yes. I think I mentioned I have a half-sister there. We had never met, and we both needed to correct the situation. I met twelve nieces and nephews and their spouses, went to the family church, ate more than I've eaten in years, and hated to leave. If it weren't so cold up there, I might consider relocation to the mountains. I'd never been in the area before."

Lynnie took a deep breath and smiled. She asked, "North Carolina. Beautiful state, the mountains in particular. Where did you stay? With family?"

"No, we stayed in a hotel in Blowing Rock. Did I tell you my father had two wives—a bigamist?"

"You did. So tell me what you found out."

"Right. Here's the story. Papa made musical instruments—banjos, dulcimers, and fiddles—and would come here to St. Petersburg by train with a load of them to sell, way back in the early years of the 1900s. He met my mother in 1916, and they had a fake wedding. She died a few days after giving birth to me, and 'Mom,' my half-sister, raised me. I didn't even know she wasn't my real mother until I grew up."

"Oh, my! What a story. So is your real last name Harvey?"

"That is my legal name, yes, but Papa's real name was Luther Willson, spelled with two *l*'s."

Lynnie gulped and took in a deep breath. She knew it was the same Willson family as Jeb's sweetheart. This had to be the same person.

If Luke had noticed her reaction, he didn't miss a beat. He went on with his story. "For years, I have swept all this under the rug, but now my family in North Carolina, along with Harry, have dug into the past. Out of nine half-siblings, I still have a half-sister alive. We went to pay her a visit. I am so glad I went. They all accepted me as family."

Lynnie had to sit on her hands to keep them from trembling. "How did you find all this out?"

"Do you recall that I got you mixed up with a woman who came and played banjo with me?"

Lynnie nodded. "Yes, I recall."

"Well, it seems she's Papa's granddaughter. She ran into Harry, my son. You met him. Her name is Susan, Susan Willson McBride. This Susan ran into Harry on her honeymoon. She had searched for years for one of those fretless banjos Papa made. Harry played some place with his banjo, and she heard him. He had been playing one of Papa's banjos. She asked him to let her see it, and she saw Papa's signature inside. When she found the banjo, it led to questions about its origin. She became suspicious that she and Harry were kin folks."

Lynnie nodded but made no comment.

"So she snooped about in the Willson family attic and found a bunch of old family letters regarding the sordid tale of our two families. She called Harry and told him about it. He went up into my attic and found our side of the story squirreled away in trunks and boxes. I had already read some of those letters years ago and found out the truth, but I chose to ignore it. Now since it came out in the open, I felt free to meet my family if they were ready to meet me."

"Incredible story."

"Yeah, I have a sister. A real sister still living. What do you think?"

"A sister. What's her name?"

"I'll not forget it. Her name is Carolina, but they call her Carrie."

Lynnie felt woozy. Carrie, indeed, had been the one she knew, and she knew there were several children in the family. One of Carrie's brothers and his wife were the ones who had adopted her baby. She swallowed but didn't respond.

By this time, Lynnie's emotions were about to get the best of her. "Luke, thank you for telling me your story. I know it must be good to get it out in the open. I…I need to get back to my room and get some music together for another concert—a soiree—I am to play for next Saturday. I had one a week ago while you were away, and it led to another engagement for next week. At least, I'm not forgotten by my fans even though I'm in retirement."

"Oooh, a soiree. Sounds like a gig my late wife would have enjoyed. I'll see you at supper, Good Lookin'."

Lynnie went through Luke's room into the hallway. She met Jasmine, one of the attendants who had come into Luke's room to check on him. "He calls all the girls Good Lookin', but I think he's got a crush on you, miss. You okay, honey? You look like you seen a ghost."

"I'll be fine, Jasmine. It's an ancient ghost I need to deal with."

Jasmine walked her back to her room. "How about a cup of tea? It always helps me. You got some tea bags?"

"I do. Will you join me?"

"No, ma'am. Makin' my rounds. I'll fix you a cup, but if you need me to stay with you…"

"No, I will be fine. Luke reminded me of some events I'd like to forget. He had no idea, and I don't intend to tell him."

Jasmine looked askance at her. "My lips are sealed."

If the girl expected some revelation, she would be disappointed. She fixed a cup of Earl Grey for Lynnie and left.

By dinnertime, Lynnie had gotten rid of her ghosts, at least for the moment.

Instead, she thought about what Molly had mentioned earlier about Luke, a.k.a. Junior, and the name change. Lynnie shrugged. *Probably more about his sister being alive—not about me.*

*Carrie. I assume she married my brother, Jeb. Lord, help me deal with this. Maybe it's time. Maybe it's time to quit hiding. Luke seems to have a new lease on life since his secrets have been brought out. What about mine? Is anyone alive, other than Carrie, who knows my secrets? What about Jeb? What about Tommy? And oh my, what about my sweet twin, Jay-Lee? Only to see them again. Just to see them once more. Lord, is it possible?*

Tears formed in her eyes as Lynnie pulled out Aunt Flossie's old Bible. It had almost fallen apart, but she wanted to reread what her aunt had written in the margin for her favorite passage in Corinthians. "God allows obstacles, but He'll show you the way in spite of them. Needful for maturity."

"It's time I mature. Luke put the challenge to my heart to redeem myself to my family. I might have to do it. Lord, please show me the way."

Later after dinner, Luke walked Lynnie back to her suite.

"Would you like to come in and visit a bit. I want to know more about your family. I made some Flossie's Famous Molasses Cookies in my tiny oven today. And, Luke, I'm sorry I had to leave you in such an abrupt manner this afternoon. I'd like to hear more about your family. Tell me about your ghosts."

He came in and sat with her on the sofa. As he munched a cookie, he told his tale. "Here's the short version. I had no idea about all this until twenty years ago when I stumbled on some letters my Papa had written to my mother and her daughter, my half-sister, Maggie. Maggie raised me from the beginning because my mother died within days of my birth. Guess I told you about it. Anyway, in those letters I learned about my North Carolina family. There were nine children in the family. My niece, Susan, stumbled on more letters of the story from their end. She set it up for me to meet my half-sister, and then we celebrated in a wonderful family gathering at the homeplace."

Lynnie took a deep breath. "Glad they aren't real ghosts. But how can men be so awful? Like your papa?"

"Don't judge every man by the bad eggs. He did repent."

"Good. Now, Luke, I have missed our music. I've played almost every evening, and I'd like to hear you on your fiddle again. Give me a little break for a change. I can see the North Carolina influence in your style. Your fiddle looks old. Where did you get it?"

"Ah. Papa made it too. He excelled as a luthier. Luther the Luthier. He made banjos, fiddles, and a few lap dulcimers. I had never heard a lap dulcimer played the proper way until I heard it in North Carolina. Beautiful but primitive. My one niece, whose name I can't recall without the cheat sheet they gave me, played at our gathering, and it hooked me on the sound."

"Did you play with her?"

"Oh yes. But we had two fiddles, two banjos, the dulcimer, a couple of guitars, a harmonica, and would you believe, bagpipes?"

Lynnie laughed, "Bagpipes?"

Lynnie wanted to know more. "Tell me about your nieces and nephews. Did you get to meet all of them? There must be a slew of them with nine of your half-brothers and sisters."

"Well, all the ones still alive. They're what Susan called the 'dozen cuzzins.'" He pulled out a list from his pocket. "I have a list of who belongs to whom. I won't bore you with the parents' names, but I met the dozen. Now here's the big shocker—Susan found out she isn't blood kin."

Lynnie caught her breath. *Susan...Susan, the name I wouldn't give her.* She didn't want to go to pieces.

"How fascinating. How did you all find out about it? In family letters?"

"No. When she and Harry were almost certain the letters were true, but they still sort of questioned the veracity, they decided to get DNA tested. What a blowout! Harry's DNA, of course, came up as a Willson, but not Susan's. Seems her real mother or father had been some kin to Carrie's husband. The last I heard, she and Mac, her husband, were on a search for her real parentage."

"How…how did this Susan take the news about not being blood kin?"

"Harry said she got all upset at first, but since the family accepted her as one of their own, she settled down. Story is she went into the bathroom and straightened her hair and put on high-heeled shoes."

Lynnie drew her brows together. "How come? What is the connection?"

"None of the other cousins were short and had curly hair. Didn't last long. She's got beautiful white curls." Luke looked at Lynnie and took a deep breath. She noticed and looked away, wondering if Luke knew the truth.

Luke went on. "Carrie said the family loved Susan in a special way because she had been chosen as part of the family. I told her since the family had adopted me, when I found my real identity, we had a recipe for a wonderful family."

"Sweet."

The way Luke looked at Lynnie unsettled her. Then he laughed and winked at her. "Suppose I'd better get back to my hole in the wall. Don't want people to talk."

After Luke left her apartment, she dashed into her bathroom and doused her face with cold water. *Does he know? I'm glad he left. If he hadn't, I would have broken down. Susan. He didn't say anything about Jay-Lee or the boys. They may all be gone. Sounds like Carrie must be a widow. Oh, Lord, please help me to keep calm and not to encourage him to talk about his family. The longing is too great, and I'm not ready to reveal my ghosts. Not yet.*

## JUNE TITUS

With the temptation he will also provide the way of escape, that you may be able to endure it…

# Chapter 38

## *"Christmas Time's a-Comin'!"*
## *by Benjamin "Tex" Logan*

*November/December 2009*

"Grab yer pardners, circle left, mind the fiddler, and do-si-do!" Luke called as he started his fiddle music.

The hoedown turned into a big success. A few couples slow-danced, including Hack and Joanne. Dr. Marshall managed to get Evelyn out on the floor for one dance. Lynnie was surprised to see Evelyn there, let alone on the dance floor. Evelyn gave her a thumbs-up when she caught her eye. Lynnie danced with another fellow named Charlie, but after one round when she tried to avoid his feet atop her toes, she sat out the rest of the dances. Most people simply tapped their toes and clapped in time to Luke's fiddling. But everyone had fun.

Legacy had a quiet Thanksgiving with several family members there for dinner. Others went home for the day with loved ones. Lynnie sat with Millie and then played the piano for an hour's entertainment. Luke's son and a young woman came in to have dinner with him. Luke introduced the girl to Lynnie.

"Lynnie, this is Harry's daughter, Gwen."

"Attractive girl. Harry has no wife?"

Luke grimaced. "She died. Sore subject with Harry."

"I understand. Now we have to concentrate on getting our Christmas program together."

Luke bubbled with excitement about Christmas. Lynnie commandeered his help with the entertainment plans. Molly had given them full rein of the music while she set up some other things such as Christmas recitations.

"Okay, Luke, you and I can play a duet. Have your son and his daughter ever heard you play your violin in the classic manner?"

"Nah. My secret. Well, Harry may remember when I played a bit of it way back when I'd play Papa's music like a real violinist just to get a rise out of Stella."

"Ah yes! Your wife?"

"Yeah. She liked high-brow music, and I knew I'd never be able to play it to suit her, so I played what I knew."

He went on to tell how he would pick up the fiddle when she had a Beethoven record playing. "Just the opposite of playing old-time music in a classical manner, I'd play Beethoven as a fiddler. I'd play along with the record 'fiddlizin'' the piece."

"Luke, you are too much. Maybe we need to try it sometime for fun but not at Christmas. But then how about you and Harry fiddlizin' and banjerizin' for the Christmas program? You and I need to play some solemn Christmas music. How about 'O Holy Night' as a duet. Do you know it?"

"I do. One of my favorites."

The next day, Luke sat with Lynnie at lunch. "Talked to Harry last night, and he's all for our plans."

"I like the idea. I look forward to hearing y'all."

"Y'all? Sounds like you're about to get in the mood for some good old-time mountain music."

# Chapter 39

## *"Let's Face the Music and Dance" by Irving Berlin*

Christmas—only five more days. Luke stopped Lynnie in the hallway outside her apartment. He was all agog.

"Guess what? My sister is here! Carrie is at my place in St. Petersburg. They'll be here for Christmas Eve. Susan and her husband—oh, what's his name? Oh yeah, Mac. Anyway, Susan and Mac brought Carrie down here from North Carolina. They'll be here for our big Christmas Eve celebration."

Lynnie gulped. Her mind went into a momentary blitz, thinking, *Now or never. Will Carrie recognize me? What will Susan be like? Is there a physical resemblance?*

Luke raised one eyebrow.

She recovered her composure, and when he made no comment to her reaction, she pursued the plans for the entertainment. "Luke, you said your niece is good on the banjo. How about if we get her to play with you and Harry? Play some of those old-time songs. I think it would be perfect."

"I'll call Harry and get him to set it up. Great idea. Will you play with us too?"

"No. A piano would ruin it. I'll play piano too but not with your family group."

"Sounds good to me. Uh, Lynnie, I need to get Carrie a Christmas present. I need a birthday present for her too. Tomorrow's her birthday. You think our gift shop would have anything appropriate? What would you suggest? Harry will be here for me tomorrow to spend some time with them, but I need to get a gift beforehand. Any suggestions?"

"Any girl, when she gets to be our age, always likes to have at least one more scarf. How old is she?"

"She will be eighty-eight tomorrow."

Lynnie laughed. "Oh, that's right. Your papa had two women in a family way at the same time? Oh dear!"

Luke shrugged. "Yup."

Lynnie shook her head as if to clear the picture. "Okay, Luke, I think we can do better than our little gift shop." She looked at the time on her cell phone. "If we hurry, the van will leave for International Plaza in half an hour. I'll check with Molly to see if there is room on the bus. Let's go Christmas shopping? I need to buy some little gifts for some of the staff who help me and for the girls who play Scrabble with me. Are you game?"

"Why not? I'll meet you at the front entrance in twenty minutes."

Luke and Lynnie joined five other shoppers going to the mall. They had two hours to shop and then were to return to the main entrance for pick up again. The other five went their own ways, but Luke and Lynnie stuck together for the most part. Lynnie, a good shopper, knew what she wanted, and she bought her gifts without any fuss.

Lynnie then helped Luke find the perfect present for Carrie. "Luke, if you want a scarf of good quality and don't mind an outrageous price, you can go to Neiman Marcus, but Dillard's will have something beautiful for a reasonable price. We're right here, so let's look."

They walked a short distance and found the right department. Lynnie suggested what she might choose for a simple and uncomplicated older lady who lives in a colder climate. "Look at this one, Luke. Do you think this would go well with her?"

The scarf, a muted gray plaid with brighter strands of blue and maroon and hints of emerald-green and gold threaded through it, had a soft, warm texture.

"This will look perfect with her gray hair and blue eyes. Thanks for your suggestion."

Luke handed the scarf and a sterling silver scarf pin to the clerk. "This is for my sister. Today is her birthday and then Christmas. Will you gift wrap them separately for me? Please?"

While the clerk wrapped Luke's gifts, Lynnie fingered a few other scarves. She held one up to her face and peered in the mirror. She smiled and put it back down.

She walked away to a different part of the store thinking, *Not today. I don't want to spend money on myself. It's a day for my friends.*

Over the next half hour, she made a few other purchases as well, while Luke looked around the store.

When Luke caught up with her at the store's entrance, he suggested a treat. "The van will not be ready to leave for another twenty minutes. I think we have time to get an ice cream cone. Are you up for it?"

"So long as it's chocolate."

They toted their packages and their ice cream cones and headed to the main entrance. Soon afterward, they boarded the van. When they arrived back at Legacy, they took their packages to their rooms.

As Lynnie wrapped her gifts, her mind went to various scenarios for when she had to face Carrie and Susan. *I know Luke will be with Carrie and the rest of the family at his place in St. Petersburg for Carrie's birthday. I shouldn't even think about facing them, but I can't help it.*

*I think Carrie might recognize me, but maybe I should lay low and see if we can avoid a big emotional scene. Since Susan has never known me, it may be better to leave things as they are. Oh, me. I never expected this moment would come. I want to reconnect with my family, to get to know Susan, but I have to admit I'm scared silly. Even more, I want to see Jay-Lee and my brothers. So I guess I need to face the music!* She laughed. "And dance!" she said aloud.

Lynnie fell to her knees beside the bed and prayed the entire time she knew Luke would be with his family. She skipped dinner. Yes, she fasted and prayed.

As the next few days led up to Christmas Eve, she went to breakfast, acted as normal, avoided Luke except to practice their duet of "O Holy Night," and sat with some of the women at the residence who were by themselves or too feeble to do much for themselves. She read to them, took them for a spin in their wheelchairs outside for fresh air, or took them to play bingo in the activity room. She spent the remainder of the evening in prayer and fasting.

When she rose from her knees long after dark on December 23, she had a calmness about her she hadn't felt since early childhood like when she and Jay-Lee would sit on the floor next to the wood stove and play with their corn-husk dolls. As wonderful as life was with Aunt Flossie, she had never felt at complete ease. *Now I know I can face Carrie, face Susan, tell the truth, and allow the full redemption of this wandering girl.*

Ready to meet the challenge ahead of her, Lynnie went to bed and slept straight through the night.

Christmas Eve at breakfast, Lynnie ate with Millie. They saw Luke come to the breakfast bar with a definite spring in his step.

"Looks like your buddy Luke is wound up. What is he up to?" Millie asked.

"He told me Sunday his family will be here for dinner, and then they will give us an old-time music concert."

"Aren't you gonna play?"

"Oh, I will. I will do several of my own arrangements of Christmas music, and Luke and I will play a duet of 'O Holy Night.' I like the way he plays. His music is textured with both fiddling and violin."

"You like him, period! Silly girl."

"Bosh! I'm a spinster and old maid, an unclaimed blessing."

"So let him claim you."

"Rubbish."

Luke heard the "rubbish," looked in her direction, and gave her a wink. Her face reddened, and she turned away.

When Lynnie got up and started back to her apartment, Luke left the table and caught up with her. "Why don't you join our family for dinner? I know you'd like them. It will be my sister, Carrie, Susan, Mac, Harry, and Gwen. Millie can join us too if she wants. Three tables pushed together will sit all eight of us."

"Oh, Luke, I don't think so. It's nice of you to think of me. The other two ladies in our Scrabble quartet have gone off with family, even Evelyn. Millie and I thought we'd do our Christmas together in her room since we have no family. I don't want to ruin your first Christmas with your family."

"The invitation is open if you want. Your call, Lynnie."

Again, the look Luke gave her disconcerted her—almost a knowing look.

Later in the afternoon, the two practiced their duet again.

"How's it sound, Lynnie? I want my violin to sound like it belongs in my hands and not some backwoods fiddler who tries to sound uptown."

Lynnie laughed at him. "Luke, if you satisfy yourself, nothing else matters. You will be relaxed, and people will all go away. It will be you and the music."

"It's the way you play, isn't it?"

"Yes. I can forget the world around me and be in the music. It has been my survival mode since childhood, orphaned and by myself. It has been my harbor, my port in every storm. It is a gift from God. Took me a long time to understand it."

Luke gave her a significant look and nodded as he put his fiddle into its case. "You will have to tell me your story someday. You know all about me and my sordid history. I'd like to get to know you better."

She knew it would be good to share it with him and the rest of the family. "Soon, perhaps. Soon."

He made no more comments on the subject. If Luke understood the turmoil she had passed through the last few days, he didn't pursue it. Instead, he picked up his fiddle and said, "I'm glad we can all be together tonight."

"Me too. You know, Luke, when I came here, I wondered if I'd have any reason to play again. Retirement hit me hard. Living here has given me another way to serve others. I don't know your beliefs, but Christmas means so much to me…the music, the joy. It is all because the Savior was born for us. We all have a story. I know mine isn't finished yet. But regardless, I trust God to direct it."

Luke's face split into a wide grin. "Interesting you should say this. We weren't much for church. I went a few times with Papa, but Mom didn't want to go to church. I never grew up with it. Yet I believe as you do. I read my Bible and pray. We all went to the family church in the mountains where Papa and my brothers and sisters are buried. I came to a better sense of what God has done for me. God adopted me, not much different from the fact my half-family adopted me, although not a legal son. If I never live beyond today, I will be with God."

Lynnie smiled. "I'm glad, Luke. We are brother and sister."

He said nothing for a loaded minute. Then, he looked at her with, perhaps, more insight than she wanted to admit. "See you tonight. You get all gussied up for our big concert. I understand about dinner."

Lynnie watched him as he trudged out the door with his fiddle under his arm. *I've never felt this close to a man before. Even in my childhood, Pa and the boys were in a different realm than Ma and Jay-Lee and me. Fears kept me from getting involved with Bobby and John. I had a schoolgirl crush from afar. Luke is different. I've been friends with men all my adult life but never in any amorous way. I'll admit—thank you, Millie—that I like him too much. Foolish old lady. But one thing at a time. I need to get through this evening.*

She laughed at herself and got dressed for the festivities. She wore a long dark-blue—not quite navy blue—velvet dress, plain and adorned with a silver lily broach and matching earrings. She looked exquisite with her snowy hair combed into a French roll. Lynnie never needed much makeup, just lipstick and a little touch of eye shadow.

# Chapter 40

## *"Will the Circle Be Unbroken?" by Ada R. Habershon and Charles H. Gabriel*

When Lynnie emerged from her apartment, Murph greeted her. "Hey there, pretty girl. Let's walk around and look at all the pretty Christmas decorations." They went by the neighbors' doors to see everyone's special decorations. She had put a nice wreath on her own door, nothing fancy. She noted Luke's door had a swag of greenery decorated with violins, banjos, harps, and bells. Decorations throughout the residence were festive, from the huge real trees in the lobby and in the dining room to a large Moravian star that gleamed and twinkled in the entertainment room. The entire place smelled like Christmas: turkey, stuffing, sweets. The aroma tantalized her nose. She and Millie would be served the same menu in Millie's room. Murph went her way when Lynnie went to Millie's rooms.

After the Scrabble ladies finished their dinner, they headed in the direction of the entertainment room where people had started to gather right after dinner. Millie made her way to the front and took her seat, but Lynnie stayed in the far back of the room. She could easily see the entertainers, but they would have to be looking for her to see her. Luke, however, caught her eye and winked.

Murph went around to everyone and sniffed out the guests. Lynnie could see the dog had made up to the lady seated by Luke. *Carrie.*

But now, everyone's attention focused on Molly as she announced the anticipated events. Luke's group would be first. "Let's welcome Papa's String Band with our own Junior Harvey, also known as Luke, and his family."

Papa's String Band performed for twenty minutes, playing mountain tunes. Carrie played a dulcimer she had brought to Luke as a Christmas present. She played "Sourwood Mountain." After a few other folk tunes, they ended the mountain program with Susan and Carrie singing a duet: "Oh Beautiful Star of Bethlehem." Susan ended with singing the old mountain version of "Brightest and Best" without the instruments.

Lynnie caught her breath while Susan sang. She could barely restrain her tears. She breathed a prayer. *Lord, help me through this night one minute at a time.*

Lynnie would be up after the next part of the entertainment, "A Pennsylvania Dutch Christmas."

Still seated in the back, when Carrie made her way back to her seat, her eyes locked with Lynnie's. Carrie gasped and leaned against Susan.

*Oh, no! Has this been all wrong? Lord, help her.* Lynnie saw Susan help her to her seat and go for some cold water for her.

But then Lynnie saw Carrie laughing at the next part of the program as though nothing had happened. Ralph the Dutchman gave his rendition of "A Visit from St. Nicholas" and "Belschnickel," the crochety old man who spies on all the children and threatens to spoil their Christmas. Everyone enjoyed his funny Pennsylvania Dutch tales, including his accent.

Once the laughter died down, Lynnie came forward and sat at the piano. When she sat down before the piano, Murph, as usual, lay down underneath. His presence calmed her. She purposely did not look at Carrie or Susan. She played her own arrangements of all the familiar Christmas carols: "Silent Night," "O Come, All Ye Faithful," "Joy to the World," and many others. Then she nodded for Luke to join her. What a surprise to his family when he played like a real violinist, vibrato and everything else.

Dr. Marshall then read the Christmas story from the Gospel of Luke. The lights had been turned low as though the audience sat on the hillside with the shepherds and in the manger with Jesus.

As soon as he had read the story, with the light still low, Millie stood with her walker and faced the group. Humoring the melody, she sang in her deep contralto "Behold, That Star." It moved the audience, especially the way Millie sang it with all the pathos of her rich church heritage.

While Millie sang, Lynnie's mind went back, not to her childhood and the Christmases in the mountains but the last Christmas with Aunt Flossie and the beautiful candlelight service at the church, when her mind could think of nothing but her own baby.

*Tonight, I get to meet her. Thank you, Lord Jesus!*

Then from the back of the room, Jasmine, the attendant, sang another spiritual that added the "amen" to the program, "Sweet Little Jesus Boy." Lynnie loved the song, and it brought a calm to her she couldn't explain. She took the sensation as a blessing from God that it would all be well when she revealed herself to her own sweet daughter.

When the lights went back up, Lynnie noted that Susan wheeled Carrie toward her. She saw a blank expression on Susan's face. She watched her lips, but she couldn't determine what words were exchanged.

Other visitors had begun to gather around Lynnie. Being polite, she spoke to each one, but her eyes were on Carrie. As Susan approached with Carrie in the wheelchair within a few feet of her, she dismissed the others and turned toward Carrie.

Lynnie remained calm, but she sensed Carrie's uneasiness. Carrie spoke first. "Your...your piano music is beautiful." Then she sighed and looked into Lynnie's eyes. "It lifted my heart. You are called Lynnie?"

Lynnie grasped Carrie's hand, but she could only say, "Carrie." Then after a deep breath, "Will you both come with me to my room?" She felt her hands trembling and clasped them together.

Susan looked puzzled as the three of them moved away from the entertainment room toward Lynnie's room. "I didn't realize you two had already met."

Neither lady answered her, but Lynnie handed her room key to Susan and took the wheelchair from her. "Come on in. We can have a quiet little visit and get to know each other."

Once inside, she invited Susan to make herself comfortable. "Please sit down, Susan. I love your voice—perfect for those old hymns. And you are so good on your banjo—really good. You are a very talented lady."

Susan sat in Aunt Flossie's rocking chair next to her Aunt Carrie. She looked about the room at the pictures on the wall, the books, and furniture.

Lynnie could see Carrie's emotions were a tender as her own, but she moved right into the matter on her mind. "Susan, you asked if we had met before. I imagine your Aunt Carrie is aware of why I brought you in here away from the rest of the family. You may wonder how we know one another. We share a difficult story. I suppose we can attribute it to Luke's fiddle and your banjo. A few weeks ago, Luke told me about your role in the location of his family, and in the process, you learned you were adopted." She shook her head, almost ashamed she had to talk about it.

"I am sure you were shocked to learn, as an older woman, the family you thought you had been born into were not your real kin. What do you know about your adoption?"

Susan frowned. Her eyes widened, her mouth agape, and jumped from the rocker. It rocked back and forth after she stood. She grabbed hold of the arms and plopped back down.

"Are...are you Jessie Lynn?" she whispered. Then with excitement, she said, "You are! You are Jessie Lynn!"

"Then you know part of the story. Yes. I gave birth to you."

A brief eerie silence hovered about the room. Lynnie's stomach churned, and she felt a little woozy. She took a deep breath.

Tears ran down Carrie's craggy cheeks. She mumbled, "I didn't tell her, Jess." Then in a normal voice, she said, "I took one look at you when you stood at the back, and I knew it was you. You still look like Junie Lee."

Lynnie sucked in a deep breath. "Oh!" she nearly screamed. "Junie Lee—Jay-Lee! Is...is she still living?"

"Oh yes. She's at the same retirement home as me. She had a hip replacement and came there for rehab—what? Six months ago. I guess she liked it well enough to stay, leastways through the winter. I think she still has her apartment in West Jefferson."

Lynnie's mind went in a tailspin, but she recovered. Now excitement set her adrenaline circulating.

"Jay-Lee! Oh, praise God! I'm so glad. So glad. But, Carrie, it's all right. It is. I am glad for this. This is God's timing. My seventy years of hiding is over. Now, Susan, tell me what you know."

Susan grasped the hands of both ladies. Tears gushed down her cheeks. She related the short version of the story.

"Harry and I had little doubt of his Willson heritage, so we decided to confirm it with a DNA test. I didn't expect Aunt Carrie's children were my only Willson first cousins, but the rest of the Willson clan are not even close. I thought, Who could my parents be? If Gladys, Will, and Gerald were cousins, could Uncle Tommy or Junie Lee have been my father or mother? I bombarded Aunt Carrie with questions, but she refused to tell me. She said, 'What was, was!'"

Carrie giggled. "I wasn't about to tell her. I promised my brother and his wife I'd never tell."

"Yes, my parents—well, who I thought were my parents. So before Mac and I came back to Macon where we live, he and I checked all the regional courthouse birth records. I found a Jessie Lynn Vance as my probable mother."

Lynnie shook her head. "You poor girl. Carrie, you could have told her. Once the cat had been let out of the bag, your promise of silence should have been over."

"So I'm a stubborn old lady. Junie Lee told her."

Susan laughed, and then with tears in her eyes, she explained how she learned the truth. "Well, I thought maybe Junie Lee had given me birth and given a different name for the birth record. I went to her and confronted her. Of course, she had to tell me the truth.

Such a sad thing had happened to you. But she told me the whole story about how she used to tease the boy and scare him away. But the day it happened, he thought you were her, and you didn't scare him away."

Lynnie's face paled, and she took a deep breath. "I don't think about it anymore, and Susan, I have forgiven him. He didn't know any better. Sweet, sweet Jay-Lee! Praise God!"

Carrie nodded. "Oh, I just remembered something." She reached into her purse and pulled out a piece of paper and handed it to her rediscovered sister-in-law. "You should call Junie Lee tomorrow. Here's her phone number. She asked me to call her on Christmas day. Your voice will be better than mine. It will be the best Christmas present she could ever have."

Susan cried now and grabbed a paper tissue from Lynnie's box of tissues beside the rocking chair where she sat.

Lynnie's tears joined Susan's. "Did Jay-Lee ever marry?"

Carrie laughed. "No. As a young 'un, she always had fellers, but none of them suited her. She says she is an unclaimed blessing."

Lynnie smiled through her tears. "I think I said the same words to someone at breakfast today."

Susan took Lynnie's hand. "What am I supposed to call you? I am so happy I can't think straight."

"Lynnie is fine. Jessie Lynn no longer exists."

"You know, it's funny I did not see Junie Lee in you. When Junie Lee told me about you, I said I would look for her in each white-haired lady I saw until I found her—you. You do have features like her, especially up close, but you wear your hair a different way, and you don't wear glasses. She likes a lot of jewelry, and her voice is deeper."

Carrie interjected, "Junie Lee's voice is the result of years of them fool cigarettes."

Lynnie laughed but made no comment. Her mind flashed back to when they both tried smoking a cigarette they had stolen from the woman they lived with. *We both got sick.*

Susan went on. "But when I saw you at the piano tonight, I thought, 'What a wonderful concert pianist!' A real treat. Gwen said a famous pianist would play. I saw an entertainer."

"Thank you, my dear Susan. My story is too long to tell you even if we should live another seventy years. We need to get back to Luke and the others. I wonder if we can get together sometime tomorrow, Susan. All the family. Would it be appropriate? I want to tell my story. I really do. I've had a wonderful, if challenged, past seventy years. Please don't pass judgment on me by what I did at age twelve. Desperation drove me to it. It may not have made sense, but I did the best thing I could think of...run off and be a wayfarer. Today, I am a redeemed wayfarer."

Susan took both of Lynnie's hands in hers and looked her in the eye. "I would never judge you. A terrible thing happened to you and made you into the wonderful person you have become."

"Thank you, Susan." Then she turned to Carrie. "You married Jeb, I assume? He's dead? Tommy too?"

"Yes, both of them are gone. Jeb died in '92, and Tommy, I guess two years ago."

"I'm glad I lived to see this day, but I'll always be sad our family circle had to be broken. I live now for the eternal Hope that I will see them with the Lord."

The three ladies stayed in Lynnie's apartment until their tears had dried and their hearts had slowed to normal. They talked about trivialities, yet the revelation of the truth surrounded each word.

"Luke and the rest of your family will wonder what in the world happened to us. Shall we join them and knock their socks off?" Lynnie threw out her hands in mock dismay.

Susan laughed. "It's good to see I came from a woman with a wonderful sense of humor. I can see myself in you—my mother."

Lynnie, tears again edging her lower lids, said, "Thank you. That is a great compliment."

Lynnie led the way back the others. Luke and company had occupied their time in conversation as Gwen petted Murph.

Luke had a sock dangling in his hand.

When the three ladies saw Luke with a sock, they went into hysterics. The four waiting family members turned toward the laughing trio.

Luke frowned. "What's so funny? You never see a feller put on his socks before?"

This caused the three women to laugh all the harder.

Carrie pointed to his feet. "We knocked your socks off."

But it wasn't time to tell them the sock-knocking news. Susan, now in control of her giggles, said, "Harry, might we invite Lynnie to have Christmas with us tomorrow?"

Luke's grin went from ear to ear as he stuck his hand inside the sock and did the sock puppet mime. "I planned to ask her anyway."

Gwen clapped her hands. "Yes! Hope you like ham."

"Love it."

Harry said he would pick up his dad and Lynnie the next day at ten.

Luke gave Lynnie a wink. "We'll be ready, won't we, Miss Lynnie? Now y'all get home and put some cookies out for ol' Santy Claus."

After the family left, Luke held out his hand to Lynnie. "Sit a few minutes with me?"

"Of course. I bet you know, don't you, Luke?"

"Know you're Susan's mother? Yeah."

"What clued you in?"

"Well, you know about gut feelings. Each time we have talked about North Carolina or said Carrie's or Susan's names, I'd see it in your eyes, a restraint maybe. I had a vibe. I'm a numbers guy, so it added up. But you know, when I first met you, I thought you were Susan. I remember when I realized you were not her, and then when I learned she was adopted, I thought you could be her mother. When I went to North Carolina and met Junie Lee, I thought she reminded me so much of you too. She's different from you, a little rougher around the edges. Then this evening, I watched you while Susan sang, and your face confirmed the truth."

"Remarkable. I think God allowed you to have those suspicions to prepare the way for tonight. I'm so glad you know. Susan will tell them in the car or maybe after they get home. And I'm glad she didn't tell them here. We didn't need a public scene. So if you had a clue, do you think the others knew?"

Luke laughed. "I kept my suspicions to myself, but Mac suggested Carrie had taken you to task and wanted to know your intentions with her little brother."

"Oh, for pity's sakes. You can't be serious."

Luke wiggled his eyebrows. "So what are your intentions?"

She glared at him. "Men! I hope my intentions are the same as yours—friendship and companionship. I like being with you, but I have no illusions."

She couldn't read his smile, but she believed he cared for her as much as she cared for him.

Luke shook his head. "Lynnie, I'm sorry I said that. I know a little bit of what you went through. You are right: I'm a man. Forgive me."

"No, Luke. There is nothing to forgive. Forgive my reaction." She went on to tell him how she had forgiven even the boy who had assaulted and raped her. "Jesus forgave me on the cross, so I forgave the boy. It didn't happen overnight, but when I came to terms with my own need for forgiveness, I knew I had to forgive him. It's the way I have survived each day since I forgave him. It's the way I have risen above my own desire to kill myself. Well, another long and hard story."

Lynnie could see tears had formed on the rims of Luke's eyes.

"Beautiful, Lynnie. I will never forget the analogy."

> As far as the east is from the west, so far has he removed our transgressions from us.

"I've heard that before. Seems not the specific sins we've done ourselves but even those done to us. God takes them all away. What has been done years ago, whether done by us, our forebears, or done to us, can be flushed down the commode. Thank you, Lynnie, for your friendship and companionship. I see it as a gift from God."

# JUNE TITUS

"It's past my bedtime, Luke. I need to call Mazie. It's already Christmas in New Guinea."

"Mazie?"

"She was my ward from the time she was thirteen—another story. She and her husband are missionaries in Papua, New Guinea."

Luke nodded. "Interesting."

"Then I will call my sister when I get up in the morning, so I won't be out for breakfast. I'll meet you in the lobby at ten. Good night, dear friend."

Luke took her hand in his and kissed it like a gallant swain.

In turn, she curtsied and headed to her apartment.

The call to New Guinea was short and sweet. Mazie and John were having a big Christmas celebration with the children in their mission. One thing Lynnie had to tell her, however, was about her true family.

"Mazie, I told you that I had a daughter when I was twelve years old and that she had been adopted."

"Right."

"Well, honey, I have met her. She is here in Tampa. I've told you about my friend Luke here at Legacy. My sister-in-law is his half sister. Susan, my daughter came with my sister-in-law to visit Luke. I can hardly wait to tell you the entire whole story, but I will write to you all about it. Now you and John have a wonderful Christmas."

They talked for another few minutes and wished each other Merry Christmas.

"Love you, Mazie."

"Love you back, Mom."

# FINALE

# Chapter 41

## *"Doxology" by Thomas Ken*

Lynnie awakened late, but her mind had no dark shadows. If she dreamed, there had been no nightmares to disturb her. A clear-eyed, peaceful image looked back at her in the mirror. To call her twin sister would be the first thing on the agenda even if she missed the breakfast bar.

As she picked up her telephone, the expected butterflies in the stomach fluttered about, but they did not deter her purpose. She dialed the number.

A gravelly voice answered, "Hello, and Merry Christmas!"

"Jay-Lee? A very merry Christmas."

"Who? Jay…Jay-Lee…Jay-Lee! Who is this?" Her voice trembled. "Jess? Jessie Lynn?"

"It is. I don't even know how to begin. All is well, Jay-Lee. Thank you for telling Susan the truth about what happened. We have met, and she knows I am her mother."

"But…but how? Where are you?"

"Sweet sister, I guess I've crawled out from under my rock. I live at the same retirement home as Luke Harvey. I don't know where to start, but maybe I can start with I am well and have had a good life. But last night, when we had our Christmas program here at Legacy, I knew Carrie had come to visit Luke, and I knew Susan could only be my daughter. I revealed myself to them after our Christmas program."

Lynnie heard deep breathing on the other end for an expectant moment, and then the telephone exploded. Joy! Laughter. Words jumbled. "Oh, my sweet dear! I wish I could have been there. Oh! Oh, I don't know what to say. We all thought you had died."

"Jay-Lee, I am so sorry I had to put you all through this. Oh, Jay-Lee! I will never see my brothers this side of heaven. But at age twelve, I didn't see any other alternative but to run. I hitched a ride, unbeknownst to the driver, in an empty watermelon truck, and ended up in Florida. Providence led me to a wonderful woman who raised me and legally adopted me. I am known as Lynelle Van Sant, or Lynnie."

"What? You are Lynelle Van Sant? Oh my goodness! I have a copy of a poem you wrote, 'The Wayfarer Returns.' I love it and have it taped to my mirror. 'Restless journey to find serenity, / Trek into a hope for someday to be free.' I think that is my life too. It never occurred to me that it could have been written by you. The title took my imagination with our childhood beggar fantasies."

"Good grief. Where did you get it? Remarkable."

"I found it in a book at a used book store. Someone must have left it in the book."

"I gave out copies of the poem with the programs at my graduate recital at the university here in Tampa. Someone must have taken it hither and yon as they left here."

"Who knows. I'm glad I have it."

"Carrie said you had a hip replacement. Are you well?"

"I am. I will stay here at the retirement home until summer, and then I may go back to my apartment in West Jefferson. Not certain what I should do at this point. So are you a concert pianist?"

"Yes...I played concerts mostly here in Tampa and the surrounding areas with an occasional trip to other places in the state. I've never accepted invitations out of state."

"Hey, Jess, that reminds me of something. Were you ever at an airport in Jacksonville?"

"Yes, several times. I gave several concerts with the Jacksonville Symphony in the early years of their existence, late fifties through the seventies. Why do you ask? Don't tell me you were there?"

"No. I used to date a Navy guy. We had already broken up, but he called me one time and said he ran into someone who looked like me. He said he went up to the lady, grabbed her, and kissed her before he realized his mistake. Talk about being embarrassed."

"Oh my goodness. Yes, my first concert there, and I had a flight back to Tampa when this Naval officer ran up to me. Yes, he grabbed me and kissed me. I could almost hear the brakes squeal on his shoes when he realized his mistake. It must have been the same person. That is so funny. It wasn't funny at the time. It nearly scared the stuffing out of me."

"I can imagine. He had no idea I had a twin, and I didn't tell him even then. But I did wonder if it was you. I never talked about you after you left. Instead, I...well, I guess I didn't want to face reality. I didn't want you to be dead, but I didn't believe you were alive."

Lynnie sighed. She wanted to cry, but at the same time, she wanted to laugh. Her emotions were all over the chart.

"Do we still look alike? Oh, Jess! I want to see you. Come home, sweet twin, come home!"

"Luke says there is a resemblance. He said you wear glasses and keep your hair short. My hair is long, and I stuff my curls into a French roll. No glasses yet. Junie Lee, I do intend to come to North Carolina as soon as I can. I have no definite plans, but I will let you know when I do. I may come along when Susan and Mac take Carrie back home."

"Oh, you must! You must come home."

The sisters talked for an hour and a half. Now Lynnie knew she had to get ready for the family dinner. Harry would soon be there, and she wouldn't be ready. "Jay-Lee, I need to hush now and get ready for the big Christmas dinner with the family. We will be at Luke's home in St. Petersburg. His granddaughter and Susan will fix a big ham dinner."

The sisters talked and talked. One sentence led to another. Lynnie looked at the clock and knew she had to hang up and get ready to go to St. Petersburg. She hated to cut off the conversation, but she finally said, "Jay-Lee, I will be coming home soon."

"I can scarcely wait. I have your phone number and you have mine. Let's plan to talk each day until you come."

"Yes. Yes! Let's do it. Love you, Jay-Lee."

"Love you more! Bye for today."

Yes, Lynnie missed the breakfast bar. She grabbed some Cheerios and a banana from her little kitchenette and got ready for the day with the family. She dressed in casual clothes—navy linen slacks, an ice-blue long-sleeved silk shell, a multi-blue scarf with her silver lily pin, and navy flats. She wanted to look her best for the family. Already, she felt as though she belonged. But she would need to get to know her beautiful and talented daughter.

The Christmas celebration, the perfect time to do this, brought the music to the final conclusion. A new song could now be written.

> Our songs are never over;
> they sing forever onward
> with multifaceted verses added
> as new and neatly penned melodies.

# Author's Notes

This story is fictional and not based on any incident. As an author, I want to address issues people experience in our culture today and at the same time demonstrate these are not restricted to current times. Lynnie's history of abuse, unplanned pregnancy, and suicide ideation and gestures are age-old problems. Setting the story in the mid-twentieth to twenty-first century presents the perspective on the problem while at the same time offers a glimpse into a historical era unfamiliar with twenty-first-century readers. I use real places in the story as well as fictional locations. There is no community in Florida named Farmer's Corner, but Jasper is real. Crossnore School is real, and at the time the fictional Lynnie would have been there, students had to live in the community. The girls' dormitory had opened when Lynnie—or Jessie Lynn—would have been in her last year at the school. The Women's Shelter is fictional. It was not until 1977 that such a shelter was established in Tampa. Legacy at Highwoods Preserve in Tampa is a real place; however, the descriptions, scenes, and events are all fictional.

# About the Author

June E. Titus, retired from a forty-five-year career as a nurse, is now an octogenarian grandmother, fiction writer, and writer of inspirational blogs. She lives with her husband in Georgia. June writes to share her interest in genealogy and history, her love of ballads and folk music, and her imaginary "friends." As a Christian writer, she reflects her beliefs in her novels and the blogs on her website and encourages others to explore their own beliefs. Her years of experience as a nurse and life in general color her work with reality. June has two current works of fiction in the Carlin Trunk Series on the market: *Harry Carlin's Coattails* (2021) and *Davey's Hat* (2022). A third book is in the works. Prior to moving to Georgia, June contributed to the *Watauga Democrat* newspaper and *All About Women* magazine in Boone, North Carolina, on a regular basis. As well, she writes for the online magazine *Devotional Diva*. June is a member of the National Society of Leadership and Success (NSLS), American Christian Fiction Writers (ACFW), and Sigma Tau Delta English honor society. She studied creative writing at Southern New Hampshire University (SNHU). For more about June, see her website: www.jetituswriter.com.

Printed in the USA
CPSIA information can be obtained
at www.ICGtesting.com
JSHW022145150224
57262JS00001B/14